# The Way to Winter

Amy Aderman

# DEDICATION

For my writing group. I wouldn't have gotten half this far without you.
Also for Anna, who knew what I needed.

# PROLOGUE

Listen: the Snow Queen lives at the roof of the world. It is always winter there: the summer sun does not shine and no flowers bloom in the ice. The snowflakes are like a hive of bees and the Snow Queen is their ruler. Her skin is white like new snow and there is a lump of ice in her chest where a heart should be. When she touches a human, she can make frost crackle across his skin and the blood freeze in his veins.

The Snow Queen flies through the air in her sled when it is time for winter in the rest of the world. She causes the snow to fall and ice to grow thick on the windows. She would like to cover the entire world with the chill of winter all year long and she is filled with rage every year when the time for spring arrives.

When at last the spring sunlight begins to weaken her grip and snowdrops creep out of the earth, she flees to her northern home and surrounds herself with the freezing cold. Remember this: always collect memories of the warmth and color of the other seasons, for soon enough winter will come and the Snow Queen will return.

# CHAPTER ONE

"Maybe the new neighbors want to open an ice hotel. It's the only reason I can think of why anybody would move here in winter," Kai mused as he sat in the town of Vasa's conservatory and drummed his fingers against a bench.

Gerda looked up from the herb bed where she was up to her wrists in masses of thyme, and grinned at her twin. "And where would they have it, in that tiny backyard? Maybe they're professional snowmen builders."

"I doubt it."

The siblings sat in the conservatory's rectangle-shaped herb room, where thick glass walls kept them warm from the cold outdoors. Kai thought about how he had walked home from his classes less than an hour ago to see the 'For Sale' sign that had been up for over a year removed from the house next door to theirs, and raced to the conservatory to tell his sister. Even though he knew it was silly, part of him leaped at seeing *anything* different after the past few months that had begun to feel dull. He watched Gerda's dark head bent over the circular herb bed that was divided into quarters, one for each kind of herb: thyme, rosemary, lemon balm, and mint. The plants had grown high and sprawled over the bricks separating each section. The mixture of fragrances was a delight but the tangled mess wasn't the tidy image that the conservatory's owners liked to present to visitors.

He remembered something else. "Once you would have said that everybody stayed away because trolls were living in the house. You believed too many of Nana's stories."

"I haven't believed in trolls in years." She gave him a scornful look. "I wonder what they'll be like?"

"The trolls?"

Gerda threw a handful of thyme at him. The lightweight clippings slapped his head with astonishing accuracy and Kai spluttered as bits of the leaves got into his mouth. She continued, "Idiot. You know I mean the new neighbors."

"Who knows? At least Nana will stop going on about how 'that empty house makes the whole neighborhood look bad.'" He snickered as he picked bits of thyme leaves out of his pale hair and examined her work. "Doesn't that get annoying? You just have to do it again every time they grow back."

She didn't pause in her work as she spoke. "I'm more patient than you. It's one of the reasons why I work here and you don't. Besides, they smell nice. Just wait a little longer and I'll be ready to leave."

Kai looked out of the windows. The fogged-up glass meant that he couldn't see through them clearly yet when he looked at the right places and squinted a certain way, he found ghostlike hints of the season outside. This afternoon, the shadows of a few snowflakes drifted to earth. People walked by in their bright coats like smudges of watercolor paints that had started to run. Indoors, his gaze turned to the potted lemon and lime trees that lined the walls, short and slim like girls waiting to dance, and the knee-high pots of lavender between each tree. He closed his eyes and breathed in the fragrances while listening to the snick of Gerda's clippers.

He didn't realize that he had started to drift off until Gerda said, "I'm finished," and he jumped at the sudden sound. When he opened his eyes, he saw that all the herbs were now properly shorn and that Gerda had already cleaned up. They donned their outer clothing: coats, gloves, hats, and scarves. At the end of the process only their faces remained bare.

The doors slammed shut behind the twins. A person unfamiliar with conservatories might have said that mere glass could never block a coming winter, but the miracles of heaters and thick glass can do a great deal. They stepped into the early December afternoon and it felt as though a spell had been broken, all the other seasons of the year vanishing behind those doors.

Even at six in the evening, the daylight was gone. The calendar in Kai's bedroom proclaimed that the season was still autumn and that the winter solstice remained weeks away. But on the shores of Lake Ontario, the snow always swept in ahead of the shortest day of the year.

Colored lights strung up outside the houses and shops helped to keep darkness at a distance. Despite the black sky, most of the town's residents continued about their daily business. Later in winter he knew they would all huddle inside and moan about the lack of sunlight, but it was still early enough to take pleasure in the newness of snow.

The cold nipped at them. Kai couldn't pull the scarf over his nose without his glasses fogging up, so he left it down and his breath was visible when he exhaled, like a dragon trailing smoke. He pursed his lips and blew out a particularly large burst.

"And just what are you thinking so hard about?" Gerda asked.

He looked around the town they had known every day of their lives. He knew every inch of it and had once won a bet with friends by proving that he could in fact walk around it blindfolded at midnight. Everything still looked the same, but... "It feels like something interesting is finally happening."

"You're still talking about the new neighbors? Yeah, it's interesting but I don't think they'll be that exciting."

"Well, it has to tide me over for at least a month. I can't wait until the next semester." He glanced in the direction of his small college campus, even though it was hidden by all the buildings in between them. He'd thought college would be a change but the first semester had been so *boring*, with all those beginning required classes and being surrounded by people he had grown up with. Some days it felt like he was still in high school. But when January came he'd finally be able to start studying astronomy for real, instead of just trying to learn on his own. "Did I tell you we'll get to out at night and look at the stars? Dr. Peters has the best telescope."

Gerda laughed. "Only a hundred times."

They walked through Vasa's main park that doubled as the town square. Evergreen hedges encrusted with layers of snow and ice served as its border. Sparrows zoomed from hedge to hedge as they sought red berries to peck at. He cupped his hands and watched the flakes settle on his gloves.

Gerda paused at the end of the park to tuck the hems of her pants farther into her boots. While she was bent over, Kai tipped his head back to look at the falling snow.

The wind blew a handful of the stuff into his face. He flinched. A burst of snow stung his cheek. Before he could turn away, something stabbed his left eye. He gave a strangled cry and snatched off his glasses.

"What's the matter?" Gerda asked.

"Something's in my eye."

"It's probably an eyelash."

"It's *cold*." He rubbed at the eyelid.

"A snowflake, then. Stop poking and let me look." She brushed his hands away and peered at his face. "I don't see anything."

"I can still feel it."

"It's only snow; you won't feel anything in a minute. Come on, let's get home."

He blinked furiously as they walked until tears streamed out of his eye. That helped, though he still felt a tiny sharpness below the lid. He shoved his fists into his pockets, resisting the compulsion to rub it away.

When they were almost home he could see the warm yellow lights that shone in the windows. All the other houses on their street were similarly welcoming, save for the house to the east of theirs. Its driveway was shoveled now and the front steps were swept clean. That morning, not even these small signs of housekeeping had been present. Yet the house still remained silent and solemn, without even one light to welcome its owner home.

Gerda paused before it. "Well, you got what you wanted: something happened."

"I'm sure the trolls will be perfectly nice neighbors," he offered as a gust of wind snuck inside the collar of his jacket.

"Oh, shut up." The wind grew colder and the two of them ran the last short distance to their house.

Kai slammed the door shut the moment they were both indoors, allowing little heat to escape the old, narrow house. They left their coats and boots strewn about. Little puddles of water dripped onto the hallway floor, ready to ambush any unwary person who walked by in stocking feet.

The fragrances of stew and biscuits filled the surrounding rooms. Their grandmother, her face soft like tissue paper, stood in the kitchen. "Did you have a good day?" she asked.

"It was all right." Gerda sniffed at the vegetables in their pot. "The steps are getting icy."

"So salt them in the morning." Nana plucked the mangled remains of a leaf from Gerda's braid. "I swear, you get messier now than when you made mud pies as a little girl."

"I do not. And it's Kai's turn for the steps," she said, sneaking the claim in before he could open his mouth. She turned to him and added, "Don't forget to tell her about your eye." Before he could object, she left the room.

"What's this?" Nana asked and turned to face him.

Kai realized too late that it would have been a better idea to ask Gerda to keep her mouth shut before she escaped up the stairs to the bathroom. He gave up trying to dust the snow out of his pale hair before it melted. He twitched as the cold water trickled down the nape of his neck. "She better not leave plant bits all over the shower again."

"She'll clean it up. Now then, stop stalling and tell me what happened."

"Nothing. A snowflake blew in my eye. It just stung for a moment, that's all."

"Let me see." She leaned closer, placing her hands on either side of his face like when he had been a child and she wanted to examine a bruise. "Does it still hurt?"

"Not really."

"I can't see anything wrong. If it still bothers you later, we'll make an appointment with the doctor."

"All right."

At dinnertime they sat at the small kitchen table as they always did; with only three people in the house, there was little need for the larger dining room. The stew was delicious and revived the teens after their walk outdoors. More than one tongue was singed by eating too fast; the taste buds would stay raw until the following morning. The meat and vegetables sat warm in their stomachs.

"How was your day?" Gerda asked as they ate.

"Just another day at the library. Some new books arrived, Danny has finally stopped shelving bodice rippers in the mystery section, and I'm *still* trying to get a hold of Carl Hensen. He's supposed to come by and play Santa next week but he won't call me back," Nana said. She smiled ruefully and smoothed her napkin over her lap. "And selling hot chocolate sounded like a good idea at the time, but now we have to keep reminding patrons not to spill it everywhere."

Kai and Gerda winced.

"And how are my favorite grandchildren today?"

"We're your only grandchildren and I played in the dirt some more," Gerda said. When she stood up to put her empty plate away, she peered through a window that faced the newly-sold house. "There aren't even any footprints. Did you see anybody moving in?"

"Not at all. Maybe somebody will turn up tomorrow. It'll be nice to not have an empty house anymore."

Kai smiled at the carrots he chased around his bowl. "Because it'll make the neighborhood look better, you mean?" he asked.

"That and I like meeting new neighbors," Nana agreed.

Even without looking up, he could tell that Gerda was also smiling at the answer.

"How was class?" Nana asked before he could get more of a response out of her.

He shrugged. "Dull. I already know everything in the core classes but they still say I can't take anything more advanced until I've 'satisfactorily finished the required courses.'"

"They just want to make sure your mind is fully developed," Nana consoled him.

"Like a ripe fruit," Gerda added from the sink, where she was rinsing her plate.

Kai made a face. She looked up in time to catch it and smiled at him.

After everybody finished eating Kai went upstairs to study. Nana settled at one end of the living room couch with the newspaper. Gerda curled up in the rocking chair nearby, playing with strands of her still-damp hair.

It only took a couple minutes before Nana stopped muttering at of the crossword puzzle and touched the girl's foot. "I see that smile on your face. What mischief are you planning now?"

"Just thinking about how winter is pretty at the beginning."

"Even when it's almost always dark and nothing is growing?" the old woman teased. They were happy about winter's arrival every year but by February Gerda would be glaring at the barren ground and taking every day that plants didn't start growing as a personal insult.

"The fir trees stay green. And something's always blooming at work." Gerda uncurled her legs. "Will you tell me a story?"

Nana smiled. "What will happen when you're too old for stories of trolls and spells and adventures?"

"I'll die of boredom."

"Well, then." Through the windows across the room, Nana watched a few snowflakes falling in the gap between the curtains. The fully dark sky and lack of a moon had turned the world pewter-gray. "I once heard of a charcoal burner who always had to rebuild his stacks of wood, as they were forever falling down. One cold evening as he sat outside his home, a beautiful woman appeared and asked if she might be allowed to warm herself by his fire.

"Being an experienced man of the forest, he suspected that the woman was a huldra, who was very beautiful from the front but possessed a bushy fox tail when seen from the back. She and her sisters often caused great amounts of mischief to human men but he thought it might be worse luck to refuse her request..."

Kai awoke with a jolt, as though a bucket of ice water had been dumped onto his face. He lay in the darkness and listened. The clock ticked and the radiator clinked in the hallway. No footsteps moved throughout the house, nor bodies shifted below their blankets. None of those had wakened him. He didn't remember having any dreams that could have woken him suddenly. Something bright streaked by his window that faced the empty house next door.

He squinted and put on his glasses. The glow reappeared, its shape blurry beyond the frost covering the outside storm window.

Still mostly asleep, he tugged his arms free of his quilt which slid onto the floor when he stumbled out of bed. He stepped around his small telescope that pointed to the sky and the books of crossword puzzles on the floor. Moving clumsily, he slid up the inside window. The once-clear outer window now coated with etchings of ice crystals that spiraled in every direction and he couldn't find any gaps in the frost.

When he tried to open the window, he discovered that it had frozen shut. Kai pressed his right hand against the glass instead. It took mere moments for his warmth to melt the thin skin of frost. It slipped away below his fingers, the water running down the glass only to quickly refreeze. He felt the pads of his fingers grow numb and pulled his hand away. Bits of frost stuck to his palm. He bent and looked through the cleared space.

The window in the other house was also full of frost that spread from corner to corner. Behind the ice, he saw the pale light. It moved in and out of the window space, turning this way and that. He held his breath and stood in his uncomfortable position without moving. The dim glow was the only illumination on the other side, just enough to brighten the frost when standing next to the glass. He couldn't make out any strong details but the light resolved itself into a tall shape as he watched. It bent down and then stood upright, moving smoothly. His left eye began to sting once more as he watched. It almost seemed to throb in rhythm with his heartbeat. He swiped at the tears that clung to the eyelashes but did not look away.

He watched until the cleared space on his window began to fill up with frost once more. The light stopped in front of the glass and remained there. He felt as though it was watching him in return, though his room remained dark and he hadn't made any sounds that could betray his presence. The light vanished. Kai realized that his hands clutched the windowsill and his fingernails dug into the wood. When he stumbled away from the window his knees collided against his bed.

It felt as though the quilt had tied itself into knots on the dark floor and he had almost decided to give up by the time he was able to tug it back onto the bed. He pulled all of the blankets and sheets over his head, and tucked the still-cold hand against his shoulder.

He dreamed sometime in the night. In the dream he stood before the window once more, but it was now open to the night air. Goosebumps covered his body. The light returned and became so bright that he shut his eyes. It managed to sneak beneath his eyelids until he was nearly blind. When he tried to move, eyes still closed, his feet collided against ice. The brittle substance cracked with ease at first but spread everywhere. In the nightmare the frost grew faster than he could break it until it surrounded him, until it nudged at his face and eyes. Somebody stood before him. He had not seen anybody before he shut his eyes, he did not hear anyone, and he did not touch anything but frost, but he could tell that something was there, watching him.

Bells rang in his ears. Light touched his eyes once more but he still couldn't move. Something was pinning his arms to his sides.

The bells rang louder as he struggled. The sound was stabbing into his ears. Kai twisted and thrashed until he fell and landed with a thud.

His eyes snapped open. He lay on the floor next to his bed, wrapped in a snarl of blankets. The ringing was his alarm clock, which had fallen with him, and he slapped it until the noise stopped.

Mind still fuzzy with sleep, he lay on the floor. The sun had melted patches of frost on the storm window and he frowned, trying to remember why he would have left the interior window open all night. The room had grown so cold. He slammed down the pane of glass.

That morning he dressed in a warm wool sweater. Its gray sleeves were too long and he rolled them into the cuffs of the shirt underneath; not even the most determined wind would creep in through there.

He remained cold throughout the day despite sweaters, cups of coffee, and thick gloves. In class he watched the snow fall outside the windows. When looking from a certain angle, he thought he could see details in the snowflakes. He wanted to open the window and let them collect on his hand. Perhaps he could borrow a microscope from one of the labs and use it to examine the crystalline edges. Out of everything in that long, dismal day, the snowflakes alone were perfect.

# CHAPTER TWO

Two days later, Kai found a scarf outside his front door: a long band of ice blue cloth tangled around the railing. Made of some translucent, smooth fabric, it rippled in the breeze. He untangled it and let the fabric puddle in his hands. It felt like cool water on his fingers.

A tall girl with hair so blond it was nearly white stepped out of the house next door and ran to the steps below him. "Sorry about that, the scarf's mine. Thanks, I've been looking everywhere for it." She held out her hands, bare in the cold air.

Kai tipped his hands. The scarf slid out of his palms and into hers. The girl looped the scarf around her neck, seemingly more as an ornament than for warmth. The light-colored fabric seemed bright against her pale face. "How'd it get over here?" he asked.

The girl shrugged. "We're still moving in and everything's a mess. Thanks again." She turned to leave and he saw that the curtains had been pulled away from the windows.

He jumped down from the steps as she began to walk away. "What's your name?" he asked. "Now that you're living here, we'll probably see each other a lot and it would feel weird if I didn't know what to call you."

She raised an eyebrow. "You *think* you'll see more of me, or you *want* to?"

Kai hoped he wasn't blushing. He could only think to say, "Well, the houses are close together so it would happen either way."

The girl smiled, a little grin of personal amusement that tugged at the corners of her wide mouth. "You can call me Eva. And you are...?"

"Kai. What brings you to Vasa?"

"This and that. It was kind of a last-minute decision."

"Do you have to get back to unpacking right away?"

"I could put it off—if something good came along. Why?"

10

He shoved his hands into his pockets. "I was going to meet my sister at work. If you want, you could come along. It would be like a tour of town. Not that there's a lot to see, but it's still more interesting than unpacking." Kai bit the inside of his cheek and the babbling stopped.

She stared at him for a moment before smiling again. "I'd love that."

Starting the day after Thanksgiving, at least a little snow had fallen every day. By early December Vasa appeared like the picturesque illustration seen on a vintage Christmas card. For a little while at least, everything looked perfect. He and Eva walked well together, their long legs matching steps. Kai felt her eyes on him even when he turned to point out landmarks. Her gaze prickled on his neck. He led her to the center of town, dodging the small crowds that gathered on Saturday afternoons. They strolled through the park, skirting that day's flock of snow angels. One person must have brought dye, for several of the newest angels possessed crimson wings and blue torsos.

Standing in that space, he remembered the feel of something striking his eye. Since that afternoon the odd sensation had come and gone many times: on some occasions, whole hours had passed without feeling anything; but it was becoming more common to feel a slight pain, as though an eyelash had worked its way under the lid and refused to leave.

He paused at the center of the park next to a life-size stone statue of a reindeer. Icicles dangled from its antlers and gleamed like crystal in the afternoon light.

"A local artist made this years ago," he said. "It's been here since before I was born. When my sister and I were little, our grandmother told us that it was alive."

Eva raised her eyebrows. "Really?"

"The story goes that if you breathe on it during the night of a full moon the stone changes to flesh and blood, and you can ride the reindeer anywhere you want for the rest of the night. But if you're not back at this exact spot by dawn, you'll both turn into stone."

Eva snapped the tip off of one of the icicles and rolled it between her gloved fingers. "Do you believe that?"

"It's just a statue."

"But didn't you ever try it as a child, to see if she's right?"

"No." He laughed and shook his head a little, patting the cold stone neck. "I suppose I didn't want to know for certain if it was made-up."

They left the statue and continued walking. They passed the Victorian-era library where Nana worked. The building was edged with snow like sugar frosting. Store owners had decorated their doors with wreaths of pine boughs that released their scents every time a customer opened the door. Even the church bells chiming the hour seemed more festive during this time of year.

Eva clapped her hands to her ears as the grand bells rang above their heads.

Kai touched her arm. "What's wrong?"

"I didn't expect the bells to be so *loud*," Eva said.

"They can be a little noisy at times," he admitted, "but it's still nice music."

She lowered her hands. "All I hear is noise."

"You'll get used to it soon," he promised.

"I doubt it."

Taken aback by the utter certainty in her tone, he cast about for a different topic. "Are you cold? I can buy us some coffee." He had noticed that Eva's coat was open at the collar. Her neck had no more protection than that wispy scarf and her ears were barely shielded from the cold by her chin-length hair. He himself had started becoming more comfortable with the cold weather over the past few days. It was like this every winter, though this year it seemed to be happening faster than usual. Still, the thought of something hot to drink sounded good.

"I'll be fine."

"Are you sure? There's a cafe at the end of the block."

"No. I don't need anything hot. Is there anything else to see here?"

"There's always the college," he said and detoured from the main streets to show her the closest of the school's brick buildings. "What's your major? Maybe we'll have some classes together."

"I'm not in college."

"Why not?" he asked, surprised by the lack of hesitation in her answer.

"I'm taking some time off. I have some other projects to work on."

"Oh. Well, they have an outdoor skating rink during the winter. We could do that sometime, if you want."

"I'd like that."

Kai had planned the walk so that they would end at the conservatory. He told Eva, "My sister works here; I told you I was going to meet her. You'll like this."

He opened the outer door. The building was laid out as a large square, each of the four sides a different room connected by doors, and hollowed out by a courtyard in the building's center. Kai remembered being mesmerized the first time he saw it. The houses in Vasa had only small yards, not room enough for gardens this extravagant. Most people made do with potted plants on porches and in windows. When he saw it as an adult it was impressive; when he was a child it had felt like magic.

The first room's contents were changed to match each season. Now that the year's end had arrived, it was filled with tiers of green-and-red poinsettias. Holly grew in enormous pots at the room's four corners. Kai and Eva's boots scraped against the brick floor. A still pool of water had been built into one corner. It didn't ripple as a fountain like the other bodies of water in the conservatory, but lay dark and quiet and you could see reflections in the water. Kai looked into the pool and saw himself surrounded by reflections of the poinsettias that circled the rim. Eva's white face appeared over his shoulder, expressionless.

Kai dug in his pockets and uncovered a couple of pennies. "Do you want to make a wish?"

Their reflections shattered, rippling into smears of color on the water as the pennies dropped to meet the other coins that lay scattered across the bottom of the pool.

"What did you wish for?" he asked.

"It's a secret," she said and smiled into his eyes. "But if it comes true, it will make me *very* happy."

"It's so hot in here," she added when they stepped into the room designed like a rainforest. Other people who had sought refuge from the cold afternoon were present. On the opposite side of the room Kai saw parents with a small child who gazed intently at turtles perched upon rocks beneath a sunlamp.

"Isn't it great?" he asked. "All you have to do is go through a door and it's like you're in another country."

Eva removed her coat. Spots of heat were bright on her cheeks. She looked over the flowering hibiscus, trailing vines, passion flowers, and glossy-leafed plants with polite interest but didn't show any passion over Kai's descriptions of the plants' origins and their Latin names.

He led her into the next room, which was a dry space filled with desert plants. The spines of the cacti warned visitors away from too-close admiration. Three saguaro cacti stood in a row, their arms curving towards the glass ceiling.

She collapsed onto a bench and fanned her face. "Do you come here often?"

"Almost every day," he said. "Do you like it?"

"It's different." She pushed up the sleeves of her green-and-white shirt. "Can you wait? I'll be ready to leave in a minute."

He sat down next to her. "Are you okay?"

"The heat surprised me. It's a shock after being outdoors so long," she said.

"I'm sorry. We can rest as long as you want."

"No, I want to keep going." She stumbled as she stood. Kai caught her by the elbow and helped her to balance.

"We can go back soon. I just want to show you the last parts," he said.

Eva barely paused to look around the room with the citrus trees and herb garden. When they returned to the lobby, Kai stopped her from going to the exit. "There's one more thing." He put his hand to a frosted glass door and stepped into the courtyard.

Gerda dropped another handful of debris into her bucket. Even with the conservatory's high walls, leaves and bits of twigs still blew over the building and dropped into the sheltered space. She began one last walk around the courtyard for anything else that needed to be cleaned up before leaving.

Gray flagstones lined the courtyard paths and climbing roses grew up all the walls. This late in the year they would look ugly to anybody else: she had pruned the branches and they looked like brittle brown sticks. The remaining stems still possessed knife-sharp thorns that could scratch fearsomely when hidden by leaves in the spring and summer. A few rose hips that she had overlooked still dangled from their bushes. Yet she reminded herself that in the summer the roses were beautiful: glossy green from the sun and hiding people in the courtyard from those on the other side of the glass.

Her gaze landed on the miniature apple trees planted in each corner. The little flowerbeds scattered throughout the space were currently covered by snow, but in the spring small flowers and shrubs would grow. A rectangular pond that housed a school of koi was placed in the center of the courtyard. The pond was still clear and when she knelt she could see the swimming fish as orange and gold blurs. Before long though, ice would creep along the water's surface and the fish would sink into hibernation.

She heard the door open and close, and Kai's voice saying, "I know it's not much to look at now, but it's great in the spring." He spotted Gerda crouched by the water and waved. "There you are. Meet Eva; she just moved in next door."

Gerda tried not to smile at the slight emphasis he placed on the last two words. There was no point in letting the new neighbor know they had been talking about who she might be, though she would find out soon enough that everyone in Vasa talked about everyone else. Eva stepped farther into the courtyard and Gerda was able to get a better look at her. "It's nice to meet you. Where did you move from?"

"Farther north." Eva was examining the seemingly-barren space as she spoke. "It's very…different here."

Gerda laughed. "You've never lived in a small town, then? Don't worry, you'll get used to it."

"Eva and I were about to walk home," Kai said. "If you're almost finished, do you want to come with us?"

"Give me a few minutes."

The three of them walked home together in the twilight, Eva in between the twins. The outdoor holiday lights had been turned on and Gerda noticed that Eva's fair hair nearly glowed underneath the colored lights, even as her own dark braid melted into the shadows.

They halted in front of Eva's home with their breaths pluming in the air. Now the formerly abandoned house had smoke trickling from the chimney and lights in several of the rooms.

Eva smiled at them but her cool eyes rested a moment longer on Kai. "Thank you for the tour. Good night." She walked into the house without looking back. The ends of her scarf fluttered behind her.

"So that's our new neighbor. Definitely not a troll," Kai said, breaking the silence as they watched.

Gerda tried not to smile too broadly. She knew his voice, expressions, and movements as well as her own, and she had noticed a lot since the two of them entered the courtyard. He'd fallen and fallen hard, even if he didn't know it yet. "She's pretty," Gerda said, looking at him sidelong.

"I know. Wait, what's that supposed to mean?" he asked.

"Nothing. I think it's nice that you have a new friend."

"Shut up." But he smiled as they crossed the snowy lawn.


The next afternoon there was a knock on the front door. When Kai opened it, he found Eva standing on the other side. "I was thinking of exploring some more. Do you want to come with me?" she asked.

"I would but I'm in the middle of something."

"What is it?"

"We're telling stories. Well, Nana's the one who tells them; Gerda and I just listen."

She raised her eyebrows. "The two of you still listen to fairy tales?"

His shoulders stiffened. "It's a tradition. We always do this, ever since I was little."

She stepped closer and looked into the hallway. "Can I join you? You make it sound like something special."

Kai let her in. Gerda and Nana sat at the kitchen table, drinking coffee and eating fruit-filled scones still hot from the oven. "So this is one of our new neighbors," Nana said. "I was hoping to meet you soon. How do you like our town?"

"It's different from any place I ever lived."

"I hope your parents are having an easy time settling in. Let them know we're available if they need anything."

"I will but they like to keep to themselves. Kai said you tell stories. May I listen?"

Nana grinned. That smile always made her look like a younger woman. "Any storyteller worth her salt can always use a new person in the audience. Make yourself comfortable."

As soon as everyone was settled, she said, "In my grandfather's day, there was a young man who lived in the countryside and supported himself by hunting. One day he saw three swans fly past him and land on the shores of a pond. Thinking of the local lord who would pay a great deal to be able to feast upon swans and stuff his pillows with their feathers, the hunter crept closer. As he hid in the rushes, the birds threw off their feathers. Three milk-white women arose and dove into the water.

"The hunter rubbed his eyes. Everybody in his village knew stories of creatures that could shed their skin and change from one shape to another, but nobody he knew had ever claimed to have seen one. His bow and arrow lay forgotten as he watched.

"The women splashed about in the water and laughed at one another. Not once did they seem to suspect that they were being watched. Even in human shape, they moved like birds: the way their arms curved, how they turned their long necks, even how they bent to drink—none of these were ways human women moved.

"After they tired of this play, the women climbed out of the pond and stepped into their feather dresses, very close to where the hunter lay. Then they changed back into swans and flew away.

"Although all three swan-maidens were beautiful, one of them in particular seemed loveliest and had caught the hunter's attention. He couldn't stop thinking of her, dreaming of her, and watching the sky for her. He couldn't even concentrate on hunting.

"Things continued like this for so long that he decided to visit an old widow who lived nearby and ask for advice. She was the type of person who knew a little about everything, and she had helped him with other problems before.

"'I have seen the most amazing thing,' he told her. 'A trio of swans came to the pond and changed into women, right before my eyes. But they went away and I'll never be happy again if I can't have the prettiest swan-maiden for my wife.'

"'If they enjoyed the pond so much the first time, they are sure to return eventually,' the widow said. 'Hide there every day and wait for the swans to arrive. When they change into women, pay attention to where your lady lays her dress. If you take it when she is not looking and keep it hidden, she will be bound to you.'

"The hunter did as she said and hid in the rushes at dawn. The mist was still thick and he couldn't see the swans until they were almost upon him. The birds landed in the same place and changed into the same three women as before, flinging themselves into the water as soon as they had changed shape.

"The hunter watched carefully. The moment the maidens' backs were turned, he snatched up the dress belonging to his swan. With all their chattering and splashing, they never heard his stealthy movements. The feathers were soft against his hands. He had held birds before but had never touched anything so fine as that dress made of feathers. He folded it up and tucked it within his jacket.

"Soon two of the swans rose from the water, donned their robes, and flew away without waiting for their companion. The third woman swam in the water a few minutes longer before leaving the pond. When she searched for her dress, she found the hunter instead. She instantly knew what had happened.

"'Give my swan-skin back to me,' she said.

"The hunter shook his head. 'You will leave if I do that. I love you and I want you to be my wife.'

"The swan-maiden continued to plead but the hunter refused. At last she agreed, 'I will be yours so long as you have my dress, but know that I am telling the truth when I say that I cannot stay bound to a human forever.'

"The hunter had brought a cloak with him when he went out that morning, and he now draped this human clothing about the swan-maiden before leading her to his home. He hid the feathers that night while she slept. It did not take long to prepare a grand wedding. The swan-maiden appeared to participate in the ceremony willingly and did not say that she wished not to wed. The couple lived happily enough, although the wife constantly longed to be near water and grew distracted whenever she heard the sounds of other birds. She gave birth to two daughters, who were never told of their mother's true nature.

"Three years after they were married, the hunter pulled the feather dress out from beneath a floorboard. It was the day following their wedding anniversary and he wanted to feel the soft feathers once more.

"His wife entered the room while he was lost in his memories. The moment she saw the feathers from her former life, the dress floated out of his hands and into hers. She changed back into a swan and flew out of the house. Their two daughters also changed into swans and flew away with their mother. The hunter could do nothing but watch his wife and children disappear. From that day on, he never stopped roaming through the woods, looking for her without success. He remained alone for the rest of his days and nobody else in that village ever saw so much as a single swan feather again." Nana folded her hands and leaned back in her chair.

"I don't understand the swan-maiden," Eva said.

Nana looked surprised. "What about her?"

"If her feathers were so important to her, why didn't she keep searching? They were married for three years and the cottage can't have been that big. She gave up too easily; she deserved to lose them."

Gerda sat up straight, her hands pressed against the table. She glared at

Eva. "Maybe the hunter kept changing the hiding place. And it's a *story*; things don't have the same logic in stories."

The pale girl waved this aside. "The hunter's stupid, too. He was so careful to hide the dress; he should have known what would happen when he took it out. He deserved to lose the swan-maiden for being so careless."

Kai began to feel as though he'd rather be at the bottom of the hunter's lake rather than sitting between the two arguing young women. "Maybe the hunter just had bad luck," he suggested. Even to his ears, the diplomatic answer sounded weak.

Eva waved a hand at this argument. "Luck isn't real; it's just something that people can blame when they fail."

Nana clasped her hands around her coffee cup. She said, "The people in stories have to have flaws, or else they're too perfect and we lose interest. Aside from entertaining us, we can learn from them."

"And what can I learn from a man who kidnapped his wife and then didn't even do a good job of it?" Eva asked.

Gerda opened her mouth and Kai stood up. He said, "Good story, Nana. I'll be back in a little while; I'm just going to see Eva home." He ushered her out of the house. The wind slammed the door shut behind them.

Having left the others behind, Eva paused at the entrance to her home and turned to look at Kai. "Do you want to come inside?"

"Sure."

She grinned and, wrapping her long fingers around his wrist, pulled him through the door. Inside, he saw that the structure was almost identical to his house, although here the floors were uncarpeted and he saw few furnishings through the doors opening off of the hallway.

"Aren't your parents home?" he asked as Eva led him up the narrow staircase.

"They're busy." She flung open a door at the end of the hallway. "This is my room."

The bedroom matched the weather outside: its walls were painted a blinding white; the windows had sheer, ice-blue curtains that matched her scarf; and silver-colored pillows sat atop the bed's ivory quilt. He heard the furnace working somewhere in the house but this room still felt cool. Eva didn't seem to notice the temperature: after closing the door, she had pulled off her sweater to reveal a white blouse with short sleeves. A full-length mirror stood in one corner. The oval glass gleamed as though she had polished it only moments before. He glanced into it and saw Eva smiling over his shoulder.

"What do you think?" she asked.

"It's very nice," he said automatically and turned away from the mirror. He sat down at a desk and she leaned against the wall next to him. "So why don't you like stories?" he asked.

"I never said that."

"Could have fooled me."

"I don't *hate* stories," she said. "I just don't understand the people in them. They know they're making mistakes or that they're going to do something wrong, but they go ahead and do it anyway."

"It's like Nana said—that's how we learn." He laughed. "Besides, if everybody did everything right all the time, nothing interesting would ever happen." She looked doubtful and he said, "You must not have heard many stories. It makes sense after a while."

"I know a few. Does your grandmother tell many stories?"

"Hundreds. She seems to know stories about everything—that's what Gerda and I thought when we were little, anyway."

"Maybe I know some you haven't heard yet," she said. She had a strange little smile on her face.

Kai shifted in the chair as she stared at him. Searching for conversation, he noticed a display of crystal figurines lined along the windowsill. "Do you collect those?" he asked.

Her pale blue eyes left his face and her smile softened. "Yes, I've had them for as long as I can remember." She picked up the tiny figurine of an owl with outstretched wings and handed it to him. The craftsmanship was so detailed that he could see the etching of each feather. He looked at the others; none stood taller than his thumb.

Glancing once more at the collection of figurines on their windowsill, Kai realized which direction the window faced. "I think you can see my bedroom window from here."

"Really? Which is yours?"

He got up and, returning the owl to its place on the sill, pulled aside the curtains. "That one."

Eva placed her hands on either side of the window frame. Her arm brushed his hand. "There's too much frost for me to get a good look." She opened the window.

Wind gushed into the room, frigid enough to make Kai's breath catch. It swirled the curtains out of his hand and blew papers onto the floor.

Eva didn't seem to notice. She leaned out the window and he put out a hand to keep her from falling. Snowflakes caught on her eyelashes. "Now I can see it. I like the telescope. Do you star-gaze often?" She glanced away from the window to look up at him.

"When I can. I like astronomy." He rubbed his arms and backed away towards the faint warmth at the far side of the room. His socks slipped on the wood floor and he knocked over the crystal owl. It broke and the shards scattered wide. He fell.

Kai swore. When he lifted his hand, fragments of the crystal stuck into his fingers and palm. He pulled the larger pieces out; the others were too small to be pulled out with his fingers. Blood smeared across the crystal and stained the pale wooden floor. He lifted his head, expecting Eva to start shrieking. "I'm so sorry, it was an accident. I'll buy you a new one, I promise."

She stared down at him, the smile and any other recognizable expression gone from her face. As he continued babbling she knelt, took hold of his face, and kissed him.

Her lips felt as cold as if she had been drinking ice water. She moved her hands to his shoulders, thumbs pressing against his collarbone. One of the snowflakes clinging to her hair dropped and landed on his cheek. As he brought his hands up another piece of glass fell; his palm brushed the hem of her white shirt and left a streak of blood. He closed his eyes and felt the now-familiar sting return to his left eye.

Eva let go. She stood up and shut the window while he remained kneeling on the floor. As soon as he had stood up, she took him by the wrist and led him from the room without even glancing at the broken figurine.

She brought him to the living room, where a solemn, bland-looking woman now sat on the couch while reading a magazine. She said, "Mom, this is Kai. There was an accident upstairs and there's glass in his hand."

The woman didn't appear surprised or alarmed. "I can fix that," she said, not even bothering to greet him. "Wait here." She left the tidy but colorless living room, returning soon with tweezers and a box of bandages. "This won't take long."

Kai sat down next to her. Eva's mother bent her head over his hands. She removed the pieces of crystal without further conversation, setting them inside the box's lid. Several more drops of blood fell, staining the pale couch, but neither Eva nor her mother commented on this.

He winced as the metal prongs prodded at his skin. Eva's mother was quick, however: she moved swiftly and removed every piece of glass. She stuck bandages over the deeper cuts. "    Thanks," he said.

"You're welcome." She picked up her things and shuffled out of the room.

"Is your mother mad at me?" he asked Eva in a low voice.

"Why should she be angry?"

"Well, I just broke something. She barely talked and she didn't even want to know who I was."

"She's just quiet."

Kai shook his head and stood up. "I should go home."

Eva accompanied him outdoors. Despite the cold, she didn't bother buttoning her coat over her blood-stained shirt.

Even though he had intended to go straight into his house, he automatically looked up. The sun had finished setting and the sky had turned black during the short time he had been in her house. It looked to be one of the clear nights that he loved and some stars were visible in the gap between their houses.

"Stars seem like just these little points of light," he said while still looking at the sky, "but they're always being born and dying, and somehow we still see their light after they're gone."

"It doesn't seem like you could see many stars here, with all these houses and lights."

"You just have to know how to look." He took Eva's hand and led her to the street, where they stood in between patches of black ice. This late on a weekend, few cars drove by. "See? You can get a better view over here."

"You're right," she said. "Which constellations do you know?"

"I can find all of the ones around here." Eva tucked her arm through his as he pointed his other hand at the sky. "There's the Big Dipper, or Ursa Major. That one's easy to find. Orion's Belt is over there."

"I don't see it."

He turned her head slightly. "Over there. Look up higher. They're the three stars in a row."

She nodded. "I can see it now. It's interesting—I spent a lot of time watching the stars before I moved here but I never really studied them. I did see the Northern Lights, though."

"I've never seen them," he said. "But I know the official name is the aurora borealis, and that they're named for a Roman goddess and the north wind."

Eva laughed. "Do you always know everything?"

"Sometimes I want to. Did you really see the Northern Lights?"

"Many times. They're one of the things I miss now that I live this far south."

"What do they look like?" he asked.

"They're perfect. There's every color you could think of and it feels like you can touch them. They're the only colorful thing that I truly like. I've never seen a person make anything as good as them. Winter is the best season."

He nudged her. "I bet you won't say that after four to six months of it."

"I do, too. I grew up farther north, remember? I say it every year and winter back home lasts much longer than it does here."

"Prove it."

"Very well." She looked him in the eye. "I bet that I won't complain about winter once during the whole time I live here."

"And I bet you will."

"What do you want to wager?" she asked.

He thought for several moments before laughing. "I can't think of anything interesting."

"How about this: the winner can ask the loser to do something they want *and* the loser can't complain. That'll give you plenty of time to think."

"It sounds like you already have something in mind."

Eva smiled. "I might."

She sounded smug. From Kai's experience with his sister, it usually didn't mean anything good when a girl used that tone of voice but he couldn't back out now. He shook her hand. "It's a deal."

"I guess you'll have to keep an eye on me in the meantime—to make sure I don't complain."

"I guess I will."

"Good. Is your hand feeling any better?"

"I'll be fine. It just stings a little bit." He pulled off his glove and wiggled his fingers. Little jolts of pain raced through his skin. "Okay, that wasn't my best idea." He replaced the glove. Turning back to the stars, Kai swiped at his eye.

"Is something wrong?"

He made a face. "It's stupid; a snowflake got into my eye a few days ago and it still feels like something's there, even though it would have melted right away. I think I must be imagining that something's still there."

"Let me look."

"Nana and Gerda already did, and they didn't see anything." Yet he still removed his glasses.

Eva pulled off her thin leather gloves and put her hands on either side of his face. She looked closely at his eye without speaking then brushed one finger alongside it. He blinked and she kissed his closed eye. "There. Feel better now?"

He put his glasses back on. "It comes and goes. Aren't you cold? You should go inside or at least wear something warmer."

She laughed. "I'm used to it. Besides, I always have trouble staying warm. This is easier."

"You'll get frostbite if you're not careful."

"You'll have to be careful for me, then."

"Maybe I can show you some more constellations another night. You can get a great view along the lake—there aren't so many lights," he offered.

"I'll look forward to it."

They walked back to the snowy driveway and Eva turned to leave.

"Hold on," he said. She raised a pale eyebrow but waited. He stepped forward and kissed her.

At first he caught only the corner of her mouth but she turned her head to meet him better. Her short hair tickled his cheek and he thought of the swan's feathers from Nana's story. Kai slipped his arms around Eva's waist beneath her coat. She broke away briefly and sighed, so quietly that he almost couldn't hear, "Why do you have to be so *warm*?" Then he kissed her again. Even in the darkness, by the time she pulled away he could see a rare flush on her pale face.

"I'll see you later," Eva said. She turned away and walked back to her house.

He paused before going inside to look at the stars once more. Instead, his gaze was caught by the icicles that had reappeared on the gutters even though Gerda had hacked the old ones off with a yardstick only days earlier. The icicles lost their harmless beauty at night. He felt their weight dangling above his upturned face, and imagined them breaking free from the roof and splintering around his feet.

Indoors, Kai called out, "I'm home," and retreated to his room before anybody could see him. When he looked outside he didn't see a light on in Eva's room. He lay down on the bed and stared at the ceiling until Nana called him for dinner.

Kai managed to hide what had happened until the end of the meal. When he reached out to clear the dishes, Gerda saw his hand. "What happened to you?" she asked.

"Nothing."

"Kai!"

"I dropped a glass at Eva's house and cut myself when I tried to clean it up," he said as Nana examined his hand. "It's fine, her mother took care of it."

"We'll see," Nana said. She peeled off every bandage and swabbed the cuts with disinfectant as Gerda continued to scowl over his bare-bones explanation of the accident.

"That stings!" he complained.

"That's what happens when you poke at sharp things with bare hands. It'll feel better in a minute."

"I'll be more careful."

"I should hope so," Nana said. "There, you're finished. Put clean bandages on before you go to bed."

"Fine. Can I go now?"

Nana released his hand. He returned to his room without saying anything more and stayed there for the rest of the night.

The following day dragged. Nana had started it off by saying to Gerda, "I won't be home for dinner; I have to stay late at work. There are Christmas cards in the living room for the two of you to sign." Kai hadn't woken up until later than usual and slipped out the door before they had a chance to say more than, "Good morning."

Gerda felt restless throughout her workday. It was difficult to stay in one room long enough to finish a task and she frequently walked around the building under the excuse of looking for items she had misplaced. Eva's remarks on stories and the people in them scratched at Gerda's mind as she automatically clipped dead flowers and twisted vines out of the paths. Hadn't the other girl ever heard or read old stories before? She had taken it apart as though it was something completely foreign. Gerda shoveled the snow in the courtyard more vigorously than was necessary when she thought about Eva's dismissive tone of voice. If Eva didn't like stories, she shouldn't have come in.

She walked home alone. Kai didn't meet her every afternoon but it would have been nice to see him. He wasn't present when she got home either, even though on this day of the week he didn't have classes past mid-afternoon. She turned on the lights and heated up a bowl of leftover chicken and wild rice soup. She sat in front of the television as she ate alone but turned it off after she realized she was flipping through all the channels for the third time.

Kai returned home before Nana. Gerda sat on the couch while addressing envelopes. "You're supposed to sign these," she said and held up one of the cards that would be sent to relatives living far away.

Her brother flung himself into the rocking chair and scowled. "Why? We haven't seen any of them in years."

"It makes Nana happy."

"But why does she care? They probably wouldn't notice if we didn't send anything. And even if they did, they wouldn't do anything about it. When's the last time you heard from any of them? They don't call on our birthday; they didn't write when we finished high school; none of them except Nana cared about us when Mom and Dad left."

"Stop it. What's the matter with you?" she asked.

He scowled. "Nothing. I don't see why everybody has to keep thinking that something must be wrong. You can sign my name on the stupid cards if you care that much." He jerked his coat back on and stomped out of the house.

Gerda slumped down on the couch and watched the cards spill onto the floor.

# CHAPTER THREE

Only Gerda was at home when Kai came downstairs the next morning. She sat at the kitchen table, drinking a cup of coffee. He felt her watching him as he cut a fruit-studded slice of bread and nibbled at it. "What is it?"

"I was just wondering when you got in. I didn't hear you come back before I went to bed."

"I don't know, sometime late. I wasn't looking at a clock." The night had felt as though it would stretch on forever. Even after returning to the quiet house, he didn't look at a clock and didn't go to bed. Sleep hadn't seemed important at the time. Now a faint headache started to grow and the food was making him feel queasy instead of helping like it usually did. He forced himself to swallow.

"You better watch out," she warned. "I don't care if you want to stay out all night, every night with your girlfriend, but Nana's worried about you."

"There's nothing to be worried about."

"Tell her that. And you're lucky—she was angry, not worried the times when I stayed out all night."

He rolled his eyes. "That's because you were fifteen. And who says I was with Eva all night, anyway?"

"Please. It doesn't take a genius to figure that out." Gerda grinned, he thought partly at the memory of her late-night antics. "I see the way you look at her."

"Believe what you want." There didn't seem to be any point in arguing about what he might or might have not been doing. Besides, whatever he got up to didn't compare to Gerda's midnight driving lessons. He yawned and it was so loud in his ears that he missed her next words. "What did you say?"

"Are you still angry?"

"About what?"

"About last night." She played with a loose thread on her sleeve.

It took a little while for him to recall squabbling over something that seemed so unimportant now. Who cared about the stupid cards? It would have taken him five minutes to sign them and then he wouldn't have had to think about their uncaring relatives for another whole year. "It's nothing. I'll sign them later."

"Too late—I already did it for you."

"You took me seriously?" He didn't think he had sounded *that* bad. Gerda should have been able to tell that he was just venting. After all, she didn't care about their relatives any more than he did. His arguments last night weren't anything that she hadn't said long before. They were used to it.

"You sounded like you meant it." The solemn look disappeared from her face and she seemed just the tiniest big smug. "And don't feel too bad. I plan to make you sign the cards for both of us next Christmas."

"Wonderful." He pushed himself away from the kitchen counter with a groan. "I really don't want to go to class today."

"Then don't. You look like hell."

He made a face at her. "You always say the nicest things." But it was true—he felt like a washed-out version of his usual self, whereas Gerda was made up of warm colors and even still bore a trace of her summer tan. He dropped what remained of his breakfast in the trash can and started up the stairs.

Gerda followed. "Can I get you anything before I leave?"

"Do you really have to treat me like an invalid?" he asked in return as he opened his bedroom door.

"It's kind of fun—wow." She paused at the doorway. One of his most complicated jigsaw puzzles, made up of over a thousand pieces but only a few colors lay upon the floor. It was almost completed, except for a few small sections in the middle. The last time he had tried it, almost a week had gone by before he got that far.

He shrugged. "I didn't feel like sleeping and it was the only thing I could concentrate on."

"I can tell. So, is there anything you want?"

"Every book on astronomy from the library."

She swatted his shoulder. "Nice try, but I can't carry all of that. What else?"

"Spice cookies from the bakery."

"I'll get them on the way home from work. At least try to get some sleep, okay?"

"I will." Kai listened to the familiar sound of Gerda's boots tramping down the stairs and out the front door. He started to feel so tired now that the night was over and even with the thermostat turned low for the daytime, he still felt overheated. He peeled off the sweater over his t-shirt and lay down.

Something tapped outside. At first he thought it might be a woodpecker but the rhythm wasn't fast enough. He sat up and looked: Eva was leaning out of her open window and called out something that he couldn't hear. He opened his own window. "What did you say?"

"I was wondering why you're still at home."

"I don't feel good."

"That's too bad." She smiled and beckoned him with one hand. "Why don't you come over here? I'll make a fuss over you and you'll feel better in no time."

He felt lightheaded when he remembered kissing her under the stars and he knew he could be at her door within moments. He felt near-feverish now and the thought of her comfortingly cool hands was almost overwhelming. Yet something compelled him to shake his head. "I don't feel like going out."

"Why don't I visit you, then? I don't have anything special going on and you know you'll be bored by yourself. Why waste a whole day when you could do something interesting instead?"

"I'm not good company today. I think I just want to rest."

"If that's what you really want…" She started to turn away.

Her offer started to sound appealing. He didn't feel *too* sick—he'd gone to school feeling worse in the past. It might be nice to have somebody around. And after all, he could always finish the puzzle another time. "Wait! Yes, I do want you to come over."

Eva looked back at him and smiled. "For a moment, I thought you were going to let me down. I'll be there soon."

Kai forced himself to move downstairs quickly. It shouldn't have taken Eva long at all to arrive, but he stood there shivering at the open door for more than five minutes before she strolled over.

"I'm glad you changed your mind," she said as she approached. She didn't enter the house right away, instead remaining on the top porch step.

"You were right," he said, "I would have been bored. Was there anything special you wanted to do?"

"I had a few ideas about how to make you feel better." She smiled as she spoke and wound her arms around his neck.

"You did? I mean, good." The headache started to disappear as they spoke. Eva tugged her arms slightly closer and he took the hint, pushing back her fine hair and kissing her.

In between kisses she asked, "Are your grandmother or sister around?"

Kai smiled and shook his head. "I have the house to myself all day."

"Then you should take the chance to rest while it's quiet. You really

27

don't look well." She loosened her grip and stepped out of reach.

He stared at her. "What do you mean?"

"I thought of something else I need to do while you were trying to decide what you wanted."

"You're leaving already? Whatever it is, can't it wait a little while?"

"No, it can't. You should have taken me up on my offer the first time. Feel better soon." She turned her back on him and walked back to her house.

"Eva?" He called her name several times but she didn't answer before shutting her own front door. He stumbled back upstairs to his room. Her bedroom window was closed now and she had pulled the curtains shut. He watched for some time, but she never reappeared.

He left the window cracked open and reclined on his bed. The air in the room continued to cool and he began to relax. He listened to the wind and the trees, and thought very little. He tried to finish the puzzle but the colors swam before his eyes. It was so much more comfortable to lay still. He dozed off and on, looking at how much farther the sunlight had passed across the walls of his room each time he awoke from half-formed dreams.

Each time after waking up he emerged from bed long enough to look out the window, yet there was still no sign of Eva. Sometime during the afternoon the dream from several nights ago returned, in which he stood before the open window and felt frost growing over his body, even as he tried to walk away. He couldn't wake up until it began to cover his eyes.

He lay in bed, breathing hard. The clock on his nightstand read late afternoon and he could hear Nana's voice downstairs. The familiar sound reminded him of how Nana would stay home from work when either he or Gerda had been sick as children.

The cold air had felt soothing that morning but now Kai began to shiver. He shut the window. Something crunched beneath his foot when he left his bedroom. Sitting on the floor, slightly squashed, was a small packet wrapped in white paper. He smelled cardamom and cinnamon: the cookies that Gerda had promised. He could still feel the warmth from the bakery's oven.

He peeled away the seal and put one of the broken cookies to his lips. He gagged, doubling over the moment it sat on his tongue. Yet his stomach growled and he forced himself to eat. By the end of the packet, they tasted like the same cookies he had eaten every winter as long as he could remember. He licked the crumbs off of his fingers. Over the past few days it had become a habit to look in the hall mirror as he passed it. Today, as all the other times, nothing appeared wrong with his eye.

Nana was clattering about in the kitchen. Gerda lounged in the living room with a magazine and looked up as he flopped down onto the other end of the couch. "Did you get the cookies?"

"Yes. Thanks."

Nana came into the room, wiping her hands on a dish towel. "Gerda said you stayed home today. Are you feeling better?"

"I think so," he said. She touched his forehead and he shifted away.

"You look a little feverish. I hope you weren't planning on going out again tonight."

"No."

"Your girlfriend will think you've abandoned her," Gerda teased.

"She'll be fine," he said, thinking about Eva's words that morning. He wondered if he should have gone after her but she had sounded so absolutely certain when she said there was something she had to do that didn't involve him. She knew he was going to be home all day. If she had changed her mind, she would have been able to reach him.

Nana only said, "It'll be nice to have you to ourselves. Dinner's ready." The three of them walked to the kitchen together.

The next couple of weeks slipped past as the days grew shorter, minutes at dawn and dusk nibbled away. Gerda said that she enjoyed being able to watch the sunset through the conservatory's glass walls.

Kai became even more anxious for the semester to end. Even in the classes that were dull, he had usually managed to concentrate on a few fragments of interesting information. Now all that seemed unimportant. Periodically he calculated how many hours it would be before his time in the classrooms before vacation was over. Even during exams his thoughts drifted again and again to the snowflakes outdoors, and wondered if Eva would be available when he was finished. It felt easier to concentrate when he was with her. He tried to spend time with Nana and Gerda, but the house felt increasingly claustrophobic. Nothing they talked about seemed to interest him, and more and more as time went on, he found it easier to speak to them only when he had to. Whenever he escaped from Nana's concerned looks by retreating to his room, he shut the door and left the window open until fresh air filled the room.

The night of the winter solstice arrived. Kai and Gerda stood in front of Eva's house. The curtains were drawn but they could see light leaking past the edges of the fabric.

"Are you sure about this?" Gerda asked. "Eva probably has other plans."

"She'll be interested," Kai said.

"Are you sure? She might just think we're being silly, like she did that time she listened to Nana's story."

"She didn't think we were being silly and she always likes it when we do something outdoors. Besides, this is the only way we can get to the lake."

He raised his fist and knocked on the door.

Several moments passed before Eva's father opened the door. "Hello."

"Is Eva home?" Kai asked. He'd met her father once or twice during his visits, but the older man never had much to say.

Her father nodded and stepped back. "Just a minute."

They waited in the front hall as he went upstairs. Kai saw Gerda looking around with barely-disguised curiosity. "Expecting to see something strange?" he muttered.

"Just curious. I haven't been inside here for a long time."

"It's no different from our house."

"There's no Christmas tree." The living room was bare of any seasonal decorations; inside the house, it could have been any time of year.

He rolled his eyes. "Maybe her family waits until the last minute. There's still a few days left. Besides, there could be plenty of other reasons why they don't have a tree."

"Kai!" Eva exclaimed from the top of the stairs. As she descended, she said, "I was just thinking of you." When she reached the floor she briefly nodded to Gerda, but then looked only at Kai.

He smiled. "We have an invitation for you. Gerda and I were thinking of driving out to the lake. I know you haven't seen it yet and it's pretty this time of year. Do you want to come with us?"

"I'd love to." She squeezed his hand.

"What Kai hasn't mentioned is that we're also asking for a favor," Gerda said.

Eva raised an eyebrow. "A favor? I'm happy to help if I can, though I don't know what I can do for you."

"We need you to drive us to the lake," he said.

"Why not drive yourselves?"

"Our grandmother went out and she has the car."

Eva laughed. "That's easy. Give me a minute to get ready and I can take you anywhere you like."


The parking lot was closed for the night. Eva parked the car by the locked gate and they scrambled down the bank. The illumination from the roadside lights reached only a short distance and clouds masked any light from the sky. Eva held a flashlight that she used to light the way. Hard-packed snow coated the frozen sand and much of the lake shore had frozen, blurring the line where land ended and water began. A few small stones littered the ground and Gerda tossed one against the ice. It clattered for a few moments before coming to a halt somewhere in the darkness. Farther down the shore, seagulls huddled together as they slept.

"I know you can't see much right now," Kai was apologizing, "but it's still interesting."

"Don't worry about it. I'm glad you asked me to come here," Eva said.

"How do you like it here, now that it's been a few weeks?" Gerda asked.

"It's different from anywhere I've ever lived. I'm not sure how long I'll be staying, though."

Kai's gaze snapped away from the dark horizon. "You're leaving?"

"I like to travel," Eva said calmly. "It was interesting when my parents moved here but I'm starting to get restless again. You know what it's like." She laid a hand on Kai's shoulder.

"Where will you go?" She sent a sympathetic look in Kai's direction but didn't think he saw it in the dark.

"Here and there. I think I'll travel north, and see what kinds of winter celebrations I can find."

"Make sure to bring plenty of warm socks," Gerda said dryly.

"I don't think that will be a problem. Kai says the two of you have always lived here. Don't you ever feel like leaving?"

"No. I like my life here."

Eva nodded. "That's right, you have your greenhouse. It must be nice to be content doing the same thing every day."

Gerda bit her lip. Kai still hadn't said anything since Eva's revelation, and she cast about for a new topic. "People will be ice fishing soon," she said. She couldn't even hear any waves in the distance on this still night. No cars drove by and there weren't any homes close enough for human noise to break the stillness of the icy night. It almost felt as though they stood upon the edge of the world.

"The lake's not frozen enough yet but later you can watch them cutting holes in the ice. Some of them sit out there all day. You should stay long enough to see that, at least," Kai added.

"Don't forget at least one person falls in each year," Gerda said. "Nobody's died in years but that doesn't make it any less risky."

Kai rolled his eyes. "Usually it's because the person's drunk."

"Not always."

"So you don't have plans to become an ice fisherman?" Eva asked.

"Not on your life," Gerda told her.

"It's not a great risk," Eva said. "Such a little thing wouldn't stop me from doing something I liked."

Gerda laughed at the confidence in the other girl's voice. "Okay, then. I dare you to walk on the ice."

"That's easy." Eva strode to where the snow-covered sand merged into uneven ice. She stepped onto the lake without hesitation. The ice creaked below her feet.

Kai jumped to the edge of the beach at the first moan of the ice. He reached out a hand, but she shook her head and laughed. She walked out a body's length onto the lake before pausing. The space was so dark that from shore it was impossible to see how close she might be to the open water. Next she began to stride up and down the lake, not slipping once even though the ice was uneven and she didn't so much as glance at her feet in their slippery-soled shoes. "Satisfied?"

"All right, you win," Gerda said.

"Why don't you give it a try?" Eva looked at both twins as she spoke. "There's nothing to it."

Kai was the first one to join her. His feet skidded during the first few steps but he didn't fall. Walking as if a tightrope stretched before him, he reached Eva without mishap and took her hand. He laughed. "It *is* exciting. I wish we'd thought to try this sooner."

Gerda smiled wryly and shook her head. Kai was too busy looking at his girlfriend to notice and Eva typically didn't pay her much attention. She had thought of trying to walk on the lake almost every winter but the creaking ice always made her keep to the shore. Now she stepped forward.

It was easier than she had imagined at first. At any rate, it wasn't any worse than trying to make her way down a frozen sidewalk. And Kai was right—it was a little exciting. She was no more than a few feet away from him and Eva.

The ice had been groaning quietly since Eva first stepped out. Gerda stepped forward once more. The groan changed to a sharp crack and before she could jump back, the ice broke beneath her feet.

She plummeted down. There wasn't even time to shriek before she landed.

Kai dropped Eva's hand and skidded forward. "Are you all right?"

Gerda shook as she caught her breath. "I think so." The lake was no deeper than her calves where she stood but it was colder than anything she had ever experienced. It felt like the dark water was made up of hands grabbing at her legs. The shards of broken ice poked her legs. She couldn't stop wondering how much deeper the water would have been if she had gone even a little farther before falling in.

He reached forward and pulled her out. The ice didn't break again and they were able to step away from the jagged hole. She laughed weakly. "So much for easy."

Eva shrugged as she joined them. "You must have landed on a weak spot. You said that at least one fisherman falls in each year."

Gerda began to shake. Her clammy pants stuck to her legs and water puddled in her shoes. "Let's go back."

Kai squeezed Eva's hand. "We can come back tomorrow," he promised.

After they returned to the car he stretched out in the back seat and closed his eyes, leaving only the front passenger seat available for Gerda. Eva steered the car onto the narrow road with its deep ditches on either side. Gerda fiddled with the temperature knobs but only a weak stream of barely-warm air emerged from the vents. It wasn't even close to what she needed to thaw her frozen feet. "Doesn't the heat work any better than this?"

Eva looked away from the road long enough to poke at the dials but the temperature didn't improve. "I've been having trouble with the heat in this car for months."

"Haven't you taken it to a mechanic?"

"Nobody's been able to fix it."

Gerda glared at the air vents. She slipped off her ruined shoes and massaged her feet. The skin felt numb but she forced her toes to keep moving. At least they weren't too far from home. "I can't believe it's not even one-thirty."

"Are you in a hurry for morning?"

"Tonight's the winter solstice. It's the reason why Kai and I wanted to go to the lake. We've been doing it every year for a long time now."

"I know it's the solstice. Why didn't Kai say anything?"

Gerda shrugged. "Maybe he thought you'd laugh."

"I never laugh about anything to do with winter," Eva promised. "It's my favorite season.

"Anyway, it's not as though this is the only time we go there all year. But I do like to stay up all night. You know how it's easy to stay awake when you aren't trying to, but the moment you make a plan of it, time drags on forever? That's how it feels right now."

"And you aren't going to sleep until you see proof that the sun has come back?"

"If I can. My feet will keep me up for a while, anyway." Gerda twisted around and looked into the backseat. "Not Kai, though. He's already asleep." He lay slightly curled up so that his long limbs fit onto the seat. His glasses were folded and hooked onto his coat collar. She saw him frown a little and fold his arms tighter across his chest.

She turned back to face the road. Black roads and black trees weighted with snow met her gaze. "But sleeping is good. Maybe he'll be in a better mood when he wakes up."

"Problems?"

"He's been in a bad mood lately."

"I haven't noticed anything wrong when he's with me," Eva said.

"I'm sure you haven't."

The narrow road stretched alongside the lake for some distance before it twisted back towards the town. So late at night, the body of water looked like nothing more than black space occasionally disturbed by drifts of snow and ice. The headlights illuminated only a short distance of the road before them. Eva drove with confidence, one hand alone directing the steering wheel while the other rested on her lap. Gerda remembered seeing cars damaged by collisions with deer and tried not to hold her breath.

"You might want to watch out for that curve ahead; it tends to be icy."

Eva drove through the area without batting an eye as Gerda tightened her hold on the door handle. "Don't worry. I've had a lot of practice with winter roads."

"I believe it. Weren't you afraid of falling into the water earlier?" Gerda asked. She still couldn't stop shivering. The fall had scared her almost more than the water had hurt her skin.

"The ice felt strong where I was. Besides, I've done that plenty of times. It's exhilarating to walk on something that would sink beneath you any other time of year. You should try it again sometime. I'd be happy to help you."

"I don't think so."

Eva chuckled at Gerda's dry tone. "Maybe Kai and I will be able to change your mind. I'm just relieved that winter is finally here."

"It's been the same outdoors for weeks, you know. There'll be cold weather after the first day of spring, too. The snow isn't different just because we cross off one more day on the calendar."

Eva looked away from the road long enough to give Gerda a rare smile. "Yes, it is. Now it's *real* winter. I can tell the difference when the snow's falling and there's ice on the trees. Winter's clean."

Comments about slushy streets and muddy snowballs sat on Gerda's tongue but she pressed her lips together. And though she never would have said it aloud, part of her agreed with Eva's strong opinions. She knew that the official change of a season didn't make a difference to how the weather behaved, but somehow those first few days following the solstice always felt magical. She turned away from Eva's satisfied face and looked out her window. The hum of the engine was the only sound between them.

No other people were out and about when the car drove through the streets of Vasa. Eva pulled the car into her driveway and Gerda shook Kai's shoulder until he woke up. He said goodnight to Eva as she put her shoes back on, then they turned away to their own home.

Lead-colored clouds lined the sky on the following day. Gerda had remained awake until dawn, sitting by an eastern window with red and green and white candles that burned brightly as a clock ticked the minutes away. Filling the bath tub with warm water and submerging her feet until the skin changed from white to pink helped to pass the time. She'd had to reheat the water three times before her shivering stopped. Some years she had been greeted by a brilliant blue-and-gold sunrise. This year it was difficult to tell when the day officially began: the sky merely lightened from black to gray and the streetlights blinked out.

After the disappointing start to the day she sat in the kitchen with Nana, sluggish from staying awake so long and considering spending the rest of the day in bed. Nana laughed at Gerda's slow movements. She seemed to be waiting for Gerda to fall asleep at the table any moment. Even the birds were plain today: they watched the brown-and-white sparrows bully each other at the bird feeder in the small backyard, but no scarlet cardinals or striking chickadees appeared to join the sparrows' company.

"Did you have a good night?" Nana asked. "I tried waiting up for the two of you after I got home, but I was just too tired."

Gerda rested her chin on her folded arms and shrugged. "Parts of it were okay."

"It's a good thing you went out and had fun yesterday." Nana shook her head a little as she paged through the newspaper. The headline on the front page blared, "First Blizzard of the Season Approaches." "There's supposed to be a nasty storm coming in before dark."

"I'll probably sleep through it." Gerda smiled halfheartedly.

Kai stumbled downstairs. He was dressed but there were circles below his eyes and his hair hadn't been combed. He walked past the others without speaking and drank a glass of water.

Nana smiled, although to Gerda it seemed more of a grimace. "Enjoying sleeping in during your winter break?"

"I wasn't sleeping."

"Oh. Were you reading, then?" Her smile became a touch more genuine. "I remember when I used to have to check every night to make sure you'd gone to sleep instead of finishing off another book."

"I wasn't reading, either. Can you just leave me alone?"

Any trace of a smile vanished. Nana's back stiffened. "I will not 'leave you alone'. It's my job to care about you and I've had enough of your moods lately. If something's wrong, tell us. But if there isn't and you keep acting this way, you'll be grounded."

Kai stared at her. "I'm too old for that!"

"Not while you're under my roof. Think about that and decide how you want to behave." With one final glare, Nana strode upstairs.

Kai sat down on the floor, his back braced against the cabinets. "She just threatened to ground me. Like a fourteen-year-old who got caught sneaking in from a party."

Gerda sat down next to him. "And you've always been the good twin, too."

He grabbed her elbow. "Don't make fun of me!"

"Stop that!" She pulled away. "Nana's right; either shut up or stop being so annoying. What's the matter with you?"

"I don't know. I'm sorry." He attempted to smile but it lasted only a moment. "Do you want to do something today?"

35

"I would have thought you'd want to go out with Eva. You promised to go back to the lake with her," Gerda said.

"It'll be better if I stayed home and pretend to behave for Nana. Eva will understand."

Of all the many words that Gerda thought could describe Eva, "understanding" was not on the list. But she merely bit her tongue and nudged him. "See? You're sounding better already. Nana won't ground you. Do you want me to make some hot chocolate? It'll help."

"You always did think every problem can be fixed by making something good to drink."

"It's not a bad idea. At least *my* solution is delicious."

Kai remained seated on the floor while she fixed hot chocolate for both of them. She snuck glances at him while she heated milk on the stove and fetched chocolate-covered peppermint sticks that she dropped into a pair of mugs. At any other time she would have been comfortable with the silence, but that day his sudden meekness was almost more alarming than his bad temper.

After the scent of cocoa filled the kitchen and she divided the drinks, they moved into the living room where Kai paced about and Gerda settled onto the couch. She picked up the remote and pretended to watch television. She remembered to keep her head turned toward the screen, even though she constantly watched her brother out of the corner of her eye. Kai drank his hot chocolate in several gulps but continued to clutch the empty mug in his hands. After several rounds of pacing he sat in the rocking chair. Yet even then he couldn't quite stay still, and kept the chair moving back and forth. He adjusted his glasses often.

"How was the hot chocolate?" she asked when she couldn't pretend any longer.

"Good."

She tried again. "It's nice to have you at home. It feels like you've been gone a lot lately, since Eva moved in."

"I was just next door."

"But it feels like your mind is always someplace else. Even when you're here, I can tell when you're not paying attention. I miss you."

Kai opened his mouth but dropped his mug onto the floor before he could respond. The chocolate silt from the bottom of the cup sank into the carpet. He yanked off his glasses and rubbed his eyes.

Gerda knelt next to the chair and grabbed his hands. "What's wrong?"

"Don't touch me!"

She didn't let go. His hands felt as cold as if they had been buried in snow.

Kai jerked out of her grasp and sprang up from the chair. He shoved his glasses back on. Gerda remained sitting, leaning on the rocking chair's arm.

"I'm fine," he said.

"Are not. Why don't you tell me what's wrong? You used to tell me everything."

"I still tell you things." The frenzy that had been in his voice earlier now settled into a dreadfully quiet and calm tone.

"Not like before."

She could practically see him deciding to ignore this comment, like he had done other times when he didn't want to talk about something. "I'm fine," he said at last. "I know you think something's wrong, but it's not. And you don't have to try to fix anything, because nothing's broken."

"You never could get away with lying to me, remember?" she asked. "I know there's something you're not telling me."

Kai smiled. On the surface the expression looked the same as ever, but something about his smile now struck Gerda as hopeless. "Everything's all right." He walked past her and up the stairs.

There was a throw pillow within reach. She grabbed it and punched the soft fabric until she stopped wanting to shake Kai by the shoulders. Moving slowly, she put the mugs in the sink and cleaned up the mess. She made her way upstairs. When she knocked on Kai's door, he didn't answer. She tried the doorknob but he had locked it.

Gerda retreated to her own room and lay down on the unmade bed. She found small comfort in familiar things: photographs of Kai and Nana on the dresser; clothes draped over a chair; scarlet geraniums, pink miniature roses, and an ivory amaryllis in pots on the window seat. She could hear Kai pacing across the hall, as even and unceasing as the ticking of a clock. The unhappy rhythm and the exhaustion that had been growing since last night sent her into sleep.

"Gerda, wake up."

Kai was shaking her arm. "What is it?" she asked and pushed tangled hair out of her eyes. Looking at her clock, she saw that hours had passed until the afternoon was far gone. The last of the weak daylight was vanishing and the sky outside had turned almost black. The wind had picked up while she slept and now sleet rasped against the frosty window.

"I'm sorry," he said and let go.

"What are you talking about?" she asked. He hadn't turned the light on, and she had to fumble with the bedside lamp before she could see that he was wearing his coat and boots. "What are you up to now?"

"I'm sorry I was awful and I made you worry, but I can't stop. Sometimes I thought I was going crazy but it was this—it makes everything horrible and it *hurts*, and I couldn't think about anything else." He pressed something sharp and small into her hand.

"What is it?" She began to open her hand but caught only a small glimpse of something that gleamed before he closed her fingers around it. The sharp edges pricked at her skin.

"Don't look. It twists everything. I've been seeing the world like that for weeks."

Gerda had never heard him ramble like this, not even when he had been on painkillers after having his appendix removed years ago. She had laughed herself sick at his random conversation then but there was nothing funny now. She saw that his left eye was blood shot and the skin around it swollen. "What did you *do*?"

"I had to get it out. I think I got it all but it's too late." His hands shook. "She's calling me and I can't stay away. You have to keep that away from me."

"Who's calling you? You're not making any sense." He was scaring her more and more every moment, but she couldn't turn away.

"I'm sorry. I just wanted to say goodbye. Tell Nana I love her." He squeezed her hand one last time and ran from the room.

"Wait!" Gerda shoved the small object into her pocket without looking at it. She ran after him, clattering down the stairs. She shoved her feet into the first shoes she found and yanked on her coat.

Nana appeared at the top of the stairs. "What's going on?"

"I don't know. Kai's acting strange. I'm going after him," Gerda said.

"Wait for me," Nana said. She started down the stairs but Gerda ran outside. The door slammed itself shut behind her. A gust of wind knocked her down as she descended the slippery porch steps and she landed in a snow bank.

She heard Nana pounding on the other side of the door but it didn't open. Gerda fell again as she tried to stand up. A crust of ice hidden in the snow scraped her chin. She saw a faint smear of blood on the white surface as she pushed herself up.

The full force of the storm Nana had expected that morning now arrived. Branches scraped against houses and bits of trees littered the ground. Gerda narrowed her eyes against the wind. The gale blew her hair into her face. The street lights winked out one by one and she heard the glass break.

Kai was out of sight but the wind hadn't blown his footprints away. They led straight to Eva's house. Gerda ran through the open door.

The storm's noise vanished when she closed the door behind herself, yet she could still see the trees waving outside. The sudden silence was more unnerving than listening to the shrieking winds.

The inside of the house was a disaster. Every window was broken from the outside as though the wind had punched them in with giant fists. The glass crunched below her shoes. The larger shards had left deep gouges in the walls and one long piece still stuck there, close to her face. Snow flew through the broken windows.

All the furniture in the living room was overturned and the couch cushions were ripped apart. The room was such a mess that it took Gerda a minute to realize the worst part: the bodies of a man and woman lay in that room. They were tangled up in the overturned furniture and glass from the broken windows was scattered over them. A small shower of it fell from the man's clothing when Gerda stumbled against his leg. His eyes stared up at her. She jumped back against a wall. A partial shriek escaped before she could shove her fist against her mouth.

She slid along the wall, unable to look away from those dead eyes. When she reached the corner she saw a trail of snow clumps leading up the stairs. It took several tries before she could turn her back on the two bodies. She forced herself up each step, gripping the banister so hard that her nails scored the wood. The upstairs hall was also quiet. The other rooms were similar disasters but she saw no other bodies. Only one door at the end of the hall was shut. She turned the ice-cold knob with both hands.

Kai stood before a tall mirror with his back to her. Instead of his reflection, she saw snow falling onto a flat land divided by a frozen river. The land seemed to stretch on forever and little light shone from the colorless sky. He showed no sign of hearing her entrance.

Eva stood next to him. She had also been looking into the mirror with one hand raised toward it when Gerda stumbled in. She turned around and smiled, showing teeth as white as her skin. "Hello, Gerda. Care to say goodbye to your brother? You almost missed us."

Gerda backed away from that smile. Eva still possessed the same body as last night but she no longer seemed human. "What are you?"

"The Snow Queen. You should have a talk with your grandmother. Kai said that she's told you hundreds of stories but it seems that she never mentioned me. Much of this is her fault, really—if she had warned you, you would have been smart enough to keep out of my way."

Kai hadn't moved as they spoke. "What did you do to him?" Gerda asked.

"I haven't done anything. Kai has a piece of my mirror inside him and I want it back. I'm bringing him home and he's going to fix my mirror. When he's finished, I will be able to make winter last forever," the Snow Queen said.

Gerda clung to one bit of logic in the growing nightmare. "It can't be one season forever. That's impossible."

"Nothing is impossible for me."

The recent sight of death downstairs distracted her from the idea of never-ending winter. She asked, "What did you do to your parents?"

The Snow Queen stepped away from Kai. She stood far too close but Gerda couldn't raise a hand to push her away. "I didn't need them anymore and they were in the way. I know you're a fool but surely even you aren't stupid enough to believe that they were my true family." She rested her fingers on Gerda's shoulder. The freezing touch shot through her layers of clothing and into her bones. The Snow Queen put her lips to Gerda's ear and spoke in a murmur as though they were close friends. "I'll tell you a secret: I killed their real daughter, too. She lies deep under ice, just as pretty as the day she died."

Gerda believed every word. "Don't take him away," she managed to say though her body ached with the cold. It became harder to stand with every moment.

The Snow Queen tipped her head a little and a considering look appeared on her face. "Beg."

Gerda didn't know whether the Snow Queen referred to letting Kai go or removing her burning cold touch. "Please. We never did anything to you. Kai *loved* you. Don't take him away." It became harder to speak as the Snow Queen's grip tightened. "I don't…I don't know what you want me to say."

"What a pity. I thought you would be more interesting." The Snow Queen let go and returned to the mirror.

Gerda stepped forward. "But what about Kai? I just—"

"I never promised to give him back. Or do anything else, for that matter. I've seen other humans do a far better job of begging, by the way, but you might improve with practice. You were wrong about another thing as well—Kai still loves me and he will forever."

"You can't do this." Gerda moved closer. "I'll find you, Kai. I promise." He showed no response but she forced herself to believe that he heard her words.

The Snow Queen pointed at her. "Remember how cold you were when you fell into the lake? Compared to what I can do, that would feel like nothing. I'm granting you the favor of your life, which is more than most humans get. Take it and stay away from us."

Gerda stood very still. The snow blowing in through the broken windows clung to her dry lips. She watched the Snow Queen set one hand on Kai's shoulder and kiss him.

The Snow Queen returned her attention to Gerda and lifted her other hand. A burst of wind slammed Gerda against the far wall and she slid to the floor.

The Snow Queen wrapped her arms around Kai and walked through the mirror.

# CHAPTER FOUR

The images in the mirror faded until it reflected only the bedroom. Gerda pulled herself to her feet and pressed against it as the Snow Queen had. Nothing happened. She shook the mirror until the glass trembled in its frame but it remained solid.

She avoided looking into the living room when she went back downstairs. Outdoors the wind had stopped but the snow continued to fall. Unlike the Snow Queen's touch, this new snow melted as it landed on Gerda's face.

It looked like Nana had just managed to force the door of their house open when Gerda returned. Her grandmother stood at the top of the steps and her face paled when she saw Gerda alone. "Where's Kai?"

Gerda looked up at her. "The Snow Queen has him."

Nana sagged against the doorframe. "That girl was her?"

For the first time that day, Gerda felt angry instead of scared and confused. Nana had known. The Snow Queen had said that Nana knew but she didn't warn them, and now Kai was gone. "Why didn't you say anything? Even *she* thinks you should have warned us. You could have protected us!"

"It was a story I didn't want you to hear." Nana reached out to her. "Come inside. Don't let the Snow Queen drive you to freezing yourself just because you're mad at me."

Indoors, the lights were out as well as the heating. Nana kindled a fire in the fireplace and lit candles throughout the living room. Gerda wrapped herself up in an afghan and tried to find comfort in the small flames that glowed against the night outside. For a moment she allowed herself to pretend that it was no more than any normal winter storm. The candles made interesting shadows and Kai would tell supposedly true stories about ghosts from books he had read while Nana made popcorn over the fire—

41

but no. Kai was gone.

"She killed them—the people who were pretending to be her parents. She froze them to death," Gerda said. Nana almost dropped a candle at the words. Gerda pulled the afghan tighter and kept talking. "She murdered their real daughter, too."

Nana sat next to her. "Did they know who she was and couldn't fight, or did they think she really was their daughter?"

"I don't know. Now you need to tell me about the Snow Queen. Why didn't you say anything? You told us stories about everything I can think of but you couldn't be bothered to mention her once?" Gerda demanded.

Any other time Nana would have told Gerda to mind her manners but now— "I didn't want to believe in her." Nana watched the flames winding around the logs in the fireplace as she spoke. "And if she was real, I didn't want to know. I always thought the creatures in stories could exist and I think I saw some of them when I was little, but I never wanted to think about the Snow Queen."

"She said she has a mirror that can make it always be winter and she needs Kai to fix it. And she said that he has a piece of it in him. Maybe that's why he was changing. Remember when we thought a snowflake got into his eye? It was really the mirror. She controls winter, right?"

"She *is* winter. She's the one who creates it every year." Nana rested her forehead in her hands.

"Do other people ever see her?"

"I didn't. And I never heard of her pretending to be human before. The most I ever heard about her at once was during one winter, when I was seven or eight. A man from the farm next to the one I grew up on disappeared during a storm. He'd left the house to check on the cows in the barn but he didn't return. That part wasn't so strange. A few people would go missing every year, when they were foolish enough to go out during a blizzard without something tying them to the house. It was awful but not strange. I remember the snow came up past the windows. The blizzard went on so hard that we couldn't look for him for several days. There wasn't a trail by that time, of course. My parents and the other neighbors searched, but they couldn't find anything. Nobody told me that he was probably dead but I could guess what they were thinking.

"He came home a couple weeks later. He wasn't an old man but all his hair had turned white while he was away. For the next few days he rambled constantly and barely ate. My mother didn't want me to see him but I was curious. I ran over whenever I could get away from chores.

"I was there with my father when the man finally seemed to wake up. He said that the Snow Queen had driven up in a sled when he was leaving the barn. She reached out a hand and he sat in the sled at her feet. He said it sounded like wind rattling through icicles when she talked. She held up a mirror and he could see winter stretching all around the world. But he said she lost interest in him before long. She drove the sled faster and faster until he fell out and she left him behind. He didn't recognize anything so he just started walking until he found his way back to the farm."

"So she let him go because she got bored with him. It probably saved his life," Gerda said.

Nana sighed. "Probably. I remember that for years afterward, his wife said that he talked about the Snow Queen's mirror in his sleep. He would even ask her to take him back. They had to stop him from wandering off every winter after that. I think they even locked the doors to keep him inside."

Gerda tried to imagine being so far under the Snow Queen's spell that a person would search for her, even though he knew he would slowly freeze to death. She shuddered. "Tell me about the mirror."

"The way the stories go, the Snow Queen was once given a mirror that twisted everything it reflected: anything beautiful believed itself to be ugly, truth turned into lies, and so on. It could also cover the world in winter forever but the mirror broke before she had the chance to do that. The pieces were scattered all over the world. Some of them landed in people's hearts and after that, they saw only evil in the world. I thought it was just an explanation for why some people can be cruel. The stories also say that if she ever fixed the mirror, winter would never end. Don't worry—we'll think of some way to get Kai back." Nana put her arms around Gerda as they huddled before the fire but the look on her face showed little hope.

They sat quietly for several minutes. At last Nana shook herself and stood up. "We can at least do something about the neighbors. They deserve that much."

Gerda sighed. "Like what? You can't arrest somebody who vanishes into a mirror."

"It's still not right to leave them lying there. And better to tell the police now, before somebody else finds out and starts asking questions."

"All right." Gerda picked up the phone but shook her head once she listened to it. "The phones aren't working, either. I guess the Snow Queen was even more annoyed than we thought." She laughed darkly at the thought of the Snow Queen thinking to affect something as normal as telephones during her grand storm. "I'll walk to the station and tell somebody."

"But you've barely slept and it's a disaster out there. I can go."

"I can still walk there and back faster than you. You're the one who knows about the Snow Queen—you think of something we can do." Gerda couldn't bring herself to say, *You're old and I don't want to lose you as well.*

"It's dangerous," Nana said. "There's too much snow and ice."

Gerda buried her face in her grandmother's shoulder. "I couldn't stop the Snow Queen before, even when I had the chance to find out what he was going through. I have to do *something* now; I can't just sit still until we have a plan."

Nana kissed the top of her head. "We'll save him, I promise." She stood up. "Get ready, then. If we're lucky, I'll have remembered something we can use against the Snow Queen by the time you get home."

Gerda pulled on wool socks and layers of clothing with shaking hands. She *was* tired; she remembered hitting her head when she Snow Queen tossed her against the wall and the sleep she had gotten during the day hadn't been enough after her vigil the night before. Part of her wanted to lie back down and pull the covers over her head. It would be so easy to pretend that Kai was still home and that he would roll his eyes at the idea that the Snow Queen was real. Gerda shook away these thoughts. She finally pulled out the object Kai had shoved into her hand: his fragment of the Snow Queen's mirror. Despite her curiosity, she remembered his frenzied voice and didn't look into it. In one of her dresser drawers she found a tiny box that had once held a pair of earrings. She dropped the shard into the box and stuffed the box into her pocket.

Nana waited by the door with a flashlight. "Be careful out there."

"It's a ten-minute walk," Gerda said.

"In the summer. And I wouldn't put it past the Snow Queen to have left some traps out there."

"I'll be back before you'll have time to worry."

"I'm already worried," Nana said.

Gerda kissed her grandmother's cheek. She paused in the doorway long enough to say, "Wish me luck," and stepped into winter.

She made her way through Vasa, the whole town dark and silent after the Snow Queen's blizzard. The glow from her flashlight bounced off of the snow banks before her. It looked as though everybody else had decided to stay indoors while the snow continued falling. She was grateful—asking how others were doing and pretending that she had only normal storm damage to deal with would have been too much. Gerda wondered if anybody else had seen something they didn't want to believe, had seen the Snow Queen's terrible beauty through gaps in the frost on their windows.

Debris was scattered all over Vasa. With every street, Gerda passed dozens of broken branches, downed power lines frayed where they had snapped, trash cans tumbled far from where they belonged, and gutters ripped from houses. As she walked she heard the sharp cracks of thick tree branches breaking under the weight of snow and ice.

She heard few other sounds. All the winter-hardy birds—sparrows, black-capped chickadees, and scarlet cardinals—remained hidden in their shelters of trees and bushes. There were only the sounds of her shuffling walk and her heavy breath below the wide scarf. Even though the walk took a long time, she never saw anybody else tramping through the snow.

Due to the treacherous footing, the short distance had stolen over a half-hour of the night. Wading through the snow drifts was slow going and her legs had started to ache within the first block, but she didn't stop. Despite the deep wind chill, sweat trickled down her back.

The storm began again as she passed the park. Gerda yelped and bent over to shield her face. The wind shook the world around her. It sent snow spinning up from the ground to sting at her eyes. The temperature dropped even farther and the hood of her coat was blown off of her head. She looked up when the wind changed direction.

A face formed above her in the clouds. Two gaps appeared that made eyes out of the black sky. In a voice that sounded as though it spoke directly next to her ear, the Snow Queen said, "Turn back. You know what I will do to you." Then the voice blew away and the clouds were only clouds once more.

Gerda's shaking hands dropped the flashlight. She searched but it had sunk deep into a snow bank. The wind blew at her from all directions now. It felt like it was trying to squeeze the breath out of her.

She began to walk again, though she could barely see. Almost nothing looked familiar. A handful of sleety snow scoured her face and she gave up on her destination. The police station could wait until she had found a bit of shelter and the storm ended. She grew so tired that she would have happily lain down beneath a bush.

She crashed into something firm. When she opened her eyes she saw that her feet had brought her to the conservatory; it was the iron door handle that had caught her in the side. The wind screamed in her ears as she fumbled with the key that was always in her pocket. Eventually the lock clicked and she slipped inside.

The door crashed shut behind her. She had passed nothing but destruction during her walk, but somehow nothing in this glass building was broken. Even the heating still worked.

In the warm entrance hall she could feel the prickings that signaled the painful thawing of her fingers and toes. At this point, it could be frostbite. Before the snow embedded in her clothing could melt, she walked straight to the courtyard and didn't stop until the toes of her boots touched the edges of the koi pond. She could still hear the wind but in this space it soared by harmlessly above the roof. The ice on the pond's surface was lumpy and several inches thick now, filled with bubbles like ancient panes of glass. The circulation pipes at one end of the pond kept the nearby water moving so that a small space would remain free of ice and the fish could be fed throughout the winter. Sheltered as they were, the fish now spent most of their time hibernating at the bottom. If she watched long enough, she imagined she could see their gilded bodies hovering and their fins drifting like seaweed.

Gerda couldn't bring herself to venture out again into the storm yet. She put her hand into the pocket of her coat and drew out the little box. She hesitated for a moment before revealing the bit of mirror.

From a distance she could almost imagine that it looked harmless, merely a piece of glass smaller than her pinky nail. But then it glimmered from some inside light and glittered like a knife ready to chop. Warily, she raised it up. She remembered Kai's warning but told herself that she needed to know what he had been going through. Soon it was before her face. She held the mirror close and peered into it.

Cold slammed through her body and forced it rigid. She could feel every part of her ache as she stood in the middle of an eternal blizzard. Through that tiny mirror-window she saw Vasa made into a ghost town. Roofs caved in from the weight of snow, trees were uprooted, and ice coated the streets. People lay in their beds and died when the cold caught them while they were sleeping. Everybody was covered in frost and looked obscenely peaceful.

She hissed and snapped her hand out of that cold spell. She retained just enough control of her body to avoid dropping the piece of mirror in the snow where it would have remained hidden like her flashlight. She pressed her free hand against against her heart, wanting to feel it beating beneath the layers of clothing. The terror faded. Refusing to let her gaze be drawn in again, she returned the fragment to its box and shoved it into her pocket.

She returned her attention to the pond and knelt beside it, her entire body slumped from exhaustion. She swayed and dreamily gazed upon the dusting of snow across the ice. Something moved beneath the surface that didn't appear to be the scarlet-and-orange body of a fish. Gerda leaned forward and wiped the snow away.

She felt as though she was looking through the ice and deep into the water. Currents rippled and the image of a crystal sled swam up through the darkness. Even though the picture was small, she could see Kai sitting beside the Snow Queen as they raced along. They vanished when she leaned closer.

Gerda rose to her feet, the lethargy wiped from her mind. She couldn't travel through a mirror like the Snow Queen but perhaps there were other ways. Her memory swept through fragments of Nana's stories in which heroes walked to the bottoms of lakes without drowning, or traveled upon underground rivers, or lived with mermaids in the depths of an ocean. Perhaps the Snow Queen wasn't the only true thing in Nana's tales.

She took a deep breath and jumped through the ice.

# CHAPTER FIVE

Kai stood in darkness. The air all around him was black, as well as whatever lay beneath his feet. In the distance he could hear a sound that might be waves and it reminded him of being at the beach with Gerda and Ev—the Snow Queen less than a full day ago, back when he didn't know anything. But here instead of a beach, there were only the sounds of shifting water and groaning ice.

Now the Snow Queen stood next to him. She shone in the darkness, pale light glowing from her hair and skin. The light grew until he could see that they stood on ice-encrusted snow. Still in a daze, he watched as she raised her hands. Ice began to build up on the ground. It grew quickly, clear as diamonds with no imperfections. The Snow Queen remained silent as her work progressed with no acknowledgment of his presence. Some small part of his mind clamored that he should take this opportunity to run away, but a greater part of him craved her attention and was willing to stand there for an eternity if need be until she looked at him once more.

The ice shifted and carved itself until he could see that it was forming a sleigh. Even its runners were crafted from ice, looking as though they ought to be too delicate to bear the weight of such a massive object. Now the Snow Queen made a sharp gesture with her hand. Gusts of wind blew loose snow together in the air until it was packed into two pure white, enormous swans leashed to the front of the sleigh.

The Snow Queen smiled with satisfaction and climbed into the sleigh. Only then did she look down at him. "It's time, Kai." She extended her hand and he took it without hesitation, despite knowing now what she was.

He sat down on the sleigh's broad bench and leaned against its high back. The swans flapped their wings and the sleigh lifted into the air, without having to run across the ground first. They were high in the air within moments. When he looked down he could see scraps of white that must be waves rippling in rows toward an unseen shore.

One of the Snow Queen's arms loosely curled around his waist, while her other hand dangled over the sleigh's side and she dabbled her fingers in the air currents. She seemed so utterly relaxed that it took a minute for him to realize that one careless move would send him plummeting through the air into that dark water. For one moment, he considered doing it on purpose. Yet he knew that the Snow Queen wouldn't risk losing him, not after she had taken so much trouble to catch him. Now that he was closer to the sleigh he could see delicate, scrolling designs carved into the ice; the part of Kai's mind not dulled by the cold searched for the overall pattern. They had risen through a layer of clouds and now the sky before them was well-lit by the moon.

"Where are we?" he asked. They were moving so fast that the freezing air streamed past in a strong wind.

"Far away from that town of yours," she said, responding as easily as if they had been chatting for hours. She smiled as she took a deep breath. "It feels wonderful to have left all those filthy cities and towns behind. There's nothing like a good winter's night. We'll have to hurry home; I spent so much time getting you ready to return with me that winter's already begun. I have a lot of work to do and so do you. I must admit though, you made the time pass quicker than I expected."

Kai watched her. She still seemed somewhat like Eva: her voice was almost the same and he couldn't easily find any differences in her body. Yet now she seemed older. She moved differently and her eyes seemed to see things that his couldn't. The Snow Queen was slowly shedding her human guise like the layers of a snake's skin.

He shivered. The air had grown so cold that his coat and gloves offered almost no protection. He looked down out of the sleigh once more and realized that he could no longer see anything past the clouds. The wind plucked the wool scarf from his neck and whipped it away into the night.

"My poor Kai!" she said as he shuddered and she pulled him closer. She sat bare-armed in that freezing wind but a length of white fur lay folded at their feet; she picked this up and wrapped it around him before sliding her hands up along his neck. "Even your eyelashes look nearly frozen. We'll have to fix that."

She removed his glasses and kissed his eyelids. Kai took a deep breath and found that he could open his eyes all the way. Once more he felt the blood moving through his hands and feet. She smiled when he began to shift out of that frozen position. Still holding his face between her pale hands, she leaned forward and kissed his mouth.

Kai grew cold, colder than he had ever been, even more than when he had fallen into an icy pond as a child. Even as he shuddered, Kai leaned towards the Snow Queen. But she ended the kiss. She had not closed her eyes during it and, leaning back, she murmured, "Enough. You make it too easy for me to forget how fragile you humans are."

Though he still quivered with cold, Kai was able to move easier. He couldn't understand why. During past winters, it had always been harder to move when the cold bit at his limbs and numbed his face. But now he felt as though he could run across a field thick with untouched snow.

"How did you do that?" he asked.

"You're mine now. You'll need cold to live, not heat." She bit her pale lip, for a moment looking like the girl he had thought he knew. "You're still too warm but even I can't make it happen all at once. If I forget and do too much before your body is ready, you'll be lost. And then I'll never have my mirror."

Kai didn't want to think about what might happen to him if the Snow Queen was careless. He said, "I still don't understand why you need a mirror."

"Not *a* mirror, *the* mirror." Her voice seemed a mockery of the tones Nana used to tell stories. "Many winters ago, there was a human who spent time with a group of goblins and eventually they accepted him as one of their own. He had a gift for crafting things, particularly from metal and glass. I visited the goblins often in those days. The human—I don't remember his name—had always been fond of winter and he wanted to impress me."

"So he made this mirror for you?" Kai asked.

"Eventually. He had many failures along the way, but they were entertaining to watch and still caused some mischief. He did manage to impress me in the end: he made a mirror that could change the nature of what it reflected. It made everything it reflected cold and pure, just the way I like it. I can make an excellent winter on my own but they always end when the other seasons start to clamor for their turn. With the mirror, I could have kept control. But it broke and the pieces were lost. I've been looking for them ever since, and you have the last one."

He frowned. "But how did you know to come for me? You arrived in Vasa on the same day that the mirror got into my eye."

"I hadn't planned that, actually. I knew that the last piece of my mirror was in your town but not the exact location. The house was merely a refuge in case the fragment took a long time to locate. *You* were a pleasant surprise." The Snow Queen stroked her thumb across the back of his hand. "I hadn't expected the mirror to fall into my hands and bring you along with it. Just think—if my mirror hadn't found you at that exact moment, we might never have met. I would have had to hunt for somebody else who could fix it and you wouldn't be a part of something so important. Soon I'll be able to capture the whole world in my mirror and everything will be perfect. Won't it be wonderful to have a world that is always cold?"

He leaned back from the Snow Queen and looked over his side of the sleigh at starry sky. She pulled him back from the edge and laced her fingers through his hair.

The clouds grew thin. As night faded, enough weak light bled into the sky so that he could see a land mass covered with snow, with no trees or signs of human life anywhere in sight.

The Snow Queen remained silent throughout the rest of their travels, although she kept a secure hold on him. The farther they went, the more relaxed she seemed. When he had just begun to wonder if they would fly in that silence forever, the sleigh began to descend. Kai leaned forward and saw that they were headed for an enormous building made entirely of snow and ice, more fantastic than anything he had ever seen. The birds dipped lower and lower, until they were even with the lower levels of the building. Yet they did not slow down.

He gripped the Snow Queen's arm. "Aren't you going to stop them?"

"Afraid, Kai?" He heard the smile in her voice. "Do you really think I would be careless with your safety now that we have come this far?" She made no movement to halt the sleigh.

He could not bear to watch any longer and shut his eyes as they flew straight at the solid ice. Yet he neither felt nor heard a crash.

"It's safe to look around now," she said after a moment.

Kai forced his eyes open. The sleigh now sat in a little, dark room. He stared about in confusion.

The Snow Queen saw the look on his face and laughed. He remembered that the sound had once made her seem human. "It's good to be done traveling," she said. She clapped her hands briskly and the birds collapsed into two piles of snow. "Come." She held out her hand once more.

When he took it she tightened her strong fingers and led him down a long hallway without doors or windows. Packed-down snow crunched below their shoes. He looked at her hands as they walked. They were paler than the lilies at funerals, and he couldn't find blue and green veins full of hot blood below the skin. The fingers were longer than they should have been. He wondered why he had not noticed these things sooner.

They came into a large, square room. Kai had never seen so much white in one space. Three walls were panes of ice. They were frozen perfectly smooth, with no bubbles or cracks, so pure that he couldn't tell whether it was an inch or a foot thick. He saw a flat, white landscape through the ice. At regular intervals in the fourth wall were five doors, all closed but for the one they had just walked through. These doors were made of pale wood, carved with the same designs as the sled.

He turned around as he took in the empty space. "Does anybody else live here?" The ice and snow muffled his voice.

"Not another soul. I get to have you all to myself. Aren't I the only person you need?" She said this last bit in an affected, coquettish tone.

Kai reminded himself that he had a family who loved him and a home that was full of warmth, even in deepest winter. Yet even after only this short time in the Snow Queen's company, it became harder to think about these things. He asked, "The mirror?"

"You remember what I told you about the little problem I had with it. And you've had part of it within you for several weeks now, so I know you can feel it."

"You want me to fix it. I remember." He shied away from thinking too hard about the piece of the mirror that had found him. He wondered if she could tell what he was thinking. It now seemed like she had been able to see straight through him in Vasa, as though he were made of transparent ice like the windows.

"I *need* my mirror. I can last through the coming year but I won't go through another winter without it," the Snow Queen said. Kai realized more with every passing moment that the hunger he saw on her face was not for him, but for winter. She stepped to one side and revealed a large chest carved from ivory. Its lid was open and he spied tiny pieces of glass that glittered in the dull light. "Everything you need is in here."

Already in his mind he could feel the familiar impulse to solve a puzzle. He forced himself to look her in the eye. "Why can't you do it?"

"It has to be a human," she said.

"Why?"

The Snow Queen clenched her hands. "A human made my mirror, so only a human can mend it. I've tried other ways. They failed and so it has to be you. Understand?"

Kai swallowed and nodded.

"You have a lot of promise," she told him. "If you prove yourself worthy and finish my mirror in time for me to use it when the next winter arrives, you can help me make the season the way it's supposed to be. I'll show you how to freeze all the water in an ocean and send the snow falling down from the tops of mountains. Would that please you?"

He nodded again. To help create a world where everything was perfect and would remain so forever… Yet even as these attractions and promises whispered in his mind, he glanced around the room that was empty of any of the things he would normally use in daily life. "How will I live while I work on it?"

"You don't have to worry about that. Remember, you're one of mine now; I've arranged things so that you won't need such human distractions." She plucked the first piece of the puzzle from the chest and set it onto his gloved palm. "I suggest you get started."

The Snow Queen glided from the room. Kai shut his eyes and tried to remember the sun.

# CHAPTER SIX

Cold water rushed across Gerda's face. She could see fish and clouds of silt. Weeds wrapped themselves around her arms as her boots and heavy coat weighed her down. Her lungs burned for air. It became harder to keep her mouth shut. Completely lost, the only thing she knew for certain was that there was a glimmer of light above. She tore free of the plants and struggled upward.

Just below the surface, something small dropped down and caught on her sleeve. Her waving arms caught a length of cord and she pulled.

Her head broke free from the water just long enough to see an astonished face inches away from hers. Startled, Gerda let go of the cord and fell back underwater.

Something reached into the water and caught hold of her arms. The one gulp of air hadn't been enough—Gerda ran out of air and started to choke. The strong grip pulled her to the surface once more and dragged her into sunlight.

Gerda coughed up mouthfuls of water. She lay on the bank of a river, her feet still dangling above the water. Instead of the midwinter courtyard she saw a forest and thick grass. Instead of the frozen fish pond, this river was fast-moving and bright with sunshine. A woman some years older than herself sat nearby, her fair hair streaming wet from the river. A fishing pole sat beside the woman, as well as a basket holding several limp fish. The thing Gerda had felt catch at her was a hook attached to a fishing pole, sunk deeply into the sodden fabric of her coat.

"I think you'll want this back," she said and started to giggle helplessly. She tried to pluck the hook free but her soggy mittens got in the way. The absurdity of the gesture made her laugh even harder. Until this moment, she still hadn't been completely certain what would happen after jumping into the conservatory's pond. Yet the water must have acted as a passageway after all, for she couldn't think of any other way to have leaped from winter into spring.

"What in the world were you doing in the river?" the woman asked. "Do you know you could have drowned if I hadn't been here?" Her voice scolded but she helpfully thumped Gerda on the back before removing the fish hook.

Gerda ignored the questions and looked around. Her sudden mirth began to fade and her throat hurt after coughing up all that water. The plants and warmth were confusing. Could Kai be in such a warm place, so soon after leaving with the Snow Queen? "Where are we?" she asked.

"We're in the southern part of the forest, just a short distance from my home. Again, what were you doing? Are you quite sure you're all right?"

"Yes, I'm fine. I'm looking for my brother. I thought I saw something in the ice in a pond, so I went through. Have you seen him? He's my age, with blond hair and glasses. His name's Kai." She stood up and peered into the water. She could see all the way to the stones scattered across its bottom, past the minnows darting about and the swaying water-weeds. Despite the sunlight, she shivered within her cold, wet clothing.

The older woman shook her head. "I haven't seen anybody until you came appeared in the river." She tugged Gerda's wrist. "Come away from there. It was hard enough making the river give you up the first time."

Gerda stood her ground. "Who are you?"

"Linnea. Who are you and why has your brother gone missing?"

"I'm Gerda. He was stolen away," she continued, curling up her gardener's hands until the short fingernails scraped her palms. "The Snow Queen took him."

Linnea's face grew ashen. "Are you sure?"

"She told me who she was right before she left. You know her, don't you?"

"I've heard of her."

"Then you know I can't waste any time. I have to find out where he went."

Linnea grabbed her hand. "Wait a moment; you don't even know where you're going. At least come to my house on the way—it's close by and you can dry off while you plan."

Gerda thought this over while squeezing water from her hair. Although a complete stranger, Linnea had kept her from drowning and she couldn't rescue Kai if she died of hypothermia on the way. She had no better choices. "Just for a little while."

Linnea led her to a wide path through the forest and away from the river. Gerda half-expected this lush, warm day to fall apart and reveal a blizzard at any moment. "I still don't know where we are," she said as they walked.

"It's spring."

Gerda frowned. "That's a time, not a place."

"I already told you, we're in the southern part of the forest."

"But which forest is it?"

Linnea looked surprised. "There's only the one."

Gerda tried to think of what to ask next. Her mind kept chanting, *Farther away, he's getting farther away and you're wasting time.* Her feet dragged while the sun warmed her chilled face. The nap in her bedroom before the storm and abduction felt as though it had taken place years ago.

They arrived in a clearing bordered with white birch trees. A cottage stood in the middle, made of dark wood with forsythia blooming bright yellow along the walls. A thick carpet of grass starred with wildflowers grew from the pointed roof. A garden stretched out all around the cottage and Gerda saw every springtime flower she could imagine. Planted around the garden was a border of rosebushes already in full bloom. "It's beautiful."

Linnea smiled. "I'm glad you like it. I can show it to you properly, if you want."

"After I've found Kai." Despite her feeling of urgency, she couldn't help pausing at the rose border and leaning forward to cup a peach-and-cream blossom that was as large as one of her hands. In the sunshine, the green leaves were glossy like emeralds. Dozens of these waist-high rosebushes circled the cottage. As far as she could see, no two had the same flowers. "He likes these," she said. "At home, I work in a conservatory with a courtyard that's covered in roses in the summer. He'd always sits in the chairs, just looking at them. I asked him about it once and he said that he loved to look at the patterns of twisting stems, imagining how he could untangle them." She wiped her eyes with her coat sleeve.

Approaching the cottage, they passed a well. Linnea took hold of a cup chained to the stone and dipped it into the water. "Why don't you rinse that river water out of your mouth?" She pressed it into Gerda's hands.

"I'm not thirsty, thanks. It feels like I swallowed half the river." She looked down at the cup. It was made of silver, embossed with a design of poppies in full bloom. The water glimmered inside it and she was surprised to find herself licking her lips. She drank. The water tasted cold and sweet. A few drops spilled over the rim and clung to her chin.

Linnea was waiting at the cottage door. Inside, Gerda heard the rustling of new leaves on the trees as they blew together outside the glassless windows. She remembered all the times those same tree sounds outside her bedroom window had lulled her to sleep in Vasa. A table stood in the middle of the room and she draped her sodden coat over one of its chairs.

"Here." Linnea pulled a bundle of fabric out of a chest and pointed to a door that stood ajar. "Use that room."

Gerda went in and shut the door. The room held a chair, a dresser, and a bed pushed below the window. A patchwork quilt was spread out tidily upon the bed, all cornflower blue, butter-yellow, and creamy white. She passed a hand over it; the fabric felt soft from many washings. A cluster of indigo hyacinths stood in a water glass atop the dresser. She peeled off the layers of heavy, wet winter clothing and dropped them onto the bare floor in a soggy heap. When she saw long white lines marked on her shoulder, she stared in confusion before realizing it was the exact spot where the Snow Queen had grabbed her. Gerda shuddered.

Unfolding the bundle, she found a pair of trousers and a white blouse with blue birds embroidered along the hem. They fit her perfectly. She reached into the pile of damp clothing, removed the little jewelry box containing the piece of mirror, and tucked it into a pocket.

When she reentered the main room Linnea stood at the table, folding down the top of a basket.

"What are you doing?" Gerda asked.

"I thought it would be a good idea to bring some food with us."

"You're coming with me?"

"For a little while. You don't know where you are or where you're going."

"I think I should go north," Gerda said.

"That's a start. But at any rate, somebody has to make sure you don't stumble into the river again," Linnea said dryly.

Gerda laughed despite herself. "I don't expect *that* to happen."

"From what you've said, it sounds as though you didn't expect it the first time." Linnea took up the basket and they left the cottage.

"I wish you had seen Kai," Gerda said as they walked along the river. She stared at the water and trees that stretched in all directions. "Does anybody else live here? Maybe they would know."

"There's nobody else for some distance and few travelers come through this area. You're the first person I've seen in months."

Gerda looked in every direction as they walked. It seemed as though any moment she would miss some clue. If she had been clever enough, she could have realized what was wrong and could have kept him from being taken away in the first place. Dried off, she had no reason to be cold on this spring day; nonetheless, she felt a chill in the air. She paused and closed her eyes. Among the fresh grass and tree sap, she smelled the faint scents of ice and snow.

"What is it?" Linnea asked but Gerda raised a hand. She breathed deeply, trying to find where that hint came from. It faded before she could choose a direction and left her with only the scent of apple blossoms.

"Nothing," she said and opened her eyes.

As they continued to walk with no more clues, Gerda wondered how difficult it would be to cross the river. It seemed narrow enough to swim across but she remembered the water's strength. "Are there any bridges? What's on the other side of the river?"

"There used to be a bridge farther downstream but I haven't been there in a long time. In any case, the other side looked just like this one." Linnea swung her arm about, indicating the flat earth and trees that grew up around them.

"I think I'll want to try that bridge if I don't see anything over here." Gerda peered into the forest as she spoke but the trees were thick enough that she couldn't see far.

"I'm sure you won't need it," Linnea said. "You'll want to be careful of the forest, too. Most of it is safe enough but there are some unfriendly things in there."

"Like what?"

"Spirits, for the most part. Some are harmless but others would try to harm you. There are deer and birds as well."

Gerda laughed. "Why would I need to watch out for those?"

"The deer usually are only what they appear to be but sometimes witches turn themselves into birds, just to see how much trouble they can cause. You should stay away from them."

"Would they know how to find Kai?"

"Maybe but they wouldn't tell you unless they were in a good mood. And even if they decide to help, they always want something in return and won't tell you what it is until after you promise to give it."

A robin sat in a nearby tree, watching them throughout the conversation. The bird fluttered several branches farther into the trees. She stepped toward it.

Linnea moved in between her and the forest. "That's the sort of thing I'm talking about. Shoo," she said and waved a hand at the bird. It flew away.

Gerda shook her head. "You really think a *robin* would get me into trouble? They never did that in my grandmother's stories." But she walked on instead of following the bird.

The miles passed. "You look tired," Linnea said. "You should rest."

"Can't. I have to catch up to the Snow Queen." She kept walking, but her pace grew slower and she became light-headed. It felt so easy for her eyes to drift shut.

"Look out!"

Linnea grabbed her arm and Gerda's eyes flew open. The ground before them dropped several feet into a stream that had carved its way into the earth. It twisted out of the forest, flowing into the river.

The older woman sighed. "That's enough. You are going to sit down for at least a few minutes before you fall over. We can have something to eat while we're at it. After all, you won't be any good to your brother if you land in the river again." She directed them upstream.

Gerda paused at the border of trees. "You told me to stay out of the forest. What changed your mind?"

"This part of the forest is safe. I know every inch of this area. Besides, I think you'll like it."

A short distance into the forest, they encountered slim trees in bloom. On both sides of the stream, Gerda saw magnolias, cherry blossoms, dogwoods, and crabapples. Flower petals fell into the water and were swept away to the river. She promised herself that she would rest only long enough to be better prepared for the search.

Linnea led her to a small clearing where the stream's source was revealed to be a shallow pool only several feet wide. Grassy turf surrounded the pool for a small space before a thick carpet of violets stretched into the forest around them. "You see? It's a perfect spot."

"But just for a little while."

"Whatever you say."

Gerda pulled off her boots and socks, and dangled her sore feet in the pool. Linnea tucked her skirt about her knees and did the same. She had brought enough cheese, fruit, and bread to satisfy the appetites of a much larger group of people.

Near the end of the meal, Gerda leaned back upon her elbows and sighed. "It's already mid-afternoon and I still haven't found anything. If you don't start heading back to your cottage soon, you won't get there before dark."

Linnea paused in the middle of taking a bite from her plum. "Are you serious? You've gone mad if you think I'll let you wander off alone at night when you don't know anything about this area."

"I'm not going back."

"You might fall into the river again. You wouldn't be able to take care of yourself in the forest."

"I'll find a way. You could come with me."

"I don't think that would be a good idea."

"Why not? You know your way around. You could make sure I don't miss anything."

"But don't you like it here?"

Gerda sighed. "If it were any other time, I'd want to spend hours in your garden. But finding Kai is more important."

Linnea picked several of the violets and began weaving the stems together. "I could never go away from here. This is my favorite time of year."

"Maybe Kai and I can stop here when we're going home. You'd like him," Gerda said. She thought Linnea must be lonely indeed if she was trying so hard to keep Gerda's company. And it was easy to make tentative promises—once she managed to rescue Kai, anything would be possible.

"Family seems very important to you," Linnea said. "Did your parents ever take you on picnics when you were little?"

"We only have our grandmother."

"I'm sorry."

The clearing was so peaceful and it felt so easy to talk of the things she almost never thought about. "We don't even know if they're alive. They just up and left one day when we were little. Probably realized they didn't want children after all. Nana doesn't talk about it."

Linnea touched her shoulder. "Anybody would be lucky to have you as a daughter. If I had a daughter like you, I'd never abandon her."

"Don't you have any family?"

"I have three sisters but we don't talk often. They all live far away."

"I'm sorry." Gerda accepted a water-skin that Linnea had filled at the well and yawned. The clearing felt so comfortable and it was far too easy to think there would be no harm in resting just a few minutes longer.

"It works out best for all of us. Do you have any plans for what to do when you find your brother?"

"Not yet but I have something that might help. The Snow Queen was looking for pieces of her mirror that got broken. Right before she arrived, one of them got into Kai's eye and made him change. I don't know how he did it, but he got it out and gave it to me right before she took him away." Gerda touched her pocket. "Maybe I can use it against her."

Linnea looked up from her violets. "That's a dangerous idea. I'd suggest thinking of something else. But in any case, if you really plan to keep traveling through the night, you should sleep first."

"I'm not tired," Gerda said, even as she continued to recline on the ground. The soft turf molded to her body and she couldn't make her legs want to move as her drowsiness increased.

"How is it going to help your brother if you collapse on the way to wherever he is? Then you'll certainly miss any trail he's left. A few minutes won't delay you too much." She tugged at Gerda until the younger woman pulled her feet out of the pool and lay down with her head in Linnea's lap.

"No more than a few minutes," Gerda said, her eyes already shut.

Linnea kissed her forehead. "I promise."

The earth was tipping beneath her and she was going to slide off any moment. Gerda clutched at handfuls of grass but they wouldn't be strong enough for her to hang onto.

Her vision spun when she opened her eyes but she saw Linnea kneeling above her. The expression on the woman's face teetered from smiling to concerned and back again, until Gerda had to shut her eyes against the whirling images.

Then Linnea was pulling her up, even as Gerda tried to sink back towards the ground. They were walking downstream and she couldn't make her body stop. "No, I can't go back," Gerda mumbled with her eyes still half-closed, "I have to find Kai. I can rest there until I feel better and then I'll go on."

"You can't. You need somebody to take care of you." The hands beneath her arms were strong. When Gerda didn't look it was easy to hear Linnea's voice blurring into the fragmented memories of her mother's voice.

It seemed that only moments passed before she lay in a bed with blankets that changed into her bed at home. She gripped the soft fabric between her fingers and the spinning ceased.

She dreamed that she walked through a palace built of ice. She sped down the halls as if she had wings while the ice creaked and groaned above her head. At the end of a hall she came to a door. When she touched it, the palace collapsed into shards of ice that cut her skin. A great mirror stood before her; from within the glass, the Snow Queen stared at her. The Snow Queen gripped Gerda's wrist and dragged her into the mirror.

Gerda cried out and jerked up. She was still in the warm bed. Mild air sweet with flowers drifted through the window instead of frosty, stinging winds. The room was so dark that she could barely see her hands before her face.

"It's only a dream. Go back to sleep," a voice said. It was Linnea's voice, and Nana's, and her mother's.

"I need to stop the Snow Queen," she said. But it felt so difficult to speak and she couldn't keep from collapsing onto the pillows. She fell back asleep as she rubbed her wrist where the dream-fingers had touched.

She slipped into a dream filled with green-gold light where she sat in the violet-covered forest clearing. Cardinals and robins were singing in the trees. Snow started to fall and the dark petals on the violets started to freeze. The Snow Queen stepped into the clearing and held Gerda down. The cold hurt so much that she couldn't move and she had to watch as the snow start to bury her.

Gerda tossed in the bed, hot and cold all at once. Every time the Snow Queen appeared in the dreams, something else pulled Gerda out. When her throat stung from screaming into the icy wind, warm drinks that tasted sweet were tipped between her lips. Her mother's voice was always there, calming Gerda when she dreamed of falling into icy water or of frost crawling across her skin.

At last she slept peacefully and dreamed only of warm sunlight.

Kai picked up another piece of the mirror. The wool gloves made his grip awkward and when the bit of the mirror fell it landed without a sound. He knelt and scanned the floor. The snow was packed down hard, as though the Snow Queen had paced it thousands of times.

The piece of mirror hadn't bounced far; he found it only a few inches away by whisking his hands across the snow until the sharp edge caught in his glove. This time he was lucky: the first time he had dropped a piece, he'd searched for what felt like hours before finding it. After staring at the floor for so long, he had seen white even behind his eyelids.

He peeled off the glove. For a short time his fingers remained flexible and he plucked out the fragment. Although he moved cautiously, one of the sharp edges pricked his finger. He placed the fragment with the other sorted pieces before putting the finger to his mouth. Sometimes his hearing buzzed from a lack of any other sounds in that room. It sounded as though the mirror whispered to him, urging him to work faster.

No sounds or currents of moving air prepared him for the Snow Queen's arrival before he felt her at his back. "And how goes your work?" she asked.

It was the first time he had seen her since she left him to his task. It could have been days or weeks: the light came from a constantly gray sky and he rarely slept. He waited to feel hungry or thirsty, but it never happened. Several times Kai thought he had heard her voice, but saw just the empty room when he turned around. He wondered if even now he was imagining her.

"Is this all?" she asked.

Kai still didn't turn around. The ivory chest remained almost full. With no guide as to how the completed mirror should look, he had to choose by instinct alone. Over one hundred pieces gleamed silver against the white snow where they were laid out upon the ground. Her tone sounded light, like a mockery of the girl she had pretended to be. When he looked up he saw only the Snow Queen, a person he could never again mistake as Eva.

"The pieces look alike," he said. "I don't know how it's supposed to turn out. And I'm cold."

The Snow Queen twisted the fingers of one hand through his hair. Her nails scratched against his scalp. "Try harder."

He nodded.

"Soon you'll understand how wonderful the cold can feel," she promised. "I can still smell the heat from other seasons on you. It reeks. In that town of yours I longed to be home every day but I had to wait until autumn's end. I could have escaped on my own but I needed the full strength of winter to bring you with me. I waited all that time because of you. The least you can to do repay me is to complete my mirror. I know you want to finish it. You're the kind who can't stand to leave a puzzle unsolved."

She pulled Kai to his feet and didn't speak again until he looked her in the eye. "What do you say to striking a bargain? You need to live and I need my mirror. For every section of my mirror that you complete or every story you tell that satisfies me, you get a kiss." A high-backed chair made of snow grew up from the floor. The Snow Queen sat down and arranged her long, gauzy skirts around her legs before settling Kai at her feet.

"Why?" he asked. "You didn't like Nana's story about the swan-maiden and you just said I need to spend more time on the mirror."

"Let us think of it as an experiment. I'm curious to learn what kinds of tales you humans spin together. If you make good progress on the mirror, I can afford to spend a few minutes here and there allowing you to entertain me. I meant to leave you alone longer to concentrate, but I had grown used to your company. You can be proud of that: out of all the humans I ever met, you are the only one who has been able to occupy my thoughts more than a few days. You may begin."

All the stories he knew came from Nana. It seemed a betrayal to speak the words she had lovingly recited in this place. However, it was becoming harder to move as the cold hours passed. As he chose a story and spoke the first lines, he shut his eyes and sought refuge in the memory of a kitchen in springtime with the windows open and a vase of tulips at the table's center.

"There was once a country where the king and queen had seven sons. When the sons became men they wanted to travel in search of brides. The king and queen made the youngest prince remain at home, for they couldn't bear to be parted from all their children at the same time and they thought he was too young to marry.

"After weeks of journeying through many countries, the princes met a king and queen who had six daughters. The couples married right away, but they were so in love that they forgot any common sense: while returning to the princes' castle they took a shortcut that went past the home of a giant in the mountains. Giants hate trespassers, especially when they are humans full of joy, music, and laughter, such as these.

"The moment the giant saw the wedding party, he waved his enormous hands and turned all of them to stone. Statues of previously unlucky victims also surrounded the giant's house.

"The princes had sent a message home when they married, but no other news had reached their parents during the long months since. The king and queen were worried sick over their missing sons. 'We are so lucky to have you with us. Our hearts would break if we had lost you as well,' the queen said to the remaining prince.

"The prince said, 'But I also want to see new places and have adventures. I might be able to learn what has happened to my brothers but if I stay at home, we will know nothing.'

"At first the king and queen refused, but their son gave them no peace until they changed their minds. The older sons had taken so many supplies when they left that only an old horse and a small bag of food remained. The youngest prince hugged his parents and rode away.

"After several days' journey, the prince rode up to a large fish flopping in the road. A stream ran alongside the road, just out of the fish's reach. 'Please toss me back into the stream,' the fish gasped, 'and I will help you when you need it most.'

"The prince laughed. 'I can't imagine how a fish would help a prince but you certainly don't belong on land.' He carried the fish back to the stream. The fish leaped into the air and turned a somersault before it dove back underwater.

"Later that day, the prince came across a raven that also lay in the road. It was so weak that it could barely move and dust covered its wings.

"'Please give me something to eat,' the raven begged. 'I've been without food for days! If you help me now, I will help you in return when you need it most.'

"The prince looked at the bird. 'I think a raven would be no more help than a fish but I hate to see an animal starve. You may have the bit of food that is left.'

"The raven filled out as it ate, and the dust fell from its wings. When it finished eating, it cawed joyously before flying away.

"The next morning, the prince encountered a wolf lying next to the road. The wolf was so starved that every rib could be counted through his skin and his fur was falling out.

"'Let me have some food,' the wolf pleaded. 'I can't remember the last time I had a meal.'

"The prince had always been wary of wolves but this one looked so sickly that the prince felt some pity. 'I would help you, but my food has been gone since yesterday.'

"'Then let me to eat your horse. If you do this, I will help you with whatever you need.'

"'Absolutely not!' the prince said. 'How am I supposed to travel if you eat my horse? And besides, what if you decide to eat me as well?'

"'I would never eat a human. Your kind doesn't taste good,' the wolf said. 'But as for the matter of traveling, you can ride me. Just tell me where you need to go. Wolves are the best trackers and I am faster than any horse.'

"Because of these promises and the truly pitiful sight of the wolf, the prince gave in. He looked the other way during the wolf's meal and tried not to listen. When the prince turned around, the wolf's ribs were hidden by his full belly, his fur was thick, and his eyes were bright. The only thing the wolf did not eat was the horse's heart which he told the prince to keep in his bag, saying that it might be useful later.

"'Tell me what you're looking for,' the wolf said and the prince spoke of his missing brothers. 'I know where to find them,' the wolf assured him. The prince climbed onto the wolf's back and held on tightly as the wolf ran.

"They traveled deep into the mountains until they arrived at the cabin where the giant lived. 'Here is your family,' the wolf said, stopping in front of the statues.

"Upon seeing this, the prince became afraid. 'How can I fight a giant who can do magic like this? I'll be of no use to my brothers if I'm turned to stone as well.'

"'Don't worry so much,' the wolf said. 'The giant goes out every day until sunset. There are hours left before he will return, so we have time to plan. Also, inside the cabin is a princess the giant kidnapped to keep house for him. Go and find out if she will help you.' The wolf retreated into the forest. The prince knocked on the cabin's door.

"'Get away, right now!' the princess warned when she opened the door and saw a fellow human standing on the large stone stoop before her. 'Whoever you are, you must leave or else the giant who lives here will kill you as soon as he smells you.'

"'I can't leave; I'm here to rescue my brothers and kill the giant,' the prince said.

"'That's a foolish thing to say. This giant doesn't keep his heart in his body, so there's no way to kill him. Others have tried but they've all been turned to stone.'

"'I have to try,' the prince argued, as stubborn as when he had persuaded his parents to let him leave.

"They argued until the day was almost gone. The prince refused to leave and sat on the doorstep with his arms crossed. He knew that he would need her help to defeat the giant.

"At last the princess sat down beside him. 'I don't know where the heart is but I will try to find out,' she said. 'If I do this for you, you have to do something for me.'

"'What is it?'

"'Let me come with you when you and your brothers leave.'

"No sooner had they agreed than they heard the giant stomping home from miles away.

"'I'll keep him from finding you,' the princess said. 'Hide under his bed and listen carefully when we talk. Be sure not to make a sound, or you will end up worse than your brothers.'

"The prince had just pulled his feet beneath the bed when the giant arrived. The moment he entered the cabin, he stopped and sniffed the air. 'Why do I smell human blood?' he asked.

"'A wolf ran by the cabin today, carrying a heart in its mouth. He probably attacked a human but I still shouted at him when I saw what he carried.'

"'Why would you do that?'

"'I know that you keep your heart someplace else and I was worried that the wolf might have found it instead of a human heart. The wolf dropped it when I yelled at him and it's still lying outside.' As the prince and princess had spoken earlier, he had revealed the horse's heart in his bag. The princess had taken it and said that she thought it could be used to trick her captor.

"At these words, the prince heard the giant run out of the cabin and lift up the stone slab. The giant soon heaved a great sigh and returned. 'There's no need to worry, it wasn't my heart the wolf found.' He didn't know that the prince was listening to every word.

"The prince crawled out from under the bed as soon as the giant left the following morning. He and the princess pulled away the stone slab and dug beneath it until both of them were covered in dirt, but the heart wasn't there. 'Not to worry, we'll try again,' the princess said. The prince began to clean up the mess but she stopped him. 'You'll never be able to hide what we were up to and I think we can use it to trick the giant again.' She also scratched her arms several times.

"When they heard the giant returning, the prince hid under the bed again. Once more, the troll complained about the human stink. This time he also asked, 'Why is there such a mess outside?'

"'It's only me,' the princess said and held out her arms. 'That wolf returned and tried to dig up the stone today. He must have been looking for your heart. I managed to drive him away but I'm sure he'll return.'

"'That wolf must still smell the other heart from yesterday. He won't find mine; I don't keep it there any longer. The blanket chest is a far better hiding place—the wolf would have a hard time getting into the cabin and even if he did, he wouldn't be able to open the chest on his own,' the giant said. Chuckling over the wolf's foolishness, the giant went to sleep. That night the prince thought he could hear the giant's heart beating in the wooden chest.

"But the next day was as unsuccessful as the first. The chest they opened held only blankets. The princess and princess shook out every blanket but there was no sign of a heart. After they put the lid back on the chest the princess set bouquets of flowers atop it.

"'Maybe the giant knows you're trying to fool him,' the prince said while they tried to think of other places where the heart could be hidden.

"The princess frowned. 'He's very powerful but I don't think he's that clever.'

"That evening the giant saw the flowers and asked, 'What are you up to now? I don't want any of those things in my home! You know the smell makes me sick.'

"'I put them there to hide the smell of your heart. I know you say the wolf can't reach it but I'd hate to risk something so important.'

"'You fool. My heart *used* to be in the blanket chest. It's better than under the stone outside but soon I realized it wasn't a good enough hiding place.'

"'Is it safe enough now? How do you know the wolf or something even more dangerous can't reach it?'

"'I know it's safe because I have the best hiding place. There is a lake on the other side of the mountains. On the lake there's an island with a church. In the church there is a well, inside the well is a goose, and inside the goose there is an egg holding my heart.'

"'Why keep it inside a church? You've complained so many times how much it pains you whenever you come inside of one.'

"'That's exactly why,' he said. 'Who would ever think to look for the heart of a giant inside a church? And no wolf could ever reach it, so I never have to worry.'

"The giant left the next morning and the prince got ready to leave as well. The wolf came out of the woods. When the prince told him about the lake the wolf said, 'I can take you there easily,' and off they went.

"When they reached the shores of the lake, the wolf said, 'Hold tight,' and swam through the cold water.

"They reached the island and found the church, but the door was locked and the key hung high up in the bell tower. The prince couldn't see any way of reaching the key but the wolf told him to call the raven. The raven flew up right away. When it heard what was needed, it snatched up the key and dropped it into the prince's hands.

"The church was abandoned. They found the well in a courtyard, where they saw the goose. When the goose swam by the prince grabbed her. But just as he was pulling the bird out of the well, the egg fell out of her and sank into the water.

"This time the wolf said, 'Call the fish.' The prince obeyed. At once the fish swam up and brought the egg to the prince.

"'Squeeze the egg tight,' the wolf said. The prince did so and even from across that great distance, he could hear the giant screaming in pain. The prince squeezed harder and heard the giant begging for his life. He promised to do anything if only the prince would let go of his heart.

"'Tell the giant you will let him live if he breaks the spell upon all of the humans he has turned to stone,' the wolf said. The prince shouted this request. 'Now quickly, break the egg or the giant will come to kill you,' the wolf said. The prince threw the egg against the floor and, with one last roar, the giant died.

"The prince and the wolf returned to the giant's cabin, where the prince's brothers and their wives were celebrating, as well as the other people the giant had turned to stone in the past. During their time as statues they had been aware of everything that happened but were unable to do anything. Everyone, including the youngest prince and the princess who had been the giant's prisoner, returned home where the king and queen had been waiting. They were so happy to see their children that they held a great banquet, and they may still be celebrating to this day."

During the story the Snow Queen had removed Kai's other glove. She stroked the knuckles of his hand like snowflakes brushing against the skin. She said, "You need to understand something. You are not a statue in a giant's garden, and no prince with more luck than intelligence is going to come for you. That fool sister of yours couldn't get as far as halfway, even if she knew where to look. You're mine."

Kai knew that there was something important he had done for Gerda but the details slipped away like a half-formed dream. Instead he asked, "You didn't like the story?"

"We made a bargain. Whatever else I may do, I always keep my promises," she said. He stood up and the Snow Queen kissed him.

Kai felt like he was burning. He had suffered from frostbite once before; when his fingers started to regain feeling, it had felt as though his skin crawled with fire. It felt the same now, except that no heat came. In the first moments he tried to break away but the Snow Queen held him tight. Then the cold spread through his body and filled him with energy. He realized that he was leaning against her chair and heedlessly kissing her back.

She put a hand over his mouth, looking amused. There was a slight rosy flush on her cheeks; he almost had forgotten what the color looked like. "I have to be careful with that heat of yours until it's gone—you could melt me if I lost caution. I expect you will be able to work more easily now." The Snow Queen left him reclining against the chair and once again departed from the room.

Kai returned to the mirror. With the Snow Queen's cold still humming through his body he pulled out another handful of mirror pieces that clicked against one another like tiles. As he examined the small surfaces, he realized that he had begun to forget the details of his grandmother's face.

# CHAPTER SEVEN

Gerda was woken by the noisy chatter of sparrows. Hiding her head under the pillow didn't block the high-pitched sounds and she sat up. She could see them hopping on the branches of the untrimmed forsythia that grew through the window. Her head spun when she stumbled out of her comfortable bed and she had to lean against the wall. For a moment it the furniture looked completely different and the window was covered with glass. She squeezed her eyes shut until the vertigo passed. When she looked again, everything had returned to normal. She pulled on a green robe that had been draped over the chair and left her bedroom.

Linnea stood at the table in the main room, cutting bread. Bundles of herbs and flowers dangled from the low ceiling above their heads. She looked up as Gerda entered. "You're finally awake! You'd been tossing and turning for so long that I didn't want to disturb you once you finally settled down." She walked over and pressed her hand to Gerda's cheek. "You still feel a little feverish, though."

Gerda's limbs felt weak. She sank into a chair. "What are you talking about?"

Linnea chuckled. "Look at that face, acting as if you don't recognize your own mother. You were sick, sweetheart. Don't you remember? We were having a picnic and you came down with a fever. You'd been tired all day and I'm sure it didn't help when you fell into that stream. You've been ill for almost a week." She kissed Gerda's forehead and walked to the stove that stood by a wall covered in pots with gleaming copper bottoms.

This room also changed. The floor was covered with some sort of tiles and she could see bare trees outside the window. Within moments the images slipped away and she was left with only a vague scent of cookies. She pressed her fingers against the sky-blue paint on the table before her. It didn't change and the wordless fear in her head began to fade.

"I was so worried," her mother continued. "You haven't been that sick since you were a little girl."

"I don't remember any of that but I know I had the strangest dreams." Gerda propped her chin in her hands.

"I'm not surprised. You kept talking in your sleep."

"What did I say?"

"Nothing important. You were mumbling, really—I couldn't make out half of it." Linnea brought more food to the table. "Here, you'll feel better after you have some breakfast. You must be hungry; you haven't been awake enough for much more than your medicine in days. What do you remember of your dreams?"

"I don't know. They kept changing. I think I was in a house made of glass. It could have been ice. I was trying to run after somebody but I couldn't move." All of the food smelled delicious. The bacon and sandwiches seemed to be the most savory things she'd ever eaten.

"Who were you running after?"

"I don't know; I couldn't see him."

"Him?"

Gerda laughed and shook her head. "I'm not sure why I thought that when I never saw him. I mostly remember that the dreams kept turning into nightmares and I was always cold."

"That must have been the fever chills." Linnea reached across the table and squeezed Gerda's hand. "You had the blankets pulled up over your head a few times. Once when it was time for your medicine, you were actually shivering."

"Did you really sit with me that whole time?" Gerda asked.

"Of course I did. I couldn't leave my daughter alone when she's ill."

As they finished eating, Linnea said, "We'll stay close to home today. I don't want you collapsing again. You should rest some more."

"I'm tired of being in bed. I'd rather be outside."

"I'll agree to that if you promise not to go any farther than the garden."

"I promise."

When she was dressed and about to leave the house, Gerda slipped her hands into her pockets and frowned. "Mother, have you seen my box?"

Linnea stepped back indoors. "What box?"

"I had a little blue box and it's not here. There was something important inside it." Her heart beat faster and she rushed back to the bedroom. She started pulling apart the bedcovers but nothing appeared.

"You never had anything like that. I think you were mumbling about a box of some sort while you were ill, though. You were saying something about storing seeds in it."

Gerda paused in the middle of searching her dresser drawers. "It was another dream?" The box hadn't seemed like something she made up. She could still feel the corners fitting into the curves of her palm and the worn nap against her skin.

"It must be." Linnea frowned. "Maybe you're not as well as I thought. We can wait until later to go outside."

"No, I don't want to sleep anymore. I'll be fine, I swear."

Once in the garden, Linnea went right to work. Gerda said, "I'm going to stretch my legs."

Her mother glanced up. "Remember that you said you'd stay by the house." She held her daughter's gaze until the younger woman nodded agreement.

Gerda strolled around the cottage. It was surrounded by flower beds divided by little pathways of grass. Dozens of flowers sprang from bulbs planted deep in the ground. The tulips were fully open, some of their colorful flowers as tiny as her thumb, while others were as large as the palm of her hand. Dew trembled on their petals and dripped onto the ground.

One area near a corner of the cottage was filled with tiny crocuses, snowdrops, and grape hyacinths. Gerda knelt to look closer at the mass of purple, white, and gold flowers. The crocus petals were so thin that she could see the sunlight through them, like bits of colored glass. She saw sunshine-bright daffodils, slender irises, and hyacinths with a fragrance so strong that it seemed to soak into her skin.

She paused at the garden's boundaries. Thick, unmarked grass stretched out to the forest and the river. Yet she knew more flowers were supposed to be there. She remembered their fragrance and the thorns that lurked beneath the glossy leaves. The flowers were different colors and opened into goblet-like shapes when they bloomed. She examined every flower in the garden yet nothing she found came even close. There weren't even any plants with thorns.

When she arrived at the rear of the garden, she found her mother kneeling among the tidy rows of an herb garden. For a moment Gerda saw them planted in the shape of a wheel, until she blinked and the plants grew in straight lines once more. "Mother?"

Linnea tipped back the brim of her straw hat and smiled. "Yes, what is it?"

Gerda shut her mouth and kept the description of the unnamed flower behind her lips. It would only continue to worry her mother. The dreams would fade soon enough. She felt stronger with every moment she was awake and she hated to spend any more time in bed. "Is there something I can do?" she asked instead.

"You can help me tidy the garden, if you're feeling well enough. Those maple tree seedlings are growing faster than I can pull them out; you know how fast weeds grow at this time of year."

Gerda pulled up dozens of the seedlings as her mother attempted to keep the mint from taking over the surrounding earth. At least the seedlings were something that she could touch. She could see the roots slip out of the ground and she could feel that the soil under her fingernails was real. The fragrance of the cut mint spread throughout the entire garden. By the morning's end, she gave up trying to remember the scent of the flowers from her dream.

Several hundred pieces of the mirror were now out of the chest, half of which were assembled. Kai had counted each one and wondered how many they would number in the end. Had each one been hiding within another human? When the edges began to blur and his eyes felt as though they itched with grains of sand, he stepped away. Yet even when he shut his eyes, visions of the mirror didn't leave his mind.

He wondered if a person could become color-blind due to a lack of color. The only hues he saw now were the white snow, the silver mirror, the gray sky, and the alabaster Snow Queen when she chose to appear. Even his clothing seemed faded. He knew the names of the colors that went with each item—blue, red, brown—but the spellings had begun to seem like nonsense. The colors didn't even sound correct when he tried to speak them aloud.

The ease of movement that the Snow Queen had granted him remained, but the energy from her kisses that had made him feel like he could run across her land without stopping faded and he felt few sensations. Pacing around the room allowed him to pretend that he could make his toes warm once more. Thanks to the perfect clarity of the ice that made the walls, he could see far onto the winter landscape. There were no landmarks to provide variety among the flat sheets of snow and ice, and he could not calculate how great the distance before him might be. Light came from somewhere—a gray, silken light—but the sun hid behind so many clouds that he couldn't find its location.

The ice was so pure that if he didn't touch it, he could pretend that the barrier didn't exist. Even though past experience said it would serve no purpose, he pushed against the ice. For a moment he imagined that his hands sank through and he could leave the palace. Yet only failure greeted him and he could almost hear the mirror jeering at his foolishness. He picked up a mirror shard and used its point to scratch a line across each panel of ice. Now they were imperfect. He would no longer have to put up with foolish dreams of a path to freedom in this room.

Kai turned his back on the barren view. The mirror waited for him but his eyes still hurt. Circling about the room, he arrived at the Snow Queen's chair.

He knew it would be foolish to sleep. Nana had told them every year when they were small: you never fall asleep while outdoors in the cold, not for one moment. It didn't matter how comfortable you felt or how tired you had become: the comfort of cold was an illusion and it would kill you if given the chance. Almost every year, at least one person forgot this warning. Somebody would go missing and a search would be organized. During the recovery process—it was never called a rescue—anybody who was not part of the trained team was kept away from the body when it was found. Once when Kai was very small, the missing person had been one of his teachers who had wandered away from his car after it broke down and never made it home. Kai had slipped past the crowd of observers.

The dead man's eyes were open. His face looked like wax and his arms were frozen in place, showing how he had hugged himself for warmth as death arrived. Kai never told Nana what he had seen. For the rest of that winter, he couldn't fall asleep if it was snowing. After he told Gerda, she sat up with him until it was safe.

During this remembrance, Kai's body started to feel heavy. The Snow Queen had said that she was making him more like her; perhaps he could sleep without danger. His head slumped towards his chest and his glasses slipped to the end of his nose. He imagined that he almost felt warm as his eyes closed. Cradled by the chair of snow, he slept.

The day passed quietly. Gerda wanted to remain outdoors but compromised with her mother's concerns by taking one more dose of medicine and resting on a sunlit patch of grass. When she awoke, her mother wasn't in sight. She wandered out of the garden to the river and sat down against one of the birch trees after walking a short distance north. She was tearing a leaf to shreds and tossing the pieces into the water when her mother arrived.

"You promised that you would remain at home. Do you have any idea how worried I was?" Linnea demanded. Her cheeks were flushed even more than usual and she bit her lip.

Gerda began to play with another leaf. "I didn't go far."

"That isn't the point. You said you would stay put. I thought I'd lost you."

"I was going to come home soon." She sighed and stared at her fidgeting hands.

"Is something wrong?"

"I don't know."

Linnea dropped to her knees and squeezed Gerda's shoulder. "You'll feel better if you tell me. That's what mothers are for."

"I know I was dreaming again when I slept earlier but I still can't remember what it was about." Gerda leaned into the comforting touch. "I don't feel sick anymore so I don't know why it keeps happening."

"Is that all? It shouldn't bother you; most people don't remember their dreams."

"But it feels like I'm supposed to remember." She couldn't even say why it was so important. All she knew was that there was a great sense of urgency she couldn't explain.

"You'll make yourself sick again if you keep fretting like that. Everything will be all right."

"I guess."

Linnea pulled Gerda to her feet. "Let's go home."


The days flowed into one another as the flowers bloomed. There was something to do in the garden each day. Gerda learned how to tie herbs into bouquets and hang them from the kitchen ceiling so they would dry properly. One morning was spent chopping juice-filled chives that had begun to flower. For the rest of that day and the following night, her hands smelled of the oniony herbs.

At the end of each day she fell asleep immediately after lying down in bed. She didn't stir until the birds and sunlight woke her each morning. Only once did she wake during the night to a feeling that she had left something undone. When she looked through her bedroom and the cottage's main room, she couldn't find anything left lying about: no clothes hanging out of dresser drawers or work half-finished.

Yet the feeling remained strong enough that she walked through the garden, the grass soft beneath her bare feet. She didn't see any of the day's gardening left unfinished, either: there were only the shadowy shapes of the flowers that never seemed to cease blooming. She ventured as far as the forest's border but she didn't see anything unusual, even though her eyes had adjusted to the night. Although she still felt restless, she couldn't think of anything that might have disturbed her and returned to the cottage.

The rest of the night was filled with tossing and turning, but the incident didn't seem important enough to mention the following morning.

She walked with her mother along the river often, watching for fish jumping above its surface. Sometimes they entered the forest, where Gerda learned how to distinguish poisonous wild plants from their nearly identical cousins that were safe to eat. These foraging trips were rare and she was never allowed to wander far past the forest's borders.

The weather grew warmer and the days lengthened. Gerda vaguely remembered cool nights when she would burrow under her quilt like a hibernating bear. Now even the night breeze that came through the windows held enough of the day's heat that she slept atop the blankets.

"Is something wrong?" she asked her mother one afternoon as they weeded the vegetable garden. Linnea had stopped working and rested with her hands pressed against the ground, her head bowed.

"No, nothing…that is, I'm only a little tired. I hadn't expected today to be so warm." Linnea's face was flushed, even beneath the shade of her broad straw hat. She loosened the collar of her dress.

They walked to the well, where Gerda filled the cup with cool water several times until Linnea had drunk her fill. Linnea dipped a handkerchief into the water and pressed it against her neck as her eyes drifted shut. "That feels better."

Gerda leaned back against the well and looked up at the bright sky. "It'll be summer soon," she noted.

Her mother's eyes snapped open. "Not yet. Summer is still a long time away."

Gerda laughed. "It won't be that much longer. There will be fireflies and we can sleep outdoors if it's not raining."

"The time can't have passed by that fast," Linnea murmured. She returned her attention to Gerda. "I'm going to lie down. We'll finish with the vegetables later."

"All right."

"That's my girl." Linnea kissed her forehead and retreated to the shadowed cottage.

Gerda couldn't summon up any interest in resting herself. The afternoon was too beautiful to waste by doing nothing.

Wandering through the garden brought her to the edge of the forest. She looked back at the cottage only once before walking farther among the trees. So long as she returned home before her mother awoke, nobody would be able to scold her. There were no trails, so she walked straight through the thin undergrowth. Insects hummed in the warm air and small animals scurried away from her approach.

Gerda heard the usual forest noises during the start of her walk: leaves blowing, birds chirping, and the rasping of squirrels' nails as they ran up and down the trees. When she paused to catch her breath she heard an unexpected sound: music. It was light like the sunshine that slipped through the trees and as rapid as the birds that zipped through the air. It made her want to dance.

Her feet tapped against the packed soil but she made herself stand still until she could decide which direction the sound came from. As soon as she resumed walking, she was rewarded with clearer and louder music. Before long she arrived at a stream that had cut deep into the forest soil. A dark-haired man playing the fiddle sat upon a mossy boulder on the opposite bank.

Gerda couldn't bring herself to interrupt the music. She waited for the tune to end before she said, "Hello."

73

The man's eyes had been shut while playing, but now he looked at her and she felt he had known she was there the whole time. He smiled slightly and answered, "Good afternoon."

"I heard your music." The statement sounded obvious and stupid to her ears but she couldn't think of anything else to say.

Either the man didn't seem to notice or he didn't care. "And you came searching to hear more of it? My thanks for the compliment." His smile widened and he began to play again, quieter now. The previous song had made her want to jump and leap about, but now the music was soothing and flowed like the stream between them. This time he kept his eyes open and watched her.

"Do you live nearby? I haven't heard you before." Gerda removed her shoes and sat down on her side of the stream to dangle her feet in the water, mirroring the musician. The water was very cold but it felt so good on her tired feet.

"You probably were not close enough to hear," he suggested. "I don't go far from this stream; it's my favorite place in the whole forest."

"Why?"

"It's a good place to practice and I find the water soothing. And it is such a lovely place to receive visitors."

She frowned. "You have visitors?"

He managed to give a slight nod while continuing to play. "Even though I do not like to travel, I still enjoy meeting other people. When they hear my music they find me and then we can have a nice time until they want to leave. I have to thank you for stopping by—I haven't met anybody new in a while and you've made a dull afternoon more interesting."

Gerda couldn't help laughing at the thought that anybody besides her mother would care so much about her company. Yet she drank in the opportunity to speak with another person. "You're welcome."

"Do you have a favorite song?" the musician asked. "I could play it for you."

She thought for a little while and frowned. Wisps of music appeared in her mind but they vanished before she could try to hum them. "I can't remember any."

"What a pity."

Gerda nodded in agreement. She leaned forward. "It's a beautiful instrument." The molasses-colored wood gleamed and it looked new, despite all his claims of practice. Yet the fiddle was strung with a dark material she couldn't quite place. "What are the strings made from?"

He grinned. "Hairs from a horse's tail."

"You're teasing me. There's no way you could use those without breaking them."

"It's truth. Come and see for yourself." He left off playing and held the fiddle out.

Gerda couldn't see well enough from where she sat and stood up. Halfway across the stream, her foot slipped on a mossy stone. The stream was deeper than she had thought and when she fell, she went completely under. She surfaced in time to see the musician jump in and she reached out a hand, willing to laugh over her clumsiness.

His hands grabbed her shoulders and pushed her back under. Gerda automatically opened her mouth in shock and water rushed in.

She choked and fought her way to the surface long enough to catch a gulp of air. Then he shoved her under again. His hands bore her to the bottom of the stream and she felt the rocks dig into her back. His grasp felt so much stronger than it had appeared. She thrashed about like a fish stuck on the end of a spear.

She was drowning. The water was pressing down on her and she couldn't escape. For a moment it seemed as though she wore heavier clothing and weeds chained her body below the surface. But that couldn't be right—she wore only a light dress and the stream was free of plants. She *knew* it; she had been able to see through the clear water earlier. Yet the strange feelings didn't leave.

The air in her lungs began to fade. While her hands still uselessly grabbed the musician's unwavering arms, her legs found his. Before her energy could disappear, she hooked one foot around his and *pulled*.

The musician fell down and she came up. Gerda sobbed with the need for air. She started to scramble back to her side of the stream.

He caught her around the knees. This time when she fell down she was able to keep her head above water. The musician pinned her against the bank, one hand clutching her shoulder and the other at her throat.

"What are you doing?" she shrieked.

"Drowning you," he said, as casually as she would talk about the weather. The calmness in his voice terrified her as much as his actions. "This is my stream and now that you have wandered into it, you're mine as well."

A memory entered Gerda's head. A woman's voice said, *"You must beware if you ever encounter a man playing the fiddle near a body of water, for he is sure to be a näck. Sometimes he takes the shape of a horse but either way you should be careful, for he loves nothing more than to lure men and women to their deaths."* Yet it was not her mother's voice. Gerda could not remember who had warned her.

She couldn't kick him again; he was sitting on her legs. No human emotion colored his eyes. She couldn't look away. One of her hands futilely shoved against him but the other one was still underwater. It scrabbled through the silt and large rocks embedded into the earth. One rock felt small enough to grasp. It came loose from the streambed.

Gerda swung up her hand and smashed the rock into the side of the näck's head.

He reared back but not enough for her to get away. Blood trickled down his face and dripped into the water. It swirled around until the current washed away the bright red color. He leaned forward. Both of his hands circled her throat now. He said, "You could have had a fast death but now you are going to regret that rock very much before we're finished."

"My mother will kill you if you do anything to me."

The näck's face was very close to hers when he laughed. His hands squeezed tighter and her vision started to darken. The näck's face blurred into that of a white horse before changing back to a human. "I am not in the habit of being intimidated by mothers. Still, why don't you tell me who she is? After you're finished, I can tell her that she shouldn't have let her daughter wander into the forest alone. If you're a good girl, perhaps I'll allow her to join you."

"Linnea," Gerda croaked as she began to slip underwater.

The expression on his face didn't change but he let go of Gerda's throat immediately. "That's impossible."

"Why?"

He ignored her question. "I'm surprised to hear that your…mother finally has a daughter. Wanting one for such a long time and now, here you are. How…*convenient* for her." Despite his bold words, he glanced repeatedly in the direction of the cottage and retreated until he was no longer touching Gerda.

"What are you talking about?" she asked.

With one last wary look, the näck snatched his fiddle and disappeared underwater.

Gerda could see to the bottom of the stream but she couldn't find any sign of the creature. She scrambled out of the water, half-expecting to be pulled down again at any moment. The moment she was on land she ran back to the cottage. From her hazy memory she didn't think that a näck was known to leave his watery home. When she dared to glance back into the forest, nothing followed. When she arrived at the cottage, she stumbled to a halt against the sun-warmed stone of the well.

She looked at her reflection in the water. She saw no bruises but it was too soon for any to appear. How would she manage to hide marks on her neck from her mother? Her dress was torn and muddy. As she continued to look into the well, she saw that some of the näck's blood had dripped onto her ashen face. Gerda shuddered. She wiped away the red smears and squeezed as much water as she could from her dress before creeping into the cottage. There was no sound from her mother's bedroom and Gerda changed as quickly as she could, hiding the dress underneath her bed. There was little that could be done about her hair, except to comb it while sitting in the sun and frantically think of excuses. The scents of hyacinths and rosemary were comforting as she waited to stop trembling.

Linnea came outdoors before long and sat beside her on the bench. "Are you feeling better?" Gerda asked.

"Much." Linnea frowned. "Why is your hair wet? And why did you change your clothing?"

Gerda forced herself to shrug lightly. "I was hot and wanted to cool myself off with water from the well. The cup slipped." Her heart still raced and the näck's parting words kept circling through her mind. "Who was my father?"

Linnea, who had been smoothing her hand over Gerda's hair, stilled. "Why do you ask?"

"We never go anywhere and nobody ever visits us. I don't even know his name. What was he like?"

"Who says you had a father?" She laughed and tweaked Gerda's braid. "Maybe I found you floating in the river like a duckling."

"Now you're just being silly."

"I couldn't help it; you get the most amusing look on your face when you're being teased. Why so curious all of a sudden?"

Gerda shrugged. "It's just something I was thinking about. I don't remember anything about him and I wondered."

"I'm not surprised you don't remember; he hasn't visited in a long time."

"Do you think he'll come here again?"

"Who knows? But I love you enough for two parents. You'll stay with your poor mother and keep me company, won't you?" Linnea teased.

"Of course."

"You're such a good daughter." Linnea wrapped her arms around Gerda.

Gerda returned the embrace but continued to watch the forest over her mother's shoulder.

Linnea stood. "I need to start preparing dinner. Why don't you pick some fruit for dessert?" She returned to the cottage.

Gerda examined all the fruit-bearing plants before deciding on strawberries. She searched for the lush red fruit among their low-growing plants. The leaves made her hands itch but she found plenty of berries ready to eat.

Near the end of one row, she found a lump in the earth. When she dug it up she found a small velvety box caked with dirt. A chill swept across her skin. Yet when she looked up, the sky was still cloudless and night hadn't begun to fall. She tucked the box into her pocket.

"Did you have any luck?" Linnea asked when Gerda entered the cottage. She didn't look up from the stove.

"I found some strawberries." Gerda set down the basket holding the fruit. She touched the lump in her pocket but said nothing else.

She was halfway through cutting the strawberries when Linnea set a cup down before her. "Drink this, darling."

"Why?"

"I saw you shivering this afternoon. You shouldn't have poured so much water from the well over you—you know how cold it is. I don't want you catching a fever."

After the past hour, Gerda had had her fill of liquid of any kind. Her mother's herbal tonics always tasted too sweet as well. But Linnea had that "Mother knows best" look on her face and it couldn't hurt to humor her mother this once.

Gerda sighed and drank.


That night a crackling noise woke Gerda from her sleep. When she opened her eyes, she saw that the forsythia was covered with frost. The tiny ice crystals spread like quicksilver over everything in sight until the weight caused the flowery branches to droop in through the window. One flower broke off and fell onto the bed. It shattered into golden fragments before her.

She could see her breath and goose bumps covered every inch of her skin. The quilt had been put away long ago and the thin sheets were no protection against the cold. No sound came from her throat when she tried to call out for her mother. As she stared into the dark room, a figure opened the door and walked in.

The dead girl who entered the room was covered with snow and ice. Bits of it fell from her clothes and hair with every step. The room had become so cold that none of it melted. Her face was chalk-white and impassive. She sat down at the foot of the bed. "What are you still doing here?"

Gerda shut her eyes. "You're just a dream." Her mother had said that her dreams weren't important and that remembering them didn't matter. Soon she would wake up, and she would be warm, and she could forget this dream like all the others.

"There is no such thing as 'just a dream.'" The girl leaned forward and grabbed Gerda's ankle. "Look at me."

Gerda shook her head. If she waited long enough, she would wake up and all of this would go away.

"*Look at me.*"

Gerda forced her eyes open. The girl looked straight at her and asked again, "What are you still doing here?"

"I don't know what you're talking about." She sat up.

"Yes, you do, you just don't remember. You don't belong here and you need to get moving." The girl sounded impatient, the first emotion she had shown since appearing.

"I *do* belong. My mother and I have always lived here."

"She has, but you haven't." She held out a hand: in it was the little box that Gerda had hidden beneath her pillow before going to sleep. "Are you really going to let the Snow Queen win?"

And with those words, she remembered. She remembered childhood birthdays, meals around the kitchen table, stories of magic from the far north, working in the conservatory while Kai sat nearby, and how it all came to an end when something pretending to be a human invaded their home and shattered their peace.

"I'm sorry," she said. She didn't realize that she had started to cry until she felt the hot tears on her cold face.

"Don't be sorry; *do* something. Will you let the Snow Queen have killed me and my family for nothing?"

She remembered the Snow Queen saying, "I killed their real daughter." Gerda shuddered. It felt as though the Snow Queen were standing in the room with them, her cold lips brushing Gerda's ear once more. "You're—"

"Eva. The real one. She froze me and I want you to stop her."

"I will," Gerda promised.

"You haven't shown any sign of it so far."

Gerda flushed with shame. It was the only warmth in that freezing room. "I didn't mean to forget."

"I know." Eva glanced in the direction of Linnea's bedroom. "But you can't stop now. I'll never be able to rest if your brother finishes that mirror."

"Why did she do it?" Gerda knew that in the end it didn't really matter—the Snow Queen did what she wanted and needed, and she wasn't the type to care about the lives of a few humans who happened to be in the way. Yet she couldn't help asking.

"I had a piece of her mirror and when she wanted it back, I said no."

"If she wanted it that much, why didn't you just give it to her?" Gerda had her brother's piece of the mirror back but she couldn't want anything less. If it weren't for Kai and the suspicion that the Snow Queen would just find it once more, she'd throw it away without a second thought.

"You can't imagine what it's like, to have that perfect cold with you all the time." An odd expression appeared on Eva's face and her voice had a kind of hunger in it. "Everything was clear and I could see what was really important. There's nothing else like it. I wouldn't have given that up for anybody."

"So she took it from you," Gerda said quietly.

"Just like she did with everyone else."

"She killed everyone who had a piece of the mirror?" A broken mirror must be made up of thousands of pieces. How many of those had been inside of people?

The dead girl laughed bitterly. "Do you really think they just handed over their pieces and she let them walk away? She treated me like I was nothing. That's what she thinks about all of us, you know: that we're nothing. She'll take what she wants from your brother and then throw him away like trash. Will you let that happen, or are you going to do something about it?"

"I'm going to get him back." It was the first thing she had been certain of since the dream began. "But the forest is so big. I don't know where to look from here."

"Go north. You'll never find her in a warm place like this."

She leaned forward. When she touched Eva's hand, the dead girl cracked apart into a pile of snow and ice.

Gerda jerked upright. The days had grown so long that now even in the middle of the night and surrounded by the forest's shadows there was still a dim light instead of true darkness. She couldn't see frost anywhere and there wasn't a broken flower on the bed. No cold water from melted ice soaked the blankets where Eva had sat.

She felt the lump of the box underneath her pillow and cupped it in her hand. A stranger would never have guessed that it contained a piece of winter that could drain away all hope and happiness. Avoiding the sharp edges, she took out the shard of mirror and held it before her eye.

She felt as though she were falling into the wintry waste she had seen the first time she looked into the mirror. The cold battered her. Yet even as the wind pushed and pulled her in every direction, she felt a difference. There was green now. She could barely see it but it was there. Green threads appeared within the ice, thin but not frayed apart. She opened her mouth. Winter air rushed in, scorching her throat and freezing her lungs. At the same time, she tasted a hint of green apples and smelled new leaves. These were only suggestions, soon snuffed out by winter's strength or warped by the mirror, but she had felt them. The first time she had looked into the mirror, she'd seen only a barren landscape. Now in the distance, she saw a lump that might be a building. She couldn't make out any details yet, but it was there.

When she wrenched away she fell out of bed, back into spring. The scents of so many flowers in one space made her head throb and she felt like she was burning up in the warm night. There were too many imperfections in the room; it would be far better to smooth everything over with a coat of ice.

Gerda curled up on the floor. "Stop that," she said. She forced herself to think of everything she loved about spring until the frantic feelings departed and she didn't smell a hint of frost. The piece of mirror lay nearby and she tumbled it back into the box.

Tears leaked from the eye that she had held the mirror up to and her fingers were cold. It had been so easy to forget the mirror. She glared at the cup of her before-bed tonic sitting on the dresser. The aftertaste sat sour on her tongue. She picked up the cup and threw the dregs out the window.

"I won't forget again," she promised herself. It took only a short time to dress before she was walking through the silent cottage.

She pushed open the door to the other bedroom, the one she had never thought to enter. The floor in there was soft soil instead of wood. Plants grew all throughout the room, so thick and high that she couldn't see the walls. The only clear space was for a path leading to the bed that was canopied with wisteria and possessed a blanket made of moss. The room smelled rich from the lilies-of-the-valley that rustled against her as she walked to the bed. Linnea, never her mother, slept on. Gerda looked upon the face of the woman who had kept her from Kai and stolen her memories, and turned away.

She was about to step out of the cottage when Linnea spoke behind her. "Where are you going?"

The door slammed itself shut and Gerda spun around. Linnea stood there in her nightdress, with violets blooming in her blonde hair. Gerda tugged at the knob but it wouldn't budge.

"You shouldn't go out alone at night," Linnea continued, "it's not safe. I know what happened this afternoon. You shouldn't have ignored my warnings. Do you have any idea what could have happened to you?"

Gerda thought she would prefer to take her chances with what might be lurking in the forest over anything in the cottage. "I do know *and* I survived. And I don't care if it's not safe. I need to leave."

"You don't *need* to. Go back to bed and it'll be nothing more than a bad dream by morning," Linnea said soothingly.

"The only bad dreams are the ones you gave me. I am not a little girl and I will not go back to bed." Gerda bit out the words. "I'm going to find Kai and I'm doing it now. Open the door!" But the knob still wouldn't turn.

Linnea looked upon her with a mixture of sorrow and exasperation. "How could you want to leave somebody who's done nothing but taken care of you and kept you safe?"

The anger Gerda had been sitting on since awakening from her dream flared through her body. "Why would I want to stay after I found out you took my memories away? That's not safety. What gives you that right?"

"I knew you wanted it. You seemed so lost when I found you in the river and I could tell you were lonely when we talked. I knew we would both be happier if you stayed. Haven't I been a good mother?"

Gerda sucked in lungful's of the flower-scented air. She remembered lying feverish in bed as she forgot who she was with every moment and with every swallow of "medicine." Kai could have died while she dreamed away her life in a garden. She said, "Good mothers don't drug their daughters. They don't twist reality until you can't even remember who you are."

"But your birth mother could not have loved you, to leave you like that. I love you more than she ever did. I've wanted a daughter for so long, to raise and cherish. And then the river brought you straight to me. Now you have a mother and I have a daughter. What more could you want?" Linnea reached out.

Gerda shook her head. "Your love is no better than the Snow Queen's."

"I did it all to protect you. You don't know what she's like."

"I watched her get her claws into my brother while her mirror took over his mind; I saw the people she killed; and I almost died in one of her storms, all because she wanted a little piece of glass. I think I have a good idea of what she's like."

"You don't. I've known her all my life and she will destroy you. But if you stay away long enough, she might forget you and then you'll be safe." Linnea stepped forward but Gerda backed away from her along the wall. "Why not stay with me, when your only other choice is her? Is a life here really that awful?"

"It's not *my* life," Gerda said.

"But there's so much more I can teach you. You knew so much about plants when you arrived but here you can gain even more knowledge. Why seek out the Snow Queen in a place where everything is dead? You've already learned a great deal since coming to me and here there's no ice or snow to stop you."

Gerda felt ill as she remembered being *happy* when her memories had been hidden away. She had actually been content while Kai was being tormented by the Snow Queen and she hadn't stopped it. That sickening guilt might never leave. She knew that she had indeed learned much more about gardening than she had before, but she shook her head. "Flowers come back. It might look like everything is dead in winter but I know it will come back to life. What you gave me doesn't make up for what you took away."

Linnea now blocked the door. Gerda wasn't sure she could overpower the other woman. An air current tickled the back of her neck as her gaze roamed around the cottage. One of the windows was now behind her and it lacked glass, just like all the others. She curled her fingers around the windowsill. She hoped that her gestures would be taken as a show of nervousness. It wouldn't be completely inaccurate.

"Goodbye," Gerda said and jumped out the window.

She just barely fit through the gap in the forsythia. Some of the twigs scratched but at least there were no thorns. One foot was caught as the shrub closed the gap in a sudden burst of growth. She pulled free and ran.

Rounding the front of the cottage, she stopped short. Among the never-wilting flowers nearly bleached of color in the dim light, the roses had sprung up and surrounded the garden once more. The glossy leaves and flowers looked as though they had been dipped into an artist's paints. It reminded her of the conservatory in summer, when all the roses bloomed at once and the scent was so strong that it filled even her dreams.

There was no wind, but all the plants and trees around her started to rustle. The rosebushes slid apart and she ran through the gap. When she glanced behind her, she saw that empty space had disappeared.

She didn't look back again as she raced down the path toward the river. If Linnea was following, Gerda couldn't hear over her pounding feet. As it was, the birches on either side waved as though a wild storm were taking place. Remaining in the middle of the path kept her just out of reach of the branches that bent down and snatched at her arms.

The ground rolled beneath her feet. She fell and closed her eyes as the grass rippled below her hands. It felt like she might fall off of the world. At last the earth stilled and she rose to continue.

The path shook twice more on her way to the river. She fell each time. Once she tried to stand up during the trembling but couldn't keep her footing. It was too difficult to crawl over the rolling earth. All she could do was press her face into the grass and wait. There were no sounds other than the noisy trees.

The ground had stopped trembling by the time she reached the river, although the trees still snatched at the air. Now she dared to look back, but didn't see anybody or anything following. She stared into the dark water while catching her breath. Most of her memory had returned but parts of it were still blank.

Eva had said to go north and Gerda had no idea how long she would have to follow the river before she reached her brother. She started to jog along the water with the dimly lit night sky to illuminate her way, leaving the cottage farther behind her with every passing minute.

# CHAPTER EIGHT

Gerda traveled throughout the night. The land remained much the same: a flat bank on either side of the river and the forest all around. The hours streamed by like the river water through her fingers when she cupped her hands to drink.

During the first hours she waited to hear Linnea's footsteps following hers. Yet as time stretched on, nobody followed and the trees did not try to grab her again. Once she heard a rustle nearby but saw only a rabbit jumping out of the brush.

Periodically, more narrow streams twisted out of the forest and into the river. She paused at the first one of these, remembering how swiftly the näck had moved in the water. She felt frozen as the minutes stretched on. But it was either this or return to the cottage and amnesia. Nothing arose from the stream when she leapt over it. Later she misjudged the distance of another stream in the dim light and had to clamber up the bank, muddying the knees of her trousers.

Nighttime forest creatures made their presence known. Some of them were merely ordinary rabbits jumping through the moonlight and the occasional hoot of an owl. But that was not all: she caught glimpses of shadows along the forest moving in un-treelike ways, flowing together and breaking apart. Everything acted as it should when she looked straight at it. When she turned away and looked at the forest with the edges of her sight however, the shadows seemed to move alongside her. The rustling of leaves sounded as though it was whispering in a language that she couldn't quite understand. Nothing approached her but she felt as though she might jump out of her skin if the strange, might-be-somethings continued for much longer.

Gerda tried to distract herself by thinking about the roses from the garden. She could still smell their perfume; it lingered alongside the scents of river water and earth. She rubbed her fingers together, remembering how the petals had felt. If the roses hadn't vanished, would she have been able to remember sooner?

The mirror in her pocket felt no heavier than any other piece of glass would. Sometimes when she paused for breath, she found her hand curled around the box and her short fingernails starting to pry the halves apart. Each time, she snatched her hand away. Even the outside of the box felt cold. There was such temptation to look into it again; she couldn't decide if this was the mirror's power, or merely her own curiosity. She wouldn't look into the mirror so often as to let it overpower her, like it had Kai. But then, he'd never been given a chance to avoid viewing the world through its tainted surface. She wondered if all the people who had held a piece of the mirror within their bodies had felt the same pain.

Even anger over her memories being stolen and worry over what the Snow Queen might be doing couldn't keep her moving without rest forever. She hesitated before venturing into the trees near dawn, remembering how the ground had rolled beneath her when she escaped the cottage surrounded by trees. Yet she couldn't avoid the massive forest forever and it wouldn't do to topple at the Snow Queen's feet the moment she arrived. After getting up the nerve to step into the forest, she found neither a flower-covered cottage nor a murderous water-horse, but a small clearing with knee-high grasses that looked as ordinary as anything she might have seen back home. The tall grass ought to hide her from any prying eyes but all the same, as she burrowed down she wondered if she would wake up underneath the blue and yellow quilt back in her cottage bedroom.

When she woke up later that morning, she found herself still in the same place. Nobody pounced upon her the moment she sat up. Although the tall plants were useful as a hiding place, they hadn't prevented a sunburn that made her face itch. Her fingers twitched as she fought to keep from scratching at it.

Gerda's stomach growled. If Kai had been there and been his old self, he would have told her that she'd been stupid not to take food from Linnea's cottage before leaving. But a brief search led her to a cluster of blackberry bushes heavy with fruit. The berries were hot from the sun and some were so ripe that they fell apart when picked, the juice staining her fingers. Their sweet flavor lingered on her lips. She couldn't entirely avoid the tiny thorns: by the time she had eaten her fill, fine scratches crossed her hands and wrists.

The next few days and nights passed similarly. She ran alongside the river when she had the strength and forced herself to keep walking fast when the muscles in her legs burned. She laughed once when she remembered turning down the opportunity to participate in track while in high school. If she'd had any clue as to what would happen, she would have run rings around the entire town every day.

Gerda had thought she remembered everything during the dream with Eva but her memories were still confused as she traveled. It seemed that her false mother's enchantment wasn't easily broken. She recited facts that she knew to be true about Nana and Vasa and she traveled during the day, but sometimes when she woke from a nap she wondered how she had ended up so far from the cottage and thought about how worried her mother must be. Other times, plucking leaves and twigs from her dark hair reminded her of how much Linnea had always enjoyed brushing and braiding it, even when she was a little girl. Gerda swore whenever she caught her thoughts heading in that direction. *That never happened*, she told herself again and again. The pretend memories faded as the space between her and the cottage grew, and she silently recited everything she knew about her true home and family until the memories felt completely real.

She had to thank Linnea for one thing, though: before the Snow Queen's arrival, Gerda had known little of which wild plants were safe to eat, despite all her time in the conservatory. Now after her time at the cottage, she was familiar with many ways to find food among the trees and near water. Her stomach was never completely full but there was enough. She smiled as she dug up roots on her second evening of travel. She didn't think Linnea had intended to make it easier for Gerda to escape, but her teachings were helpful all the same.

She didn't allow herself to sleep away an entire night. Too much time had been wasted already. She would travel until she felt she couldn't move any longer before finding a place in the forest where she could hide for a few hours of deep, dreamless sleep.

After one such nap, she saw the morning sun flash off of something pale among the trees. She had walked farther into the forest than usual before finding a resting place in between the roots of several enormous trees. Her curiosity got the better of her and she walked to the edge of a large clearing. If she had been asked she might have said that she expected to find a house but she discovered a palace built entirely of white stone. She looked over the palace as she hid behind a tree. Dozens of balconies protruded from the outer walls, and masses of flowers and vines trailed over their railings. No sounds came from the palace, despite the lateness of the morning.

A raven flew out of one of the windows as she watched. It landed not far from where she stood, threw off its feathers, and turned into a girl. The girl draped a cloak of feathers over a low tree branch to reveal a black dress cut in feathery layers that had a dull sheen in the sunlight.

Gerda's near-death at the hands of the shape-shifting näck still haunted her and she almost ran away. This bird-turned-human however, was no taller than Gerda's chin and did not act as though she was trying to hunt anybody. Gerda dug her fingernails into the tree's bark and continued to watch.

The girl walked up and down the clearing, peering under bushes at the edge of the forest. Watching the girl search, Gerda remembered Nana's stories of swan-maidens. Even Linnea had said that most of the birds knew a lot of useful information. She sidled out from behind the tree and grabbed the cloak. It barely had any weight and was as soft as rose petals. The girl didn't even notice.

Gerda cleared her throat. "What are you doing?" she asked. It felt like a silly way to start a conversation, but she wasn't interested in proposing marriage like most of the characters in Nana's swan-maiden stories.

The girl shrieked in surprise when Gerda spoke and tumbled headfirst into the bushes. When she climbed out and saw what had happened to her cloak, she yelped again. "Give that back!"

Gerda grasped the cloak in both hands. "Not yet. First, I want you to tell me if you've seen a young man with blond hair and glasses." Eva hadn't said how far north she would need to travel and this was the first sign of human life she had seen in days. True, the Snow Queen would never willingly be in a place like this but she couldn't help hoping that Kai had found a way to break free. Part of her mind said that she was being foolish but she couldn't stop.

"Many people with blond hair live here," the raven girl said. She sidled forward as she spoke and leaped at the cloak.

They fell to the ground. The raven girl was persistent but Gerda managed to roll away without letting go of the cloak. She jumped up and backed away. "But do you know anybody like that?"

"Why, did your husband run off and leave you?" the girl snapped. Her cheeks were flushed from the struggle and small leaves from the bushes clung to her curly black hair.

"He's my *brother*. He was taken away and I'm trying to find him." Mentioning the Snow Queen around this flighty creature seemed as though it would cause more trouble rather than help.

"I'm sorry." The girl even sounded as if she meant it, although her eyes kept flickering to the cloak as she spoke. "A fair-haired man did arrive recently. Our queen lives in the castle and she's very clever, almost as clever as a raven." She talked faster as she warmed to her subject. "She's read every book ever written and knows the answer to every riddle. She decided she wanted a husband and sent us birds as far as we could fly to spread the news. Many men came here but the queen turned them away because they weren't smart enough—"

"Just cut to the end," Gerda interrupted, forcing her way into the endless string of words.

The girl huffed and ruffled her feathery dress. "This one is so intelligent that the queen fell in love right away and married him. He has glasses and pale hair, and he says he came from far away where it was much colder."

"I want to see him." It was almost impossible for this man to be Kai. The twin she knew hadn't been in the mood to marry anybody, even if by some miracle he had gotten away from the Snow Queen. Yet who knew how much he had changed while she was dreaming her life away in Linnea's garden? She didn't know for certain if Eva was right about everything. Even if he wasn't here, maybe this brilliant queen could tell Gerda something useful.

In the blink of an eye, the girl changed again from gossipy to scandalized. "You can't! It's the first day of summer and everyone is still asleep after the wedding last night. Celebrating the queen's marriage is a lot of work, you know. You'll have to wait until she wakes. Then you can make a proper request for an invitation. I've answered your questions, now give my cloak back."

Gerda wound it around her arm and stayed out of reach. "Not yet."

"You have to! I need it!" The raven girl hopped up and down.

"I can't wait until everybody wakes up to find out if it's my brother," Gerda said. "You'll have to find a way to get me in." It had been too long already and she couldn't bear to wait however long it would be until she could "properly request" to come in.

"But I'll lose my position if they find out I let just anybody in," the raven girl protested.

In her life before the Snow Queen, Gerda thought she would have felt worse about what she was doing now but she couldn't stop thinking about what she might have accomplished if her memories hadn't been locked away. "If anybody finds out, I'll say that I made you let me in because of your cloak and you didn't have a choice. It's the truth, after all. You can blame everything on me. And as soon as I see the man you described, you'll get your cloak back."

"Do you promise?" The girl looked wary. Gerda wondered if anybody else had stolen her cloak and made promises in the past.

"On my brother's life."

The girl started walking toward the castle and Gerda followed. As they circled the building she asked, "What were you looking for, anyway?"

"One of the ladies lost her slippers during the dancing and I was sent to find them. Now be quiet." They had come to a portion of wall covered in ivy that hung from a balcony. "We have to be very careful."

"Why? You said everybody's asleep."

The girl looked scornful. "Their dreams keep watch. Don't you know anything?"

"Where I come from, our dreams stay put," Gerda said dryly.

The raven girl shook her head. "How dull." She slipped behind the ivy curtain with barely a rustle.

When Gerda stepped forward she found a small door hidden behind the vines that led to a narrow hallway. The girl walked silently but Gerda's first steps echoed off the high ceiling. The girl spun around with a look of such great scorn that Gerda blushed before removing her shoes and tucking them under her arm.

The girl paused at the end of the hall and glanced around before they entered a courtyard barely large enough to hold a slim chestnut tree with a stone bench crafted around its trunk. "Be very careful," she said, so quietly that Gerda had to lean forward until their faces were almost touching. "If any of the dreams see or hear us, they'll race ahead and let the entire palace know there's an intruder."

They took a winding route through the building. The raven girl paused at the threshold to each room before letting Gerda enter. They took so many turns that Gerda could never have found the way back by herself. The building was honeycombed with courtyards of all sizes, each possessing its own style. She was reminded of the conservatory and the sudden desire to be back at home was so strong, she felt almost sick.

They had just left another courtyard when the raven girl stopped so abruptly that Gerda collided against her back. "Over there," the raven girl said, "quickly!" She shooed them into an alcove behind a partially-drawn curtain. A pair of wineglasses and a shawl lay on the alcove's bench.

A cluster of shadows rushed down the hall. Gerda saw finely dressed men and women racing across the plain white walls on slender horses with ribbons flowing from their manes. The people laughed and sang silently; she couldn't hear the drumming of the horses' hooves or the bells that dangled from their bridles. The hunting party didn't pause as it passed the alcove and the shadows disappeared down a staircase.

Gerda slipped out of hiding and stared after the vanished shadows. "That was a dream?"

The raven girl nodded. "Whenever anybody here dreams, they come to life and everybody else can see them."

"Do your dreams appear, too?"

She laughed, her cawing shattering the stillness momentarily before she clapped a hand over her mouth. When nobody responded to the noise, she removed her hand and shook her head. "I'm only a bird. You really don't know anything, do you?"

Gerda ignored this. "How much longer until we get to the queen's husband?"

"We'll be there soon. If this is taking too long for you, you could always return my cloak and leave."

"Keep moving."

Now they walked down a long hallway, its outer wall lined with windows like the ones Gerda had noticed from outside. The fabric of the curtains was so sheer that she could see the forest through the gauze. A breeze brushed the curtains against her legs. She kept the feather cloak wrapped around her arm in case the raven girl made an attempt to take it back.

Twice more, they hid from dreams. Gerda never heard anything coming but somehow the raven girl sensed them early enough to find a hiding space each time. The first time, the shadows took the shape of waves lapping against the wall. Large fish leapt out of the inky waters, never making a sound as each landed with a splash. A ship sailed across the wall. Its sails rippled in a wind that Gerda couldn't feel. She found herself wondering what would happen to the ship if she were to touch the dream-shadows.

The second time, a man and woman danced down the hall, moving to unheard music. As the dancers were rounding the corner, Gerda stuck her head out. Just before they vanished from sight, the male dancer lifted his head. The black silhouette seemed to be staring at her. She grabbed the raven girl's arm.

The girl looked and groaned. "You fool, you've gotten us caught. They'll tell everybody now. Run!"

They raced down the hall. Gerda's socks slipped on the smooth floors. The raven girl pulled Gerda along, her fingers strong for a person who looked to be little older than a child. The lack of sound around them made Gerda start to feel as though she were in a dream of her own, the kind where she would run and run yet never get anywhere. When she glanced back, the dream-dancers had vanished.

"Cloak or no, I'll lose my position for certain now," the raven girl muttered. "You just *had* to insist on seeing the queen and her husband without waiting."

Gerda saw a wooden door inlaid with gold at the end of the hall. She was within an arm's length of reaching it when she heard feet pounding behind them. "Stop her!" somebody shouted. Then somebody slammed into Gerda and she fell to the floor.

Voices clamored all around. As Gerda attempted to catch her breath, the door opened and a pair of embroidered slippers appeared before her face.

"Would anybody care to explain why there is a social gathering taking place outside my bedroom?" a woman's voice asked.

"We caught this woman sneaking into the palace, Your Majesty," one of the people on top of Gerda said.

"Let her up."

The other people moved away and Gerda was able to breathe easier. She stood up and looked around. Only four people surrounded her, though it had felt like more. Rika huddled against a wall. The queen had long auburn hair. She looked very stern but there were creases around her eyes that could belong only to a person who smiled often.

The door opened wider and a man stepped next to the queen. Gerda's heart fell. He looked nothing like Kai. This person had pale blond hair, but everything else about him was different. He yawned and asked, "Suvi, what's going on?"

"I'm about to find out." She looked closely at Gerda. "I will deal with this; everybody else may leave."

The other people backed away, although a woman wearing a beribboned nightdress directed an appalled look at Gerda's muddy and grass-stained clothes.

"Not you, Rika," Suvi added as the raven girl attempted to sneak away. "Stay here, please."

Gerda and the raven girl entered the large bedchamber. It was filled with roses. Clay pots holding climbing roses stood by each of the bedposts and the flowers twined up around them. The bed itself possessed a coverlet crafted from blood-red rose petals. Even from a distance, Gerda could almost feel their velvety texture beneath her rough gardener's fingers.

The queen shut the door. Gerda imagined the others listening at the keyhole. She fought the urge to laugh at the vision of all those finely dressed people practically stacked on top of one another in the hallway.

"Did you let this woman into the palace?" Suvi asked.

"She made me!" Rika protested, fully embracing Gerda's offer to take all the blame. "She stole my cloak."

"It's true," Gerda admitted. She held out the cloak of feathers to Rika. "You can have this back now."

The raven girl grabbed her cloak and clutched it to her chest. Gerda was surprised that she didn't choose to immediately change into a bird and fly away.

"You'll want to be more careful with that in the future," the queen said. "Next time, the person who steals it may have something more in mind than a temporary favor."

Rika bobbed a curtsey in response and continued running her fingers through the feathers.

"I'm sorry," Gerda said as the queen turned to her. "I'll leave right away; I just had to see if my brother Kai was here."

"Is that it?" Rika demanded. "All you had to do was tell me the name of the person you were looking for, and I could have told you that he wasn't here, and then we wouldn't have gotten into trouble! Why couldn't you have said that?"

Gerda opened her mouth. "I did—" and shut it. She had thought of Kai's name so many times before and said it to Linnea so often in the beginning that she couldn't remember whether or not this time she had said his name. "I don't know."

"Stupid human," Rika muttered. "You'd never hear of a *raven* doing that."

Gerda sighed. Despite her nap that morning, she felt weary. She turned to the queen. "I'm sorry about this," she said. "If you can show me the way out, I'll be going now."

The queen smiled. "Nonsense. I'm relieved that you're finally here; I was starting to wonder what had delayed you."

Out of all the reactions Gerda had imagined since everybody woke up, this one hadn't even come close to entering her mind. "Excuse me?"

"I expected you to arrive a long time ago. What kept you?"

"You've been waiting for me? How did you know? And why didn't you tell *them* so I didn't have to sneak in?" Gerda pointed to the door the group of people had exited through.

"In answer to your question on why she didn't say anything, it's partly because she felt like it," the man said dryly. "You would never know it just from looking at her, but my wife takes great pleasure from teasing people."

"Lukas!"

"Darling, you decided to choose a husband through a competition. Your desire for intelligence aside, that says a great deal about your character."

"I'll explain everything soon," Suvi told Gerda. To the raven girl she said, "Rika, you are not in any trouble. I want you to go throughout the palace and let everybody know that this woman is to be treated as a guest while she remains here."

Rika donned her feather cloak and leapt out of the window. Gerda found herself gently but firmly shooed from the room.

Within minutes the newly-married couple was walking with Gerda down a hallway.

"You said you were waiting for me," Gerda reminded Suvi. "How did you know?"

"A bird visited me some time ago. She described what you were up to and suggested that I help you."

"But I didn't talk to any birds before Rika."

"The robin who came to see me was very specific. She didn't know many details, but she insisted that she had seen a woman who looked like you traveling along the river, looking for somebody who had been taken by the Snow Queen."

Another memory stirred in Gerda, of when she had first come to this world. Linnea had been warning her about dangers in the forest, and she had seen a robin... "I was told that it was a witch and it would try to trick me if I asked it for help."

"Sometimes both witches and birds are more than they seem. And regardless of what my husband says," she shot him a look that was part-love, part-exasperation, "I had no idea when you would arrive. As more time went on, I started to worry that you might never come. I would have asked the robin to look for you, but witches can be difficult to find when they wish to be left alone."

"I don't know how much the robin overheard, but it's all true," Gerda said. In some ways it was difficult to speak of what happened—the last time she had shared her plans, she had been made to forget everything. Yet the queen spoke as though she expected Gerda to continue traveling. "The Snow Queen wants my brother to fix her mirror. I forgot about him until a few nights ago. A girl she killed appeared in a dream and told me to keep going north. I'm going to find him."

"You were right to listen," Suvi said. "The dead don't always stay quiet. Both they and the living can do many things in our dreams. Our souls can travel to the end of the earth and home again, in the moment between one breath and the next."

"I wasn't sure how much I should believe. With everything that's happened, I don't think I trusted myself to decide that it was all real."

"I suspect it was all the truth. If you had dreams here like we do, you would have more confidence in them. There's something I want you to see." The queen led them into a windowless chamber larger than Linnea's entire cottage and garden put together.

Gerda gasped. The room was an enormous map with each wall devoted to a different season. The walls were covered with shimmering gold and paints as bright as jewels. The sapphire-colored river flowed from each wall to the next and trees dotted either side of the water. The first wall she looked at was a familiar sight: springtime trees were filled to bursting with blossoms and little fish jumped out of the river. A multitude of colors in one spot drew the eye and she found the image of a little cottage adorned with forsythia around its windows.

On the second wall all the trees were green, so lush that she almost forgot they were only paint. There were fields with crops growing high. Among the trees she found suggestions of small faces peeping out from behind tree trunks. She also saw the flower-adorned palace painted exactly as it appeared in real life.

As she moved closer to the next wall the leaves gradually turned red and gold. They lay in hummocks on the forest floor, leaving the brown branches bare against the gold background. She could see thick-furred deer and among the trees with long shadows. Deep within the forest there was a lumpy, gray stone building among a series of hills.

The image of winter was on the wall they had entered through. Even the door was painted to match. The wall was still golden but paler than the other seasons. Nearly all the trees were gone and the river changed from blue water to diamond-like ice. The artist had dotted snowflakes across the landscape and as she looked farther across the wall, more and more of the ground was thickly covered with white. The river and trees ended. Almost indistinct from its pale surroundings, she saw an enormous building as beautiful and threatening as an iceberg. She could feel the box in her pocket grow colder.

Throughout the map she also saw areas where the forest was cleared away and many buildings were grouped together. She could see farms, towns, and roads. No people were painted on the map but she still had a sense of great activity happening in all of these places.

When she looked up, she found that even the ceiling was decorated. On the eastern side it was painted the bright colors of dawn as the sun stepped forward. The light changed for each hour of the day until it began to disappear in a muddle of red and violet halfway across the ceiling. The sky was now ebony-dark and the moon replaced the sun. Although she had never studied the skies as closely as Kai did, she could still find several constellations in the painted stars. Once the first rush of amazement passed, she saw that the stars were made from chips of crystal embedded in the ceiling.

"I had it made many years ago but it's still accurate," Suvi said as Gerda finished her examination. "You can see that as long as you follow the river, you shouldn't get lost."

Gerda examined the long distances laid out before her. "She'll have frozen him completely by the time I walk all that way."

"Perhaps not. I've been working on a solution to that problem," Suvi said.

"What do you mean?"

The queen took Gerda's hand and they left the map room. "Come and see."

The palace bustled with activity now: Gerda could hear voices and footsteps in every direction. Many doors were open and she looked inside as they passed. In one room a trio of people played string instruments. In another, a group of women chattered and laughed as they sewed lengths of bright fabric.

They all seemed so carefree. Aside from the queen and her husband, the only thing anybody here appeared to be concerned with was enjoying themselves. Gerda found herself wanting to shake one of the smiling people and demand how they could be so happy when at the same time as all this warmth, the Snow Queen was trying to cover everything in their lives with ice. How could anybody be so ignorant?

Suvi led them into the lower levels of the palace. "It still needs some work," she said before opening a door, "but I think this will help you reach your brother faster."

A partially-completed boat sat in the middle of the room. Gerda didn't have much experience with watercraft but she could see that it appeared to be a small rowboat, just large enough for one person to sit at either end. The outside of it was covered with gold. "That's for me?"

"I had it begun after the robin's visit. She thought you would likely want to continue following the river, and this seemed like a practical step."

"But I don't know anything about using boats."

Once again Suvi looked amused, as she had when she revealed that she had been waiting for Gerda. "You have so little faith in me. There's more than one way to solve a problem. I can work around that."

"If you say so."

Suvi ran a hand across the boat. "It's not complete yet; there are a few details to finish. It took so long for you to arrive that the workers had started to slow down and became distracted by other projects. But it will be ready by tomorrow."

"Can I help finish it today?"

"I don't believe so. There is only a bit more that needs to be done but I have professional craftsmen who should complete it."

Gerda started to pace. "I could start walking upriver now and you could send the boat after me when it's finished. The river's so fast, it wouldn't be hard for the boat to catch up."

The queen caught Gerda's hands and stopped her restless circling. "Listen to yourself. You won't have gotten far by then and it is easier to see you off properly here. It's only one day."

"Tell that to Kai."

"I am *not* going to send you away ill-prepared. Please wait. Tomorrow will be here before you know it."

"That's the problem." Gerda tried to break away but Suvi had a strong grip. "Do you have any idea how many 'tomorrows' came and went because I wasn't paying attention? If I hadn't wasted so much time, I could have reached him already and we would be home."

"Only until tomorrow morning. I promise."

"Then give me something to do. I have to do *something* useful or I'll go crazy."

"What are you good at?" Lukas asked.

Gerda fought the urge to snap that she was terrific at walking if only they would let her leave already. She forced herself to breathe slower. "Gardening. It's about all I'm good for."

"That would be helpful," Suvi agreed. "It's not just a distraction."

"Fine, I'll garden. But I'm leaving first thing in the morning." Gerda pulled her hands free and walked out of the room.

Partway down the hall she realized that Lukas was following. "She's not lying to you," he said. "It's true that she loves games and riddles, but she wouldn't pretend about this."

"I'm so tired of waiting." Her mind kept saying, *You should have done better. You should have been a better sister.*

"I'll wait with you," Lukas said.

He led her to one of the larger courtyards filled entirely with flowers. The plants had grown so large that they had started to overflow their containers. Although it all looked beautiful, her experienced eye could see many dead blossoms that needed to be trimmed and weeds. As she walked past a bench, her foot struck an empty basket and a pair of scissors hidden below. She seized the objects and knelt at the closest flowers that needed tending. Here was something that she could fix.

"You're very fond of plants," Lukas observed as he leaned against the arch-shaped courtyard entrance.

She laughed helplessly. "Kai teased me because I always had dirt under my fingernails."

"I prefer the smoothness of a new book."

"I made Rika let me in because I thought you might be him. It would have been so much easier if you were. You even talk a little alike." Gerda sighed, even as her scissors continued to slice through dry stems.

"If he's the sort of person who wants to know everything, it helps to explain why he attracted the Snow Queen's attention."

"It's not his fault! A piece of her mirror got into him." The withered blossoms of dried pansies crumbled between her fingers. Even as the sun's heat wove through her clothing, she never forgot the feeling of the Snow Queen's touch.

"I didn't mean it that way. But the Snow Queen wants to know everything and she's drawn to those who want to as well."

Gerda's hands shook and she almost spilled the basket of cut flower blossoms. "Sometimes I wish he wasn't so bright. Maybe she wouldn't have noticed him."

"She still would have wanted the piece of her mirror returned," he said gently. "And it could help him now; if he's as clever as you say, he will find a way to survive until you get there."

"You didn't have to watch what she did to him. I wonder how long it'll take the Snow Queen to try and stop me. She warned me to stay away but she hasn't done anything yet," Gerda said. Finished deadheading the one patch of pansies, she moved on to the tall delphiniums and columbines. A honeybee crawled over a still-blooming flower and she moved around it.

"She likely doesn't know you've gotten this far. If she had, she would have tried something obvious to keep you away."

"How do you know?"

"I grew up on the borders of her lands," he said and sat down on a nearby bench. "It's winter for most of the year there but we have a few months of warmth. That far north, they tell us about the Snow Queen before we can walk."

Gerda smiled before she could stop herself. "The winter part sounds like home. Did you ever see her?"

"She never came to our village. We were told that she didn't like to be near many people or the heat of our buildings, even during the cold season when there's more ice than fire. I did go north with some friends once. We wanted to see how far into her land we could travel."

Gerda stared at him. "Why would you think that was a good idea?"

He shrugged. "We were young and foolish. It sounded like an adventure."

"What happened?"

"During the first few days, nothing. We were used to normal winter weather and it seemed like any other journey. A blizzard struck on the fourth day. All of us knew how to watch for storms but it still managed to surprise us. We got the tent up and hid inside. I think the blizzard continued for several days but it was difficult to tell. One of my friends looked out the tent flap and said that he saw the Snow Queen standing there.

"I don't know why she chose not to kill us. It would have been easy to do. But the blizzard died down just before we ran out of food. Maybe something distracted her or she thought of a new amusement."

"And then what?" Gerda asked. She had left off deadheading plants while Lukas told his story. She held a blossom of columbine that had withered shut and the seeds rattled inside as she tossed it from hand to hand.

"We went home," he said simply. "We weren't foolish enough to stay after that. It seemed to be forever until I was warm again. I couldn't bear another full winter once we'd returned. My friends stayed home but I left to find someplace warm. I'd been traveling here and there for over a year when I heard about Suvi's challenge."

Gerda smiled at the happiness in his voice but her expression quickly faded. "I wonder what the Snow Queen will try to do to me."

"You can't obsess over it," he told her. "It's true you'd be a fool not to think ahead but you can't let it be the only thing you think about, or else you'll be caught up in 'what if's' forever."

"Maybe," she said. It was easy advice to give but difficult to follow. Still, Lukas had survived the Snow Queen's realm and so Gerda cast about for a distraction. "I've never seen anything like that map. And it seemed like spring would never end before I started traveling again. Do all the seasons last so long?"

"They never end." She stared at him and he continued with a slight smile. "If you had stayed where you were and waited for spring to end, it would never have happened. Each season has a place in our world where it lasts forever. True, the farther you get away from the center of each season, you have areas where the seasons change, but it's less common than you might think."

He leaned his shoulders against the wall, and remained silent while she puzzled over this newest revelation.

The day stretched out in the seemingly unending way of summer, like a length of cloth unfolded again and again. Gerda continued tending to the plants in the garden with grim determination. She found a patch of clover growing in one of the flowerbeds and passed some time by making a chain out of the globe-shaped flowers.

She wove clover chains until the lengths puddled in her lap. When she ran out of flowers she plucked at the clover leaves, recalling Linnea telling her once that a two-leaf clover signaled the coming of a lover, a three-leaf should be worn for protection, and that a four-leaf was the luckiest of all. Lukas remained with her during those hours and she was grateful that he did not try to distract her by claiming that of course everything would be all right.

And all the while that she sat in that courtyard, surrounded by warm grass and flowers and sunlight, she thought of winter.


Kai's hands rested in his lap. He had not bothered to put his gloves back on before he returned to assembling the mirror. His skin was now dotted with spots of dried blood, and thin scars covered the pads of his fingers and his palms.

Something in his mind said that he should refuse to help the Snow Queen but the voice grew fainter every hour. He couldn't help wanting to solve the mirror. She was right: it went against his nature to leave any puzzle unfinished. Large sections of the mirror were now completed and lay in silver puddles on the snowy floor. The edges melted together when he put the correct pieces next to one another. He could not have broken them apart again even if he wanted to.

He told himself that he did not belong here. Even as his fingers sorted pieces, he tried to remember details of the years before the Snow Queen came. He knew that he had a family, yet he could not recall details of their home. The color of the house paint faded and he wasn't sure what kind of tree stood in the backyard, or if there had even been a tree at all.

But in the end, why should such insignificant details of a house matter? The mirror was the important thing. The Snow Queen had been absent a long time. Had anybody else left him alone for so long he would have said she had forgotten him entirely, but the Snow Queen couldn't be judged by human characteristics. He stood up and walked to the closest door, flexing his fingers. There was no handle on the door, but he pushed against one side and it opened.

The door led into a dark room. Kai stepped forward and tripped, landing on a staircase. Although his eyes did not adjust to the darkness, when he spread out his arms he found a narrow stair leading up. He found his footing and began to climb.

The stairwell was crafted in tight curves, the base of the next level of stairs always just a few inches above his head. He lost count of the number of times he turned in a full circle. His footsteps echoed and every new stair added to the layers of noises throbbing in his ears.

He had started to think that the stairs would never end when he arrived in a round room. He stumbled on the even floor and swayed from the effects of the long, circling staircase. When he shut his dizzy eyes, a pair of hands held him upright until his legs steadied.

The Snow Queen said, "I am curious to learn why you aren't working on my mirror."

Her voice was emotionless. When Kai opened his eyes, he couldn't tell whether or not her face would turn to anger. "I wanted to see you."

"I would rather see you at work but it certainly is flattering to have such devotion. In some rare moments you make me think humans are almost worthwhile after all." She linked her arm through his and led him around the room as though they were any two mortal lovers taking a stroll. "You're the first human to set foot here. Isn't the view wonderful?"

It reminded him of the top room in a lighthouse. The walls here were floor-to-ceiling windows made of ice, as well as the roof. Stars speckled the nighttime sky. Now that his eyes had become accustomed to looking at only winter, he began to see variations in the land: far below them in the distance was a dark silver streak in the earth. When it began to approach the palace, it was smeared over with snow and disappeared from view.

The Snow Queen paused next to one of the windows. "I can see every inch of ground and every flake of snow from here. We're at the top world, Kai. Once you've completed my mirror, I can make the rest of it as beautiful as this."

"It's clean," he said.

"I knew you'd understand. I remember when you were showing me the stars at your home. All that time, I wanted to show you this instead." She pointed outside. "There you can see the snow fox. The frost rose is next to it."

"You told me you had never studied the stars," Kai said. Thoughts of his family and former home might fade, but the memory of standing with her in the middle of the road remained strong.

The Snow Queen shrugged. "A white lie. It wouldn't have been a good idea to show off too much at the time. I did enjoy hearing your knowledge, even though it was incomplete."

He pressed his free hand to the window. The coldness of the ice shot through his skin. The stillness of the room and the unchanging scenery had begun to seem like a dream, and the pain woke him.

"Careful." The Snow Queen slid his hand from the window. "You're still too warm to do that sort of thing often. You need to be a bit colder yet before you can play with ice the way I do."

"When?"

"I'll teach you as soon as the mirror is finished. Why don't you tell me another story?"

Kai looked onto the frozen world while he searched his memory. The sound of Nana's voice had begun to fade from his mind. Eventually he remembered the first words of a story and the rest of it followed.

"Many years ago there was a young man who was apprenticed to a doctor. He studied very hard and became skilled, although not as much as his master. When the young man's apprenticeship was over and it was time for him to head out into the world, he bought a barrel of the best ale around to celebrate.

"The young man set out, carrying the barrel on his shoulder. It became very heavy very quickly but he still had a long way to go before he would come to any inns or taverns where he could sit a while. He began to watch for other travelers to share the ale with, so that the barrel would be lighter and easier to carry. Also, the man enjoyed good company and disliked the idea of drinking alone. Yet the road was quiet and it wasn't until the afternoon that he crossed paths with an old man who had a fearsome look on his face.

"'Hello,' said the old man.

"'A good day to you as well, sir,' the young man replied.

"'Why are you sitting here in the road?' the old man asked.

"'I was walking from my former master's, but the barrel of ale I bought is heavy and now I'm looking for someone to share it with.'

"'May I drink with you? I have been traveling a long time as well and would welcome a cup of ale.'

"'First, tell me who you are and where you come from.' The young man was always curious about his drinking companions.

"'I'm the Devil and I come from Hell,' the old man said.

"'Then I will not drink with you. All the unhappiness and sadness in the world is your fault. Share my ale with you? You don't deserve so much as a drop of water,' the young man said. He picked the barrel back up and left the Devil behind, who was cursing after him.

"Yet for all the young man's firm words, the barrel felt heavier than ever after walking for several more hours. He felt that he could not possibly travel any farther unless he found someone else to share the ale with and lighten his load. As he rounded a curve in the road, he found another old man. This one was sitting on a rock and looked much kinder than the first.

"'Hello, sir,' the young man said and tipped his hat.

"'Hello to you as well,' the old man said with a smile. 'Why are you traveling with such a large barrel? I have been watching travelers all day but haven't seen anybody with a load as great as yours.'

"'I have just finished my apprenticeship with a doctor and bought a barrel of fine ale to celebrate. Yet it's heavier than I thought it would be, and I would like to share it with somebody.'

"'Would you be kind enough to share it with me? The sun has been hot today and it's given me a strong thirst.'

"'I will, if you first tell me who you are,' the young man said. He would have asked the question in any case, but after meeting the Devil he had also become somewhat suspicious. He wouldn't have been at all surprised if the Devil had disguised himself as another old man, trying to trick the former apprentice.

"'I am God, come down from Heaven.'

"This was no better than when the Devil had approached him! 'I will not drink with you either, for you refuse to undo the harm that the Devil has done. You allow evil people to become rich, while many good people remain poor and suffer misfortune. I will certainly not drink with you,' the young man said and, picking up the barrel, strode down the road.

The day was almost over and the young man was sure that he could walk no farther with the barrel as full as it was. He had also still not found an inn or farm where he could spend the night. After some searching, he was able to find a cave just a little ways off the road. The young man settled down in his shelter and cracked open the ale barrel.

He was about to lift the first cup to his lips when there was a *tap-tap-tap* at the mouth of the cave. A third old man peered inside, this one with a long beard and hobbling along on a cane. 'Hello,' said the old man. 'May I share your shelter for the evening?'

"'There's not much worth sharing here, but you're welcome to it, sir,' the young man replied. He was tired from carrying the barrel and reaching the end of his patience after turning down both the Lord and the Devil on the same day, but he still had a bit of politeness left.

"As soon as the old man was settled he asked, 'What are you doing, all alone on the road this night?'

"'I ended my apprenticeship this morning and was paid with a barrel of good ale, but it's heavy and I haven't found a place to settle yet.'

"'May I drink with you? I have been told that I'm an excellent drinking companion.'

"'First, tell me who you are.'

"'I am Death,' the old man said.

"The young man said, 'Just the person for me. I will be happy to share my ale with you, for at least you treat all people equally in the end.' He handed his cup to Death with a light heart.

"They toasted each other and drank all night. The young man was astonished to realize that Death was the best drinking companion he'd ever met. It seemed that no time at all had passed until the sun rose and the ale was nearly gone. The barrel was now so light that barely a cupful remained.

"Death said, 'I have never drunk such good ale and I would like to thank you for sharing it with me. Though there is very little ale left this barrel will never be empty, no matter how much is drunk. It will heal whoever drinks it, and will be more powerful than any medicine you ever learned about. You will see me whenever you come into a room where there is a sick person. If I stand at the person's pillow, you may cure him with a drink. However, if I stand at the person's foot of the bed, he belongs to me and you may not interfere.'

"The young man gave his thanks and Death went on his way. It wasn't long before the young man began to make his fortune. Soon he became a doctor even more famous than his former master and traveled all around the country with his ale barrel, curing many who had been thought past help. When he came into the room he would see where Death stood, and then make his prediction for either life or death. He became rich and powerful, for he was always right.

"Many years after meeting Death, the doctor was summoned to save the only daughter of the king. The princess had fallen ill after she was bitten by a poisonous snake and no other doctor had been able to cure her.

"When the doctor stepped into the princess's room, Death stood at the foot of her bed. Yet he drifted between waking and sleeping, and while he slept she felt stronger.

"'She is nearly dead already and the end will not be long coming,' the doctor said.

"'You have to heal her,' the king said. 'I have no other children and I cannot bear to lose her so soon. If you heal her I will reward you, but if you do not I will throw you into prison and leave you there to die.'

"'Very well,' the doctor said. The next time Death fell asleep, the doctor gestured for the bed to be turned around so that Death stood at the princess's head instead of her feet. The doctor let her drink the ale and she was immediately cured.

"Death was furious when he awoke and saw what had happened. 'You cheated me of somebody who was almost mine. We are even no longer and I take back my gift. And now you are mine.'

"'Will you at least give me time to read the Lord's Prayer before my life is ended?' the doctor pleaded.

"Death agreed to this last request but the doctor was very careful *not* to say the Lord's Prayer. He went to church every week, and read all the others except for that one, and so he thought he had outwitted Death. But Death is patient and not so easily avoided. Several years passed and the doctor became less careful. One night, Death crept into the man's house and set a large sign with the Lord's Prayer written on it at the foot of the bed. When the doctor awoke he sleepily read the sign. He did not realize what was happening until he came to the last words but at that point it was too late, and Death had won after all."

A light snow had begun to fall as Kai told the story. It sifted down both outside the palace and within the room, unhindered by the paper-thin roof of ice over their heads.

"I didn't expect to be fond of the human in that story," the Snow Queen mused. "Even though he knows that no person can outwit Death forever, he still tries. He reminds me a bit of you, my clever puzzle-solver."

Kai frowned. "But we're nothing alike."

"You are. I remember how that piece of my mirror troubled you when you didn't know what it was, and I was so irritated whenever your family got in the way. But I am like Death—I always get what I want. I wanted you and now I have you all to myself. I want my mirror and you will complete it. You're even learning to love winter."

"I know."

The Snow Queen's ice-hard glow illuminated the room and chased away the shadows. She reminded Kai of the full moon on nights when it looked to be made of pure crystal. Though he became more accustomed to winter's sights every minute, he turned once more to the shadowy land so that he was not looking directly into her cold light.

She caught hold of his hands. "I know my mirror has a bite to it," she said, running her fingers over his fresh scars, "but it's only in play. It's a small price for the new world you and I are making. When we're done there will be no Heaven or Hell, only ice and snow, and everything will be perfect for eternity." She pushed back the sleeves of his coat. "You've earned two kisses this time: one for making progress on my mirror—" she pressed her lips to the inside of his left wrist "—and one for the story." She kissed the other.

His body shuddered at her touch. Every sense sharpened: he felt the falling snow slip beneath the collar of his coat; the taste of night air filled his mouth; he smelled the fresh snow that lay all around them; and he heard every moan in the wind.

Kai cradled his hands to his chest under the weight of kisses that burned like dry ice and stood unresisting in the Snow Queen's embrace.

# CHAPTER NINE

It seemed as though the bright summer day would never end; even when Lukas said, "It should be time for supper now," the sunset had still not come.

"Would you like to eat with everybody else?" he asked as they left the courtyard. "I think many people would be interested in meeting you."

Gerda shook her head. "I'll just start snapping at people if I have to sit around and make polite chit-chat with a bunch of strangers who just want to ask a million nosy questions."

"All right." He led her to a more secluded room, where Rika was the only person waiting for them.

"Where's the queen?" Gerda asked. "I want to know if she's done with the boat yet."

"I'll find her. Not to worry, I promise to hurry her along if work is going slowly." Lukas squeezed Gerda's shoulder before leaving the room.

Rika remained with her, unable to sit still for long periods of time and frequently changing shape. Even though Gerda watched closely, she could never find the exact moment when the small shape of feathers and wings became a person with solid bones and human skin.

For such a hapless-seeming creature, she turned out to be skilled at keeping curious people from intruding. Shortly after Lukas departed, there was a knock at the door and a young man entered with a plate of rolls still hot from the oven.

"Where is the rest of the food?" Rika asked.

The man shrugged and tried to sidle farther into the room. "Everything else isn't ready yet." He also wore feather-like clothing in shades of blue that were layered atop one another. Short white hair stuck out around his head like dandelion fluff.

"Then why didn't you wait until it *was* ready?" Rika demanded. She started to tap one foot in its beaded slipper.

"I thought you might be hungry now," he said and peered at Gerda over the raven girl's shoulder. "Did you really sneak into the palace? One of the queen's maids said to the head gardener who said to the junior cook that you flew here on an enormous kite—"

"Goodbye," Rika interrupted. She seized the plate of bread and shoved him out the door. "Such rudeness, only coming here to spy and gossip," she huffed.

Despite her preoccupations, Gerda laughed at Rika's attitude. "You've been talking my ear off ever since I snuck up on you and you want to know everything about me."

"That's different. I met you first."

Gerda raised her eyebrows, and bit into a chive-and-rosemary flavored roll.

The second server didn't even bother inventing an excuse. Her feathery dress was brown and cream, and she carried only one glass of wine. "Are you really going north to face the Snow Queen?" she asked Gerda without preamble. "You must be very silly if you are. Just thinking about her makes all my feathers want to fall off."

"Hanna, stop pestering."

"But we always tell each other everything," the other girl complained. "You're no fun today."

"I'll tell you later but just leave her alone for now," Rika said.

"Just one more question," Hanna pleaded.

"It's all right," Gerda said to her small, self-appointed guardian.

Hanna grinned and bounced a little. "Did you really steal her cloak? Because one time, she and her sisters were swimming and this human boy—"

"Good night!" Rika shoved her friend out of the room.

"I didn't know ravens could blush," Gerda said, examining the flush that spread all the way to the raven girl's collar.

Rika donned her bird shape and flew off to the windowsill. Despite the lack of expressions on a bird's face, Gerda had the distinct impression that the girl was sulking.

This pattern continued, each server claiming that "just one more thing" had been forgotten in the kitchens and trying to get a good look at Gerda. During the fourth incident Rika said, "The kitchen seems to be having a lot of trouble tonight. Do I need to tell the queen that the cooks and servers have suddenly become incompetent?"

The interruptions ceased.

For all her stern words against the constant questions of others, Rika herself prattled on throughout the meal, seemingly content to talk with few responses. As the meal went on Gerda found it restful to listen to the flow of words. She was surprised to find that after all of Rika's early distress, the girl appeared to have either forgotten or stopped caring that Gerda had stolen her feather cloak. When in bird form, she occasionally swooped down and snatched bites of food from the dinner. Gerda managed to tweak the bird's tail feathers once or twice. Even in the middle of all her worries, she found herself smiling when she imagined how her grandmother would have been amused by this girl.

The meal itself was exquisite—salads, chilled soups, and fruit-flavored wine—but Gerda ate little. Like her mind, her stomach had difficulty settling down. After she pushed away the plates, Rika showed her to a bedchamber. The outer wall was one large window that led to a narrow but long balcony with climbing roses growing up its sides. The night had come at last, creeping through the forest and slipping up to the palace.

She tried her best to sleep but her feet didn't want to remain still. Her mind also did not seem to be able to quiet down. Kai and his logic would have said that she needed to be well-rested for traveling, and Nana would have said that she should take better care of herself, but she couldn't obey.

After tossing and turning so much that the bed sheets became twisted every which way, she gave up and began to roam about the palace. The building was as silent as when she had entered it that morning. Several times she saw dreams leak like smoke through the keyholes of closed doors and gather themselves into recognizable shapes on the walls. One of the dreams became a pair of swans that swam languidly on a dream-lake before taking flight across the hallways and ceiling. Even though Gerda remembered being chased by an irate swan as a child, she was mesmerized by these birds. They flew without tiring and circled one another. She watched until they flew out of a window towards the forest. She wondered if the dreams belonging to different people could talk to one another, so that friends could spend time together even when they slept.

She paced along corridors, walked up and down staircases, and gazed through windows at the dark forest. Fireflies hovered at some of the windows. For a little while, she distracted herself by catching them and watching the golden light leak through the gaps between her cupped hands. After many turns, she found herself in a courtyard with orange and lemon trees planted in small terraces that lined the walls. Several benches were located at the bottom. Though she knew summer was too late in the year for trees to flower, the air smelled as fragrant as though they still bloomed. Ripe fruit hung from the slender branches, the oranges as round as the full moon above her head. The oval lemons appeared nearly black.

Only the pocket against her hip felt cool. Gerda scowled. The box and layers of clothing kept the cold from injuring her but she always felt its presence, a hint of a chill even on this warm summer night. She wondered if the mirror somehow knew what she was doing, if it wanted her to reach the Snow Queen so that it could be reunited with the other pieces.

Dried violets rested in the pocket that held the mirror, little bits of purple and white at the ends of long stems toughened after drying. Sitting down next to one of the orange trees, she put the flowers back in her pocket but continued to hold the box in her lap. After several minutes of drumming her fingers on the hinge she lifted the lid and shook the mirror fragment out onto her palm. It lay in the dark like a star fallen to earth. The mirror bit into her skin like frostbite before numbing it. Gerda raised her cold arm and bent her face near.

It felt as though she were tumbling through icicles and frost. The wind pushed the snow through her open lips when she gasped, trickling down her throat. It froze even her voice. When she looked up the sky was the same shade of gray she recognized from when the depths of winter in Vasa, when the season had been settled in for months and a person would be willing to pay anything in exchange for one hour of real sunlight.

Part of the ground shone beneath snowdrifts when she looked down and she realized it was the river. She was standing on the frozen river and she could see the same building in the distance. It was closer than the first time she had looked into the mirror and she could now see that it was made of snow and ice. It still seemed too far away to walk to before dying of cold.

Once the immediate shock of winter subsided, Gerda saw that the land had continued to change since the last time she looked at it. Even though they were still almost invisible against the whiteness, she saw traces of color. In the frozen river, more threads of color laced through the ice. Only dull silver when she had first looked upon it, and only near-invisible hints of green the second time, now these tiny wisps of red, gold, and green ran everywhere below the surface.

Somehow this land had begun to change, even if it was only within the mirror, and winter didn't have to mean a lack of life. She looked intently at the land and imagined plants growing up from the snow, ones that could survive winter: small holly shrubs with their sharp-smelling leaves and red berries; hellebore that remained green throughout frosts and that flowered before spring came; witch hazel shrubs that showed their yellow flowers when snow remained on the ground; and yew hedges, with its berries and seeds that birds eagerly consumed by birds every year.

The edge of the shard cut into her palm. When she broke free of winter, she found herself curled up against the orange tree. She had difficulty moving the hand that held the mirror and almost dropped the little piece several times before she could return it to the box. This time the multitude of scents did not make her feel ill, but she continued to imagine snow beneath her hands. She leaned against the tree until she neither felt nor tasted winter. By the time she could flex her fingers, there was only the scent of citrus trees bearing fruit.

She stood up and reached one arm into the tree's branches. The orange she picked was so large that she had to cup it in both hands. When she used the small knife from her other pocket she cut too far into the orange skin and juice leaked onto her hands. She licked her fingers and readjusted her grip. Even with only the moon for light, she was able to peel away the rind in one piece, around and around so that it curled in the air. When she neared the end she fumbled and the knife slipped across her thumb. She swore and wrapped it in a handkerchief.

Gerda strolled through the palace as she ate. When she passed through a courtyard with a fountain, she paused to wash her hands. As she straightened, she saw a flicker of light in a high window. Within moments she spotted another flicker and next a flash of light reflecting off of something metallic. She went to find it.

She took wrong turns in the hallways several times but managed to keep going higher in the building. Finally she saw the night sky through an open door at the top of a staircase. There she found Suvi, who stood on a platform looking into a golden telescope. The sky above them was crammed so full with stars that it seemed about to overflow.

The queen looked up and smiled. "Impressed?"

"It's beautiful."

"You will be happy to know that you can leave early tomorrow morning as planned. The boat has been completed and I left orders for supplies to be assembled," Suvi said. "The river will eventually freeze of course, but you should be able to travel quickly until then."

"Thank you." Gerda bit her lip. "I didn't think you were really going to help me."

Suvi raised her eyebrows. "What made you believe that?"

"I appreciate everything, I promise, but I worried I was going to be tricked again."

"What do you mean?"

"Before I got here I was…stopped from looking for Kai. Somebody took my memories away because she said it would keep me safe. She didn't think I could save him. That's why I was so late."

"And you thought I would be the same."

Gerda paced around the tower. "You asked me to wait just a little longer before leaving. That's what *she* said. She kept finding ways to delay me and tricking me into agreeing. I told her I had a piece of the Snow Queen's mirror and I was going to use it to get Kai back. She hid it and pretended to be my mother. I should have known better." She smacked one fist against the stone walls as she walked.

"You can't blame yourself for everything. Nobody can carry that much guilt." Suvi took Gerda's hand and made her stop beating it against the stone.

"But it *is* my fault!"

"For stopping your search or for not keeping him safe from the Snow Queen?" Suvi asked gently.

Gerda sighed. "Both."

"You have to stop hating yourself."

"I don't think I can."

"Listen to me," Suvi said. "I know the Snow Queen. She's had ages upon ages to practice her cleverness and she's very skilled at playing with humans. She could have fooled you into believing anything she wanted. And I can guess who stole your memories: Linnea is my sister. She means well and I'm certain she cares for you, but she always wants to protect everybody instead of letting them do things for themselves."

"So you think I can do it?" Gerda asked.

"I think you have to. Even if you decided not to look for your brother, the Snow Queen would still learn that he cannot complete the mirror and she will begin searching for that last piece."

"I still can't believe that somebody could always want it to be winter."

Suvi smiled ruefully. "She's never understood that there is a proper time and place for everything. I told her that once and she tried to bury me in ice as a result."

Gerda shivered at the queen's matter-of-fact recounting. "Has she always been like that? It seems like she'd rather break the world than let winter end."

Suvi turned from Gerda then, and stared into the warm night. "We all have our favorite seasons and it's only natural to want them to last. Out of all of us she was always the most extreme and fierce about her time, though she used to accept that there was a need for change during the year in the other world. As time went on, she cared about the other seasons less and less, and she has wanted an unending winter for many years now. Sometimes I think she may have looked into her mirror too long."

"I used to look forward to winter every year. She ruined that."

"You can't think that way. If you let her make you hate or fear something, that gives her control over you."

"But she *does* scare me." The summer night felt cold now and Gerda's arms were covered with goose bumps. Pulling her hands free, she slid down the wall and brought her knees to her chest. "You weren't there when I tried to stop her from taking Kai. She almost killed me."

Suvi knelt beside her. The fine fabric of her dress hissed against the stones. "Listen to me: I know you're strong. If you were not, you wouldn't have gone searching for your brother after he was taken. You would have mourned him and tried to go on with your life. Yet you're still here, even though you know what she can do. And so I have to believe and hope that you will succeed." She pulled Gerda to her feet. "At least try to rest." The queen paused. "Out of curiosity, what changed your mind about me?"

"You had the boat." Gerda looked at the divide in the forest where the river was located. "It was something I could see and touch. Even if you were lying about why you had it, I could have changed my mind earlier and kept walking instead of staying."

"I'm glad you stayed." As they descended the stairs Suvi asked, "May I see your piece of the mirror?"

"I'd rather you didn't." Gerda wondered if even the Summer Queen could remain completely unaffected by the allure of winter held in that little bit of glass. "It's changed, though. I don't know why but each time I've looked through it, I can see more of the other seasons."

"It has?" Suvi's eyes lit up. "It's understandable that the abilities of each piece would be weaker when they were scattered, but I'm sure my sister started reuniting them as soon as she was able. Since this is the last one, perhaps it can't resist being influenced by all the seasons. That could be useful."

"Do you have any ideas?"

"No but it certainly opens the door to possibilities. Perhaps that piece of the mirror will never be able to return to its original state."

"Which means that the Snow Queen can't use it," Gerda said. Lightness grew in her body and banished the last of the chill that had overcome her.

"It's possible. I certainly don't like to think about what would happen if you tested it and turned out to be wrong, but you never know." Suvi shrugged. "Maybe something can come of the Snow Queen's dislike of seasons other than her own."

"Maybe."

"One last thing."

Gerda looked up at the queen, who still stood several steps above her. "What is it?"

"Even after everything she's done, she's still my sister. I know you might want revenge but I still love her. Do you think you would kill your brother if he turned out like the Snow Queen? Keep that in mind when you find them." She slipped past Gerda and down the hall.

Gerda returned to her borrowed bedroom and slipped into a cool nightgown. She could still smell the comforting fragrance of roses as she fell asleep.

That night Gerda dreamed she was part of a flock of ravens that soared along the walls and ceiling of the hall outside her bedroom. She couldn't hear their wings beating or any cawing, although she felt her own beak open and close.

Other dreams entered and exited the rooms as the flock of birds passed. She saw a dream-cat lying on a chair. One of her fellow birds broke away from the flock and tweaked the cat's ears. The cat hissed silently and jumped straight up, missing the bird by mere inches. The birds flew around the cat as it jumped and spun. Gerda laughed as they tired of the sport and left the irate feline behind.

She liked watching the dark shadows move against the pale stone of the palace. Without warning the other ravens began to vanish, snuffed out one by one like puffs soot. Her own wings faded and she stood in her human body once more. The palace walls melted away and changed into the winter courtyard at Vasa's conservatory.

There was no sound of the wind whistling overhead or the crunching snow beneath her feet. The air smelled of sweet roses. She blinked and found herself kneeling at the edge of the pool. Even with her thin nightgown and the snow all around, she didn't feel cold.

And as in the last time she had knelt here, a picture appeared within the ice. She saw Suvi and the Snow Queen facing each other. Suvi's mouth moved but no sound emerged. The Snow Queen also spoke silently and shook her head.

She watched them argue for a long time before Suvi tried to take her sister's hand. The Snow Queen slapped the touch away and raised her arms. A layer of ice began to grow up from the Summer Queen's feet.

"She did that to me," a voice said.

Gerda looked up. Eva knelt on her left and Kai crouched on her right. Both of them watched the queens of summer and winter.

"You have to get rid of her," Eva said.

"Suvi asked you not to," Kai said.

"She needs killing."

"She's necessary."

"You have to do it—there's no other way."

The growing ice had almost reached Suvi's waist when her skin glowed with a golden light and the ice melted. The Snow Queen snarled one last comment and strode away.

Kai put his hand on Gerda's arm. "Would you kill me if I became like her?"

It was the most terrifying thing she could imagine, even more than what she had already seen the Snow Queen do. Yet there was only one answer she could give. "Never."

The conservatory disappeared. Gerda awoke with a jolt. She lay in the soft bed at the summer palace and there was nothing else in the room with her: no shadow ravens, Eva, or Kai, only the sound of crickets chirping in the forest. She closed her eyes and remembered no other dreams for the rest of the night.

Rika knocked on the door soon after dawn, as Gerda was dressing in her new clothing that lacked mud and grass stains. "They all wanted to come," the raven girl said as soon as she entered the room, without even saying, "Good morning."

"Who wanted to come where?" Gerda asked.

"Everybody in the palace wanted to come with you on your quest."

Gerda imagined the entire palace population following her, even the people she had never seen. "Oh, no."

Rika giggled. "Don't worry. The queen put a stop to it as soon as she heard the first rumors. She's told everybody to stay put."

"Do they think I'm just going on a picnic?" Gerda demanded. "The Snow Queen would know we were coming from miles away, if they didn't get tired and wander off first."

Rika shrugged. "Sometimes the people here get bored."

"Where is the queen?"

"She and her consort are likely at the river by now. I was sent to fetch you as soon as you're ready."

Gerda and Rika crossed the short distance through the forest to where Suvi and Lukas waited with the now-complete golden boat moored to the riverbank. Leather packs containing supplies were tucked underneath the bench. Patterns of ivy had been embossed into the sides of the boat, even including the detail of veins within the leaves. Chips of jewels were embedded at the leaves' tips. In the morning sunlight, the boat caught the eye like fire.

"It's beautiful," Gerda said. "But how do I use it?"

"For a direction, all you have to do is stay on the river. As far as sailing, the boat will move whenever it is free in the water. If you wish to stop, lean in the direction you want and simply tie it up once you reach the riverbank," Suvi said.

Gerda hugged her. "Thank you."

The older woman smiled and cupped Gerda's face in her hands. "Good luck."

Lukas helped Gerda climb into the boat. He said, "Think about coming by with your brother once you get him back. I'd be interested in meeting this person you mistook for me."

"Maybe."

"Stay on the river as much as possible," Suvi said. "There are some robbers who live farther north but you should be able to avoid them as long as you keep to the water."

Gerda nodded. "I'll remember."

Lukas untied the boat and tossed the rope to her. The current immediately pulled the boat out to the center of the river. He and Suvi waved at her from the bank, and Gerda waved back. Rika changed back into her raven form and soared above Gerda, cawing loudly. She flew in spirals and dove through the bright sky. The large black bird even perched on the prow of the boat for a moment before settling in one of the trees and watching as Gerda sailed past.

To her astonishment, Gerda found herself smiling. She was out in the wide world once more and she would find Kai at its end.

# CHAPTER TEN

Being told that the boat would sail itself and experiencing it were two different things. Gerda held on tight as it swayed about in the current at first, but soon it was bobbing down the river steadily.

She didn't see any signs of human life as she traveled. She heard birds in the trees and saw small animals moving in the undergrowth, but there were no other people. She watched for Kai, even though now she did not expect to find him before arriving in the Snow Queen's lands.

When the worry threatened to overwhelm her, she distracted herself by looking through the supplies that Suvi had provided. The leather bags were filled until they nearly burst: not a feather more could have been slipped inside. Suvi hadn't lied when she said Gerda would be well-prepared: the bags contained food, winter clothing, and the sorts of odds and ends that are useful when traveling, like candles, matches, and a knife.

At the palace she had been anxious for the long day to end so that it would almost be time to leave; now the night seemed to come too soon. It was still twilight when her yawns became more frequent and the horizon ahead began to blur. The thought of traveling throughout the night tempted her but the fear that the boat might capsize while she slept was stronger. She moored the boat to a clump of tree roots that protruded from the bank and curled up for the night. She lay in the gently rocking boat and hummed one of Nana's lullabies to herself until she fell asleep.

She continued traveling on the river for over a week. The weather remained hot and dry, but she noticed that twilight came creeping along a little sooner each day. Much of the forest around her remained green but some of the leaves had started to take on a golden hue.

It was on a rare cloudy morning when she ventured ashore to look for late-season nuts or berries. She remembered Suvi's warnings to stay on the water, but she still hadn't seen any signs of human life and it would be only a short trip ashore. The forest's offerings were sparse but she found a cluster of hazelnut shrubs not too far out of sight of her boat.

As she was about to fill her pockets, the skin crawled on the back of her neck. She looked around and realized that the forest was near-silent. No birds sang and the constant chattering of squirrels had ceased. The only sound was the river in the distance.

She stood up slowly and started to walk back. Her skin still prickled. The boat seemed so much farther away now. The forest felt darker, despite the brightness of trees changing to their autumn colors. Silence grew all around until it felt louder than any storm, but she kept to a walking pace until a branch snapped behind her. Then she ran.

She raced through the forest, jumping over tree roots and swerving around bushes. Over the loudness of her breathing, she heard footsteps pounding in the leaves behind her.

Small twigs and dried leaves crackled. With every step, she fought the urge to turn and see what was chasing her. All she had to do was get to the water and she would be safe.

Just as she caught a glimpse of the golden boat shining between the trees, she stepped where she should have jumped. A stick slipped beneath her foot and she couldn't catch her balance. Something slammed into her back, and she tumbled head over feet.

As Gerda lay face down among the undergrowth with her heart still racing, she heard a woman's voice purr, "Good morning, princess."

"Sounds like you're having fun," a rough voice called from the direction of the river. "Need any help, Kristina?"

Kristina laughed. "When have I ever needed your help? There's no trouble to speak of."

Gerda tried to squirm away but she didn't get far. She was flipped onto her back and got a look at her attacker for the first time. The other woman was perhaps the same age as her, with red-brown hair falling out from under a cap, and ink-dark eyes.

Kristina knelt on Gerda's arm and pressed a knife to her throat. "I'd settle down if I were you. I hadn't planned on shedding any blood this morning, but that doesn't mean I won't do it if I have to."

Gerda obeyed. The cold blade rose and fell on her neck as she tried to slow her breathing. It was so much like when she had been caught sneaking into the summer palace but this time, there was no benevolent queen to say there had been a mistake.

Kristina grinned. "Much better."

"Would you stop playing already?" another voice asked, also coming from the river. "There's a good haul here. The princess has some nice trinkets."

"We're coming." Before Gerda could think of how to get away from that knife, she was hauled to her feet and Kristina bound her hands before her.

The robber tapped the knife against Gerda's shoulder and grinned. "Time to see what you're worth, princess."

When they arrived at the river Gerda saw five other robbers standing by her boat, which had been unmoored from its cluster of willow trees and pulled out of the water. Although she wouldn't have guessed it from the voices alone, she had listened to enough of Nana's stories to recognize trolls when she saw them. They appeared to be male, short and thick-bodied. Wide belts with knives circled their heavy coats and they wore chunky boots. Pointed ears poked out from beneath their wild, pale hair and all of them had thick beards. Their skin was greenish-gray. Each troll had a long tail that twitched about and trailed to the ground.

"I'm not a princess," was the only thing she could think to say.

"'Course you are," one of the trolls said. "Got a golden boat, don't you?"

Gerda just shook her head.

Kristina tapped her foot. "He has a point. Why travel with such riches if you're not royalty?"

"The boat was a gift. If you let me leave, I'll give it to you," Gerda said. These robbers were nothing like Linnea but she felt the same panic that she had experienced upon realizing how much time she had wasted at the cottage. She could almost hear the minutes ticking away. She couldn't be delayed again, not after having come so far.

The trolls laughed. "Don't you know anything?" one of them asked. "You can't *give* it to us. We've already taken it."

A troll wearing a red hat nudged him. "If she's not a princess, doesn't that mean nobody'll pay for her?"

"That's exactly what it means," Gerda told him. If only she could convince the robbers that there was nothing more to gain. A boat covered with gold ought to be enough of a prize for even the greediest troll. "So you might as well take the boat and leave me alone."

Kristina grinned. "Not a chance. We haven't had a visitor in a while and you'll be useful for some fun."

"Is that a good idea?" the troll in the red hat asked hesitantly. "Things didn't turn out so well that time you decided to keep that prince."

"That was a once-in-a-lifetime mistake!" Kristina scowled and started walking deeper into the forest, towing Gerda behind her. Gerda wondered what kind of trouble the prince had caused and whether he'd escaped alive. The trolls followed, carrying the boat on their shoulders.

Her knowledge about trolls should have been an advantage, but it didn't feel like one: she knew dozens of stories and none of the trolls in them were kind. They turned humans into statues, or ate them, or made them into slaves. Nana's stories had helped her to strike a deal with Rika but she couldn't think of any ways to outwit these robbers. Trolls' prisoners were usually princesses who were rescued by princes or knights. She was trying to save Kai but there was nobody to rescue her. Nana had said that sometimes trolls turned into stone when touched by daylight but these robbers only squinted in the light.

She tried using anger to push aside her terror. Each reluctant step into the forest took her farther away from the river and farther from Kai. She wondered if he would haunt her dreams once more.

They left summer farther behind with every passing moment. The light grew dim under the forest canopy. The willow trees by the river still had green leaves, but the leaves around her changed color as she watched: copper, gold, red, brown, and green shot through with scarlet.

She scuffed her feet as they walked. The trail likely wouldn't last long but it was the only thing she could do. They followed no path that she could see but Kristina led the way without pausing, turning confidently at places where Gerda couldn't see any landmarks. There was just enough space between the trees for the trolls to pass through with the boat, although sometimes they collided against the trunks. She winced at the careless treatment of the queen's gift.

Kristina spoke again. "So if you aren't a princess—and I'm not saying that I believe that, mind you—just what *are* you up to?"

"I'm rescuing my brother."

"And just what did he do, get himself captured by a giant or did he do something even stupider?"

If Kristina wanted the truth, she'd get it. "He's with the Snow Queen."

All the robbers stopped walking and stared at her.

"You're the one who asked," she said, almost cheerfully. "She kidnapped him and wants him to fix her mirror so that she can make it winter forever. And I'm going after them."

"You're going after the Snow Queen," Kristina said flatly.

"That's right. So if you think about it, I'm more trouble than I'm worth. You might as well let me go."

"Keep moving." Kristina ordered the trolls. She tugged on the rope that bound Gerda and continued walking. "The Snow Queen's more powerful than some traveler who gets herself captured in five minutes."

"What if she knows that I'm looking for my brother and decides to come after me? All of you could be in danger."

"She never comes here. Mother sees to that. So if *you* think about it, we're doing you a favor by keeping you away from her."

Gerda made a face. At least she still had the piece of the mirror in her pocket. Maybe it could help her escape somehow.

Before long the clouds opened up and rain poured down onto them, adding to her bad mood. She swore but the trolls made no response to the change in weather: when she looked back she saw that their thick hair and beards were filled with glimmering droplets. Their pointed ears flicked in the wind and they hitched their tails over their arms.

She watched rivulets of water skim across the packed earth and change it into thick mud. It sucked and squelched at her feet like a living creature; in one deep puddle, the mud almost pulled off one of her shoes. A trail of water snaked down the front of her shirt. The mud splashed up to her knees and the soggy rope chafed her skin. The only blessing was that she could still see; Kai had always complained about being blinded whenever the rain washed over his glasses. He would have been able to think of another argument for freedom. She pretended that he stood next to her, griping about the weather and taunting Kristina until she let them leave just to get him to be quiet.

They had traveled far enough that she could no longer hear the river. Now she listened to the wind making the tree branches creak against one another. It blew the leaves about after the rain knocked them out of their trees. The leaves spiraled through the air and landed with little slaps in the mud, leaving more space in the canopy for the rain to leak through. Where the leaves overlapped they created a slick, lacquered path.

She slipped once. Her clothing was soaking wet and she barely managed to keep her face out of the mud. Kristina helped her up without taunting, even when both of them almost fell down again. The trolls now had difficulty as well: despite the handholds on the sides of the boat, the rain made the gold slippery and the boat slithered in the trolls' grasp. They bumped into trees often and she could hear them muttering to each other. She was too tired to feel much glee at their discomfort.

The unceasing rain made the minutes blur together like colors running in cheaply dyed cloth. At last Kristina halted. Gerda lifted her head. That stood by a cluster of massive oak trees that grew at the base of an ancient fortress that had fallen almost entirely apart.

"This is how things are going to be," Kristina said to the group. She pointed at Gerda. "We're telling the others that she's a princess. You," she said to the troll in the red hat, "are going to leave tomorrow to find her family and ask for a ransom."

"But it doesn't sound like she is a princess anymore."

Kristina sighed. "You're not going to tell anybody that. None of you are. If you do, I'll see to it that you'll be outdoors from sunrise until sunset on a very, very sunny day."

"But I won't be able to find her family! What will Hedvig do when I don't come home with anything?"

"Try to rob somebody else in the meantime. If you still can't find anything, come to me first and I'll tell you what to do."

"Why are you doing this?" Gerda asked.

"You'll find out. Now, go on." Kristina pushed Gerda to a gap in the nearest tree. To her amazement, Gerda found a staircase descending into the earth. The watery daylight seeped in a short distance and then there was only the dark.

"Keep moving," Kristina told her, one hand tight on Gerda's shoulder. Gerda could hear the trolls grumbling over the weight of the golden boat.

"I can't see anything."

Kristina sighed but released Gerda long enough to pull a small lantern from a niche in the earthen wall. A match sizzled and lit a stubby candle. Old wax covered the lantern's base. Gerda wanted to cup her hands around the flame and let the heat lick at her until she was warm all the way through. Kristina stepped ahead and led her down the stairs.

The tunnel had been carved wide enough for two people to walk side-by-side, but it did not feel spacious: tree roots hung from the earthen roof and brushed the tops of their heads like dangling spider legs. Although dry, the tunnel was cool and her clammy hands began to shake.

Kristina rapped on a plank of wood at the end of the tunnel. It swung in and they stepped through.

Somehow that simple piece of wood had completely blocked the noise of the room that Gerda was led into. Many voices spoke loudly and feet stamped on the stone floor. The space seemed to be an enormous cavern. It was a dim room, despite candles on the earthen walls and a fire blazing in a pit at the room's center. The whole space smelled of smoke and wet hair. She wanted to walk straight to the fire. Her wet clothes stuck to her body. If being dry meant that she would reek of smoke and have to sit shoulder-to-shoulder with trolls, there were worse fates.

Each face she saw belonged to a troll. The men and women appeared much the same, except that the women didn't have beards. Their hair was just as wild however, sticking out in all directions with shining beads tied in amongst the tangles. Each troll wore a thick jacket and either trousers or a skirt, all in the bold colors of the autumn forest.

She had only a few moments to herself before Kristina sliced through the rope around her wrists and led the group to a battered chair the size of a throne placed before the fire. The seams of the leather covering were half-ripped open and stuffing leaked out. A troll woman sat in the chair and watched them approach. A dented crown carved of horn was tangled in her graying hair and she wore thick chains of gold about her neck. Her belt was full of knives.

"Good pickings today?" the troll queen asked, eyeing the golden boat that shone even brighter in the firelight.

"Good enough, Mother," Kristina said in a fond tone. Gerda started. She knew a few stories in which trolls stole children, but none where the trolls took them as family. "We caught a princess today with plenty of riches." The trolls set the boat down and rolled their shoulders.

The queen looked Gerda up and down. "She's not dressed like a princess."

Kristina rolled her eyes. "The silly thing thought she would go adventuring and tried to be in disguise. It's just like a princess, to take off her fancy gown and not think that a golden boat would stand out. Fredrik has already volunteered to leave tomorrow and go to her family for a ransom."

The troll with the red hat nodded. "That's right, Hedvig, I'll go and ask them for...all kinds of good things."

"But will they pay enough?" Hedvig mused. "The boat is a pretty prize. It might be simpler to just toss her in the pot. Do it now, and she'll be tender in time for supper."

Gerda flinched at the look on the queen's face. She worried that she wouldn't be able to do anything but squeak but her voice came out strong enough when she said, "I didn't go out adventuring just to end up as a snack for somebody who can't be bothered to go out and find her own meals. Try to turn me into a meal and I'll take you with me."

"Good attitude. That would add a bit of spice to the stew." Hedvig hopped down from her throne and squeezed Gerda's arm. "A bit scrawny, but I've had worse."

Kristina sighed. "Think ahead, Mother. If you eat her now, she's good for one meal at most. But if Fredrik tells her parents that she's in danger..." She gave Gerda a sharp look.

"Oh, I'm sure they'll ransom me. We have a lot of farmland so there's a lot of sheep, and chickens, and...other delicious things. You could eat well for a year."

"I'll keep her with me until them. I need some new entertainment and she can be trained to be useful."

Hedvig waved a thick hand with jeweled rings on every finger. "Keep your new pet, then. But she's your responsibility."

Kristina blew a kiss to her mother and ushered Gerda away from the fire. As they walked away, Gerda saw Hedvig inspecting the golden boat. Several of the other robbers began to spill the contents of the bags onto the floor. One of them attempted to pry the gems loose from her boat but his knife kept slipping. The others laughed.

"This way," Kristina said. They walked down a hall that twisted and turned away from the cavern. The sounds of the trolls' laughter drifted behind them. They passed many other rooms and halls until Gerda was completely turned around. Eventually they came to a room that, unlike most of the others, was closed off by a door. Kristina pulled out a ring with dozens of keys chiming against one another and unlocked the door.

Inside the room, Gerda saw furs, large wooden chests carved with patterns of animals, plates of half-eaten food, and dried leaves scattered everywhere. A large mound of leaves was gathered in the middle of the room, with furs spread over it and scattered with lumpy pillows. The roots of a large tree had spread all the way across the ceiling, and a cage holding small, fluttering birds dangled from one root.

An assortment of candles and lamps were piled atop a small table. Kristina lit several lamps, holding each match until its flame nearly kissed her calloused fingertips. She spread the lamps throughout the room. Deep shadows still filled the room's corners, but there was enough light for them to move without stumbling.

"Thanks for back there," Gerda said.

"Don't make me regret it. Turn on me and I'll toss you into the deepest hole I can find." Kristina tossed over a coarse towel. "Dry off before you freeze. There's clothing in the largest chest and you can use the pitcher." The robber wasted no time in unwinding the damp scarf from around her neck and pulling off her soaked jacket.

Gerda's teeth chattered. The hot bath she had taken at Suvi's palace dinner felt as though it had happened years ago. The water in a pitcher standing near her was frigid, but she scrubbed the worst of the mud off of her skin and wrapped herself in a tattered quilt while searching through the chest. The clothes were also likely stolen, judging by the variety of sizes and styles. Most of them were in men's styles (useful for running after people and robbing them, her mind whispered) but she spotted several bright silk dresses. She suppressed a smirk at the thought of the trolls tramping around their underground home in any of those outfits. She didn't expect to see her supplies from Suvi ever again, but during her search for clothing that would fit her she noticed several coats that looked like they would be suitable for winter. They'd come in handy soon enough.

As Kristina fingered the buttons of the embroidered vest she wore, she said, "Empty your pockets."

Gerda paused in the middle of donning a pair of wonderfully dry socks. "What?"

"Empty the pockets in your old clothes. I want anything valuable."

Gerda scowled but Kristina had picked up another knife and was tossing it from hand to hand. She knelt by her pile of clothing and pulled out the bits of flowers that hadn't been dissolved by the rain. There were wizened violets, columbine flowers leaking seeds, rose petals as thin as onionskin, a clover chain, sharp rosemary leaves, and crumpled apple blossoms. A stranger might have thought they were love tokens, sending a different message through each flower.

The knife stilled. "What was that?"

"Flowers. See?" Gerda spread her hands.

"No, the other thing."

"Do you really think I'd be able to hide anything?" Gerda asked, lacing her voice with annoyance. She huffed and started to gather up the bundle of wet clothes.

"Apparently not." Kristina plucked the little box containing the mirror fragment from where Gerda had tucked it into the pile of fabric. "Not a bad plan for a beginner but you could have done better. We'll work on that. You can put the rabbit food away." She waved at the little heap of herbs and flowers.

Gerda wrapped up her plants. Only the rosemary still carried any scent that lingered over the smells of mud and rain. She saw Kristina about to pry the box apart. "Don't open that!"

"Why?" Kristina laughed and rattled the box. She pursed her lips and assumed an exaggeratedly thoughtful pose. "Is there some kind of trap in it that will spring out at me?"

Perhaps Gerda could have escaped if the robber succumbed to the distraction of the mirror, but she couldn't bring herself to want anybody to fall to the mirror's influence. "It's a piece of the Snow Queen's mirror."

"*What?*" Kristina opened the box and peered inside then, but she snapped it shut almost instantly. Looking shaken, she fell back onto a pile of furs with the box still in hand. "Not-princess, I think you ought to tell me your name and the rest of your story."

Gerda told her a shortened version. The robber remained seated but turned to watch as Gerda paced the room throughout her recitation. She grew cold while speaking of the Snow Queen and wrapped the quilt around herself once more. The end trailed behind her and her elbow rubbed against a patch nearly worn through.

She had made her way to the bird cage by the time she ended her story. The tiny, captive birds chirped and pecked at a small dish filled with orange-red berries. Watching them, she could almost pretend that she was spying on the birds at home in Vasa.

"You mean to tell me that your only plan is to keep walking until you find the Snow Queen, without any idea of what you'll do once you face her?" Kristina demanded.

The illusion of being at home cracked. "More or less," Gerda said. Talking with Suvi had allowed her to consider using the mirror against the Snow Queen but she hadn't yet been able to pull her wispy ideas together into a real plan.

Kristina snorted. "You're an idiot."

"Then I'm an idiot who's going to save her brother," Gerda said sharply. "I already told you why I had to leave when you found me. "You're the one who wanted to know what I was doing. Now you see why I have to leave."

The robber waved this aside. "It's best to leave the Snow Queen alone. Your brother needs to learn how to take care of himself. Besides, he won't be able to fix her mirror if he doesn't have this."

"I promised to rescue him."

"The Snow Queen would freeze you. Better that you stay here and out of her way."

"But what's happened isn't his fault! It wasn't his idea to be stuck with that part of the mirror inside him. If that hadn't happened, he never would have gone with her. Would you be so calm if your mother were the one who'd been...*changed* by that thing?" Kristina sat between her and the door. Even if Gerda managed to shove past, she would still have to get through all the trolls.

"Mother would never end up in that situation. In any case, do you really think a human can stop the Snow Queen?"

"I do." She had to keep thinking that it *might* be possible, or the doubts would crush her.

"I was able to take you prisoner and you didn't suspect a thing until I was almost standing beside you," Kristina pointed out. "You wouldn't last five minutes against her—and that's if she's in the mood to play a little before freezing you."

"What about when she decides to go hunting for this piece of the mirror? She's killed people for the other pieces. Even if you don't care about me or my brother, the safest thing for all of you is to let me get far away from here."

"We can take care of ourselves."

"But what will your mother say when she finds out you're holding onto something that could make the Snow Queen come after you?"

"I'm good at hiding things. Even if the Snow Queen did think to come here, which I doubt, she wouldn't be able to find it."

As Gerda tried to come up with another argument, Kristina rummaged through a box containing bits of jewelry. "I forgot something earlier. Here." The robber clasped a thick gold bracelet around Gerda's wrist.

Gerda frowned at both the change in conversation and the unexpected action. "Thank you?"

Kristina grinned. "Lesson one: beware of robbers giving gifts. That bracelet is one of a pair and it'll let me know if you try to run off." She pushed up her own sleeve to reveal an identical gold band.

"And just how is it supposed to do that?"

"It's a secret."

Gerda found the thin line where the bracelet clasped but couldn't pry the ends apart.

"It's no good doing that," Kristina said, "there's a trick to it."

Gerda clenched her hands into fists. She wanted to slap the robber. "If you're that desperate to keep me here, why not throw me into a dungeon and be done with it?"

"That wouldn't be as much fun."

Gerda noticed that the other woman's hands were now empty. "What did you do with the mirror?"

"I hid it, like I said I would."

"Give it back!"

"No."

Gerda started to walk to the jewelry box—it seemed the most logical hiding place—but Kristina grabbed her shoulder. "It's not in there. Lesson two: don't be so easily distracted. I could have hidden it any number of places while you were busy with your pretty new bracelet. So, are you ready to go back?"

"Not while your mother's still thinking about cooking me up for supper."

"Don't worry; she'll have forgotten already."

"I'm more worried that she'll have the idea again."

Kristina slung an arm around Gerda's neck. "She'll be too busy thinking about what she might get from your 'family.' They won't do anything to you so long as I'm around."

"Are you sure?"

"I promise. Remember, I'm the one you need to worry about." Kristina tapped her bracelet. She then reached into one of her trunks and pulled out a long instrument case. The leather was cracked from age but the clasps gleamed silver, showing not the slightest hint of tarnish.

Gerda stepped back without meaning to. "What's in there?"

"My nyckelharpa."

"Not a fiddle?"

"Never touched one." Kristina looked sharply at her. "What is the matter now? You've gone white as a ghost—and I've seen a few of them in my time."

"The last musician I met tried to drown me," Gerda said. That alluring fiddle music echoed in her head. She could almost feel the näck's hands around her neck once more.

Kristina stared at her then slowly grinned. "You know the most interesting people. You don't seem drowned, so how did you get away?"

Gerda looked her straight in the eye. "I hit him with a rock."

The robber laughed as loudly as any of the trolls. "Oh, you're definitely staying. And wait until you hear me play—I'm far better than any other musician. Come along, now." She ushered Gerda out of the room.

The main cave was still chaotic when they returned. Kristina led her down a hallway to a large kitchen and served them each a portion of thick, hot stew in wooden bowls. She cut off thick slices from a loaf of rye bread. A pitcher contained cold cider. She showed Gerda the way back to the main room, and then made her way to the troll queen's side.

Gerda sat on a scarred wooden bench in the shadows with her back to the wall near the entrance to another hallway. She watched the robbers as she ate. The golden boat still lay next to the fire but now several of the trolls used it as a place to sit. She didn't see any of her supplies.

Shortly after she sat down, two female trolls sat down on either side of her. She didn't recognize them from the group that had abducted her. "So you're Kristina's newest find," the one on Gerda's left said cheerfully. She wore a green dress and tapped a clay pipe against her knee. Ashes smudged the front of her skirt. "It'll be fun to have a princess around. We haven't had one of those in a long time."

Gerda looked at her bowl and didn't say anything. Her knuckles turned white as she gripped its wooden rim.

The one on her right laughed. "Quiet thing, isn't she? I wouldn't have expected that after her entrance. Do you think—" she started to add but fell silent.

Gerda looked up. Across the room she saw Kristina giving the troll a forbidding look and a minute shake of her head.

"Have a good evening, princess," the troll on Gerda's right said before both robbers stood up and sauntered away. None of the trolls made an effort to approach her after that. They looked at her often and she could see them talking to one another, but none of them came so close to her again.

Hedvig held court at her chair by the fire. Just as Kristina had said, she seemed to have forgotten about Gerda entirely. The heat of the flames and a cup of ale turned the troll queen's face bright red. She could often be heard laughing over the noise of the room, amused by the antics of the other robbers. At one point Gerda watched two trolls who had been arguing over some trifle fall to wrestling. The smaller one was soon pushed back and fell down by the fire. He bounced up with a roar; she could see that the seat of his trousers was singed. His friends doused him with water to put out the sparks. Hedvig laughed so hard that Gerda thought the robber queen might lose control and fall into the fire herself.

She also watched Kristina. Although the woman wasn't physically a troll, she acted much like them: she drank as much, talked as loudly, and swaggered more than all the rest. She lounged atop a barrel with her long legs dangling. She appeared to be careful only of the instrument case, keeping it out of reach of careless feet and tails.

As Gerda ate, she looked around the room. She was certain she sat near the tunnel that had led them in from the forest but when she looked for the door she found only dirt walls. She sidled out of the room, taking the dishes with her. No one followed.

She returned the items to the kitchen and explored. It seemed impossible that there was just the one exit to the forest, but she couldn't find evidence that proved otherwise. The trolls' home was much larger than she had expected, and it started to feel like she was wandering through a honeycomb of underground rooms. Many of them appeared to be used for storing the trolls' stolen goods. None of the rooms looked as though they led back to the earth's surface. She scratched her initial on a wall in every room she examined.

Near the end of one corridor, she heard a scraping noise. She froze. When the sound happened again, it seemed to be coming from one of the rooms ahead. She slowly advanced until she thought she found the room it was coming from. Its entrance was barred by an iron gate but the gate had no lock.

A reindeer stood in the room. The noise she had heard was the scraping of the thick chain that connected one of his legs to the wall. Out of all the things she had guessed that might be kept by robbers—birds, small animals, other humans—a large reindeer hadn't entered her mind. "Did they try to cook you, too?" she asked.

The reindeer blinked its long-lashed eyes and watched her, neither moving closer nor shying away. There were wide antlers atop his head, not yet shed for the winter months. Just enough light came from a lantern in the corridor for her to see that his fur was colored like cream and pale earth.

The only reindeer Gerda had ever been close to was the statue in the park. This one was enormous, much larger than any of the pictures she had ever seen. She took one step forward. He didn't move. She took another and he still remained motionless. Gerda stretched out one arm. Her fingers hovered in the air, undecided, until she braved the chance of resting a hand on the reindeer's high shoulder. He flinched but didn't try to move away.

The thick fur was soft and warm on her fingers. She watched her hand rise and fall as he breathed. "I wonder how they managed to catch you," she said, though she didn't expect a response. "I'd have thought you could outrun even a whole group of trolls."

"He got separated from his herd and the queen's daughter found him. Snuck up on him while he was sleeping, though it took a dozen of the robbers to get him back here. My friend put up such a struggle, it took a whole week for them to untangle their beards," a light voice said.

Gerda gave a strangled yelp and jumped. The reindeer shied away at the sudden movement and she had to dodge his antlers. Yet nobody stood in the doorway.

The voice chuckled. "Over here. And don't make such a fuss; you don't want to catch *their* attention, do you?"

She peered around the dim room until she found the voice's owner sitting in a crack in the wall by the reindeer's head. He was less than a foot tall and slim as a reed. His gray clothing helped him blend into the wall but he wore a cap as red as maple leaves. A fringe of colorless hair stuck out below the cap, fine as dandelion fluff.

"You're a tomte, aren't you?" she asked.

"Of course I am," he said and chuckled. "What did you think I was, a small troll?"

"I'd never seen one of you before. My grandmother told me about you, though. She claimed her mother left food out for you."

"Very wise of her. And will you be setting food out for us?"

His cheek finally made her laugh. "I don't think so. You'll have to ask the trolls."

"I would rather try to catch a full-grown trout by myself," he muttered.

Gerda returned her attention to the reindeer, dropping to her knees to examine the clasp around his leg. Flakes of rust crumbled away and stained her hands. The base of the chain appeared to be fixed deep in the wall but she tugged at it anyway. Returning to the clasp, she found a keyhole and thought of the full key ring in Kristina's pocket.

"Do you know if Kristina has the key with her?" she asked.

"She might," the tomte said, "but that one hides things away like a squirrel with acorns. It could be in any of a dozen hiding places. I know all the good spots and I've still seen no sign of it. I am Nils, by the by." He jumped lightly onto the reindeer's head, where he wiggled into a good position to scratch behind the animal's ears. "And you are called Gerda, correct?"

"How do you know that?"

"I know almost everything that happens here. My family and I have been here since long before the trolls."

"Are there many of you?" she asked. "Nana says that you like to be near people who are tidy and kind, and that you prefer farms. I've never heard of you living underground. And don't trolls hate you?"

"It's true, we prefer to remain aboveground, but a few of my family remain here in the fortress. The others all left long ago but who are the trolls, to drive me out of my home? The queen's daughter knows of our presence but it amuses her to keep silent and watch."

"That part doesn't surprise me," Gerda muttered. She sighed and stroked the reindeer's leg. His eyes drifted half-shut in pleasure from Nils's scratching. "Has he been here long?"

"A few months."

"I'd go crazy if I were his size and cooped up in a little room like this. You say you've lived here a long time—can you help me escape?"

He looked amused and sad all at once. "I know dozens of ways in and out of here, ones that even the trolls are ignorant of. But you are too big; you would need to be no larger than myself to get out my way."

"Aren't there any others?"

"If you were in the building aboveground you could get out easily enough, but they blocked up all the entrances they could find when they built their home."

"Why do they even bother keeping the fortress if they don't use it?"

Nils laughed. "It's what they do. Surely you've noticed that they like to take things for themselves, whether they need them or not? They don't need my home, at least not right now, but that doesn't mean they want to let others use it. I haven't found any ways to the forest under the earth, except for that door that the trolls can make disappear."

"Can you keep trying?"

Nils furrowed his pale eyebrows. "I will if you take my friend when you leave. He's likely to waste away from being held indoors." He continued to stroke the reindeer's ears.

"I wonder why Kristina's kept him so long," she said.

"She's not the sort to give anything up. She comes by once in a while and taunts him with the idea of freedom. The rest of the time, I think she's content to know that he belongs to her alone," Nils said.

"I'll help him get freedom," Gerda promised.

"Good." The tomte's gaze sharpened and his ears twitched. "You may want to be getting back to those trolls."

"I'll come back here when I get the chance." Standing up, she stroked the reindeer's shoulder once more before running down the hall.

Despite Nils's warning, little seemed to have changed at the trolls' revels by the time she returned. In that room full of the scent of wood smoke and the sounds of logs crisping, she settled back into her corner. Kristina's considering gaze landed on her moments later and Gerda hid her rust-stained hands in her pockets. She eyed the bracelet sticking out from the cuff of her sweater.

"What are you waiting for, my girl?" Hedvig cried out. "We need some music."

Kristina laughed and took the nyckelharpa out of its case. She eased a strap over her shoulder and cradled the rectangular piece of wood against her body. The wider end was tucked beneath her right arm and she held a bow in that hand. A series of strings ran down the instrument until its far end, where they were caught up with tuning pegs. Her left arm curved beneath it and her fingers pressed against what looked like wooden pegs. She briefly tightened the strings and made a couple of passes with the bow. Then the music began.

At first the instrument sounded just like a fiddle. Gerda was frozen by the memory of losing her breath as water pressed down on her. She focused on the feel of her fingers clenched on the stone bench, the smoke of the fire, and the lack of any sound remotely resembling a stream's current.

Without intending to, she found herself tapping a foot to the rapid beat. Kristina played as though she was racing against the music and the tunes passed from one into another without pausing. The trolls who hadn't yet collapsed from drink clapped their hands in time to the songs. Several shouted encouragement to play even faster.

Some of the trolls paired off and began to dance. They waltzed and leapt around the fire, never missing a beat. They seemed as though they could dance without ceasing until the sun rose.

Gerda let her head fall back against the wall and closed her eyes. She wondered if Nils and the reindeer were listening. She pretended that streams of color grew from the nyckelharpa and circled around the listeners' heads. All the shades of the autumn forest were there but it was red that she saw most: the reds of roses, clay, crimson leaves, rosy old bricks, scarlet cardinals, translucent ruby wine, and vermilion flowers that grew in thick bunches.

The näck's music had mesmerized her but listening to this music, she realized that there had been no heart to it. His notes had been perfect but he used the music only for luring people to their deaths. Though Gerda had never attempted to learn an instrument, even she could tell that Kristina put all of herself into the music. It was the same way on the rare occasions that Nana played the old piano that lurked in a corner of their dining room. Her grandmother was not a master musician, but she always gave her heart to the music.

Gerda opened her eyes and saw Kristina's true smile for the first time. The robber's gaze was distant as she played madly away upon her nyckelharpa. Everybody else in the room could have disappeared, the fortress could have fallen to pieces above them, and she would have played on.

# CHAPTER ELEVEN

At first Kai had thought the mirror would be round or oval, as so many mirrors are but eventually a corner had appeared. The other three edges took shape as he had continued to work with the border pieces. All the other mirrors he had known possessed frames but this one had no such protective edging. Only by carefully gripping the edges did he avoid slicing his hands to the bone.

He lifted the mirror off of the floor. It should have been heavy; instead it seemed to have no more weight than a feather. Light ran along the surface, slipping from one completed section to another. The shine left him watching spots of light before his eyes.

There was nowhere to stand it up properly. At last he settled it against the ice window opposite the doors. Kai held out his hands as stepped back, ready to catch the mirror if it fell. He saw it fall a hundred times in his mind. A thousand times he heard every piece break apart. A million times he imagined the shards raining down upon his head and hands.

The mirror did not fall. It stood there as though it had been in place for years. He looked at his reflection. He had solved over three-fourths of the mirror and he could see almost his entire body. Through the remaining holes he saw the emptiness of the winter landscape past the windows. He used his sleeve to polish his fingerprints off of the glass.

The reflection watched him. It moved when he did, made the same turns of the head, but was still *different*. He could no longer remember what he looked like in mirrors that showed exactly what was present and nothing more. The reflection grinned at him, baring its teeth. Its lips were cracked from winter's dry air. The image was very pale, with dark circles around the eyes and frost stuck to its cheeks. He put a hand to his face but his fingers remained numb and he couldn't feel the texture of his skin. The reflection's body was rail-thin; its movements lacked any grace. The familiar glasses remained but its pupils grew large until only a thin circle of gray iris surrounded them. Those unblinking, narrowed eyes watched him.

A door opened in the room's reflection. Kai turned around and stepped across the threshold.

His feet sank deep into reindeer furs that carpeted the floor. The wall on his right was a pane of ice stretching from floor to ceiling; the wall on his left was covered with mirrors.

Images of Kai flashed in every mirror. As he did with the mirror shards in the other room, he began to count these mirrors. They weren't hung in rows and columns that could easily be multiplied, but he managed. He counted at least fifteen across the top. The cluster nearest him brought the total up to twenty-three; a handful was arranged close to the floor; tucked away in the far corner was a small one that he hadn't seen earlier... He lost count after fifty and suspected that he may have noted some of the mirrors more than once.

He saw several hand mirrors, stuck to the wall with their handles still attached. Those looked oldest. The ancient circles of copper and bronze had been polished until they shone brightly, even though any reflection would be distorted and faint. One mirror the size of his head was crafted in the shape of an octagon and surrounded by ivory. Another had a wide frame painted with indigo octopi, fish, and dolphins. A square mirror the size of his hand possessed enameled edging, made from small tiles of white, lavender, and pale blue. None of these mirrors were cracked.

The Snow Queen stood with her back to Kai when he reentered the main room. He held his breath as she ran a hand across the completed portions of the mirror, her fingers caressing the hard surface. The remaining pieces of the mirror that he hadn't yet fitted together were spread around her feet.

"You are a wonder," she said, either to Kai or the mirror, or perhaps to both as she gazed upon herself.

"I am glad that you are working faster," she said. For a moment it seemed as though her breathing sped up. "Even here, I feel the seasons pass. This must be ready for me to spread winter when the proper time arrives."

He watched his reflection place a hand on her shoulder, near the frost-white neck exposed by her short hair. "It'll be finished soon," he promised. "It's easier to see how things fit together now."

Her reflection smiled at him. The Snow Queen turned him so that he faced her instead of staring directly into the mirror. "Be careful what you look at. Human eyes aren't meant to see everything in my mirror. The man who made it learned that lesson well. I should hate to lose you before you've gotten to the end."

He nodded. Her fingers played with his exposed skin: tracing his cheeks, brushing his eyebrows, stepping across his lips, dipping below the collar of his jacket. Kai shivered.

"Tell me another story," she said. Her voice was almost gentle.

"I don't remember any more."

"Search for one, Kai. You must give me something."

"Once upon a time," he murmured, stumbling over the filmy memories, "once upon a time, she told us stories."

"Who told you stories?"

"I don't remember."

The Snow Queen smiled briefly. "What were they about?" she prompted.

"On a summer night many years ago, a group of fishermen settled down for the night in a cabin outside their village, which was on the shores of a vast sea. They would be setting out to fish early the next morning and did not want to have to travel far to their boats. While they were talking quietly around the fire, a woman's pale arm stretched in through the door, dripping with seawater and wrapped around with kelp. A woman's voice also began to sing outside and it was the most beautiful music any of them had ever heard. They knew right away that their visitor was a mermaid, who used her beauty and music to drag men into the sea and drown them. They pretended not to see her and the mermaid eventually withdrew.

"This happened every night for a week. Each night, it was harder and harder for the men to resist leaving the cabin. At the end of the week, they were joined by a group of men from a neighboring village. One of them was a young man who laughed at their warnings, and teased them for being afraid of a woman's arm and singing.

"'I would never be afraid of such things,' he said. 'You've given too much power to your nightmares and they've made you as timid as old women.'

"'But you're to be married soon,' the fishermen said. 'Surely you wouldn't betray your bride-to-be for a creature who would drown you as soon as you gave her the chance.'

"'I love my sweetheart dearly,' the young man admitted, 'but I still should not be afraid of an arm, even if it does belong to a mermaid.'

"Yet nothing appeared that evening. All of the fishermen except the young man were asleep when the cabin door opened and the white arm beckoned. The singing was very quiet, almost like a lullaby. The young man left the fireside and took the pale hand in his. He may have had fear in his heart, but he didn't let himself turn back after bragging of his bravery to the older men.

"He was pulled out of the cabin at once. The other fishermen didn't discover that he was missing until they woke up in the morning, when they saw his empty bed and the still-open cabin door. Everybody in the surrounding villages searched for him but he wasn't to be found anywhere, either on land or at sea. The villagers were not surprised, as creatures that come from the sea dislike giving up their prizes. Some blamed the fishermen for not acting sooner, but the young man had admitted that he knew what might happen and none of the men had been aware of his disappearance until hours later.

"A handful of years passed and still nobody found a trace of the missing fisherman. His sweetheart mourned when she looked out onto the sea, but she was still young. She met another man who was devoted to her and knew enough not to take a mermaid's hand. On the night of her wedding, less than an hour after the vows had been spoken, the families were celebrating when a strange man appeared outside the doorway of the bride and groom's home. He was finally recognized as the missing fisherman. Everybody was shocked and demanded to hear his story.

"Still standing outside the house, he said, 'I have been living with the mermaid all these years. She pulled me into the sea but didn't try to drown me; instead, she brought me to her palace and made me her lover. I forgot everything there: my family, my sweetheart, even that I had once lived on land.'

"'But how did you return?' asked one of the fishermen who had been present in the cabin on the night that the man had disappeared.

"'One day a seal visited the mermaid's palace and told her that there was going to be a grand celebration on the land. I remembered my former life and asked what had happened to my loved ones. She told me that my sweetheart was going to marry and I begged to be released for a mere hour to see her once more. The mermaid did not want to let me go for even that brief time but she finally agreed.'

"What the man didn't say was that the mermaid had allowed him to come ashore on the condition that he must not enter the house. The man had agreed, yet his former sweetheart looked so beautiful dressed as a bride that he couldn't resist walking toward her.

"The moment he stepped across the threshold, he collapsed and died."

"And did they return his body to the sea?" the Snow Queen asked. "I should think the mermaid would still want him back, even if that was all that was left."

"I don't remember."

She smiled. "Shall I be the mermaid and you the fisherman? I warn you, I won't let you go as easily as she did."

Kai frowned. "But I can't leave. I have to finish the mirror."

"That's right. My dear one, I knew I did right in choosing you." The Snow Queen leaned forward and kissed him.

Gerda had no idea what time it was when Kristina roused her. Without any traces of sunlight or fresh air, it could have been an hour or a day since she had fallen asleep in Kristina's room.

Most of the trolls remained in the main room. They slept together in little groups, curled up in balls like hedgehogs. Two of them had squeezed into the golden boat. Hedvig slumped on her throne as she snored, the crown nearly falling off of her head. Gerda couldn't spot Fredrik and wondered if he had already left on his fake ransom trip.

One short, round troll remained awake and stood against a wall. He wore a blue coat and his beard was completely white. He nodded respectfully as Kristina approached.

"We're going out, Arvid," she told him. "Let my mother know if she wakes before we return."

"I will." He passed one hand over the section of wall he had been leaning against. The earthen wall faded and the wooden door reappeared.

Gerda and Kristina walked down the tunnel they had used only yesterday. Gerda blinked in the sunlight once they arrived in the forest. The light felt like a thick blanket on her shoulders.

"What are we doing here?" she asked. Her legs ached to start running but Kristina and her knives were too close for Gerda to make a real escape attempt.

"We're finding somebody to waylay. I'm going to turn you into a proper robber; it's pathetic how easily you were caught."

"But I don't want to be a robber."

"You will," Kristina assured her. "It's great fun. You don't always have to kill them," she added casually. "If you're feeling squeamish, you can just truss them up and leave them in the road for somebody else to find. And besides, if you kill a person you can only steal from them once. If you leave them alive, there's always the chance to rob them again."

"Then why didn't you leave me in the road? For all you know, I might have gone back to the summer palace and returned with another golden boat, and you wouldn't have had to make up a story."

"This is more fun."

"But I don't care about stealing from people."

A crack appeared in Kristina's good humor. "You'll do it if I tell you to. Don't worry, you'll come to like it after a while. We just need somebody for you to practice on."

As they walked through the forest, Gerda gave in to the urge to annoy the other woman. "It's too bad that you only care about stealing. You're missing the finer things in life. Stopping to smell the flowers, that sort of thing."

Kristina stared at her. "You want me to sniff a plant?"

"You should learn to relax. Also, what's the point of having so many possessions if you just hide them away?"

"I do enjoy myself. And I don't hide everything away." She patted the shining knife in her belt. "I took this from a merchant who didn't even know how to use it." She touched the bracelet on Gerda's wrist. "These came from a caravan." She pulled up one sleeve to reveal a second knife. "And I sharpen this one every day. Now stop dawdling."

Gerda saw an autumn-colored movement that seemed to be more than just falling leaves. When she slowed and looked down, she found a hole that was nearly invisible behind the litter of branches and twigs piled up at the bottom of a hill. She saw a narrow face and long nose surrounded by leaves. The fox crouched at the burrow's entrance, peering with amber eyes at the two women. The animal remained silent, barely moving its head to watch the humans pass by so close to its burrow.

When she looked up, she saw that Kristina had continued ahead. Several more heartbeats passed by and the robber continued walking without looking back. By taking a few steps, Gerda was able to hide behind a cluster of bushes. She couldn't run away without the mirror but finding out if the bracelet really could stop her would get rid of at least one obstacle. She sidled off.

Less than a minute later, Kristina ran up behind her. "Just what do you think you're doing?"

Gerda tried to look innocently surprised. Given that she hadn't heard Kristina's footsteps, the latter wasn't too difficult. As far as seeming innocent, she remembered how Kai would act whenever he claimed that he hadn't *meant* to drink the last of the coffee, it just happened. For once, thinking about him made her want to laugh instead of weep. "Doing what?"

"You were headed in the opposite direction," Kristina snapped. "What else could you be doing but trying to run off?"

"I got distracted," Gerda said. "I was looking to see if any flowers were still blooming. You know how much I like rabbit food." Luckily for her, clumps of wildflowers still bloomed around their feet this early in autumn.

"Just try not to get 'distracted' again."

Kristina kept a closer watch on Gerda after that. The robber brought them to the top of a wide hill studded with birch trees that reminded Gerda of the forest around Linnea's cottage. She wondered which was worse: to have no knowledge of who she was and what she was meant to be doing, or to remember everything and be forced to do nothing.

"This is a good place to wait. Somebody almost always comes along and they never suspect a thing," Kristina said.

"But don't people know about it, if you rob travelers here so often?"

"Some of them are too stupid to remember. The others think they're too smart to be caught."

Kristina lay down on her stomach, only the top of her head visible over the hilltop. Gerda knelt by her side. A short span of earth was cleared of trees on both sides of the wide road. The narrow road had become pressed down into the ground through the years, trod by hundreds of pairs of feet. Sharp curves and the hills hid what lay ahead. Even Gerda's novice eyes could see how easy it would be to attack an unwary person.

"Stay quiet," Kristina said, "and keep out of sight. When somebody comes along, jump into the road. You'll be the distraction until I can restrain him." She glared until Gerda nodded.

Gerda clenched her fists as she tried to think of ways to prevent harm to any travelers without getting herself into more trouble. Yet despite Kristina's assurances that this was a prime location for discovering people so rich that they drank from golden cups at every meal, no one appeared.

An hour passed. Kristina swore under her breath as they lay upon the hillside, fuming over travelers who didn't know she was angry with them. Gerda wondered if this was because the other woman truly wished to rob someone that day or if she wanted to show off.

Gerda started to relax as the time passed and nothing happened. With any luck, Kristina would soon grow bored: they would return to the fortress and she could search for the mirror.

Yet the minutes passed and Kristina showed no signs of desiring to leave. She remained frozen in her position; only her eyes moved as she searched the road, reminding Gerda of a bird perched on a scarecrow. She turned away from the road and stretched out until she lay flat on her back. The earth had dried after yesterday's rain and the sun rose higher. This early in autumn, they were still closer to summer than winter.

"How did you end up living with the trolls?" she asked, still puzzling over Kristina's obvious sense of comfort despite being a human among trolls.

"The queen is my mother," Kristina said without ceasing her scrutiny of the road.

"Not by birth, she isn't."

"She's my mother in every way that matters. She found me when I was a baby and took me home."

"Did she steal you? A plump, defenseless baby might have been attractive to her kind."

Kristina lashed out at Gerda and pinned her to the hillside. "Never say that again. She found me, and raised me, and loves me. She *chose* me."

Gerda lay very still. "You're lucky. Our parents didn't want Kai or me."

"Oh." To Gerda's amazement, Kristina moved back with flushed cheeks. "Do you know why?"

"I have no idea. We only have our grandmother. Once I met somebody who said she was my mother but she lied," Gerda said.

"What a mess. We're much more sensible about these things. I've never spent much time around other humans and now I have another reason why."

"Just long enough to steal from them?" Gerda asked.

"Typically, that's the only thing they're good for." Kristina tipped her head. "Are they all like you?"

"I may be more stubborn than most."

Kristina rolled her eyes. "I already know *that*."

Gerda propped herself up on her elbows. "Can we go yet? I doubt anybody's coming by today."

"We'll try one more place first."

She shook the bits of leaves and grass out of her hair as Kristina led her through the forest. They passed from birch trees to oak groves with their leaves that reminded her of hands, long green palms with the stubby fingers. The ground was thick with large acorns, each one round as a child's top with a nubby cap. Even though the squirrels had begun their harvest, she still saw hundreds of the nuts remaining. Their feet slid in the uneven carpet of slippery acorns.

The second location where they lurked was at a cluster of hills surrounding a path. Kristina became very still, almost invisible behind thick bushes. Gerda swung up onto the low branches of a rowan tree. Overripe berries fell as she climbed to a comfortable perch. She was able to see far but couldn't see any indication of the river. Even when the birds paused their songs, she heard only rustling leaves instead of the river's pounding.

Despite examining all directions, she couldn't see an end to the forest. She wondered how far the trolls' home spread underground, if it reached even this far. The tree's branches tossed above her like waves upon the ocean. The rustling of their leaves almost sounded like words whispered in her ears.

Kristina made a disgusted noise in her throat after they had waited over a half-hour in solitude. She shook her head and said, "What a waste of a perfect morning for practice. We'll just have to try again tomorrow."

"Maybe the travelers knew your plan and don't want me to become a robber, either," Gerda suggested. Her mind raced with thoughts of where the mirror might be hidden. If she could find it by tomorrow, it would be the prefect chance to run away. Then she remembered her promise to the reindeer.

"Don't you start." Kristina scowled and played with the hilt of her knife.

Gerda paused on the walk back to the trolls' fortress. They had entered a clearing containing several fallen trees whose bark had rotted away, leaving the insides gaping open. Woodpeckers and insects had made holes in the trunks until the remaining bark appeared like lace. Thick, rippling layers of mushrooms covered the side of one tree stump. Gerda knelt and began to pick mushrooms, snapping each one off at its base and filling the pockets of her coat.

"No wonder you have such horrible thievery instincts," Kristina said as Gerda worked. "You should be watching for people weighted down with gold, not grubbing about in the earth. However have you managed to survive this long on your own?"

Gerda ignored the question and continued to examine the forest's offerings. "I told you from the start I was a gardener. If you think I'm such a horrible robber, maybe you shouldn't bother keeping me around."

"Not that again." One of the feet in Gerda's line of vision started to tap. "Aren't you done yet?"

"In a minute. Look at it this way: at least I'm grubbing over something you can eat."

"What are those ones good for?" Kristina asked. She poked at one of the mushrooms. Light brown on top, it was creamy white underneath the cap and had wavy edges. She ran her fingers over the smooth surface.

"These ones are safe. They won't taste good raw, but cook them with a little butter and even your mother will be in a good mood. Mushrooms grow in groups. Look around and see if there's anything else."

They found several other varieties growing in the damp ground. One had a broad, nearly flat cap with thin spikes growing underneath. Gerda picked several of these gold and white plants.

"What of this?" Kristina asked. She pointed her foot at a ring of mushrooms growing upon slim stems. The slightly rounded caps were several inches wide, tinged green like spoiled eggs. For a moment the fungi smelled sweet like honey but then the underlying scent of surfaced.

"You want to stay away from those," Gerda said. "Remember what it looks like. Just one nibble of this can kill you. There are others that look almost the same and are safe to eat." She saw a clump of near-identical mushrooms with pink gills and a wider stem several paces away. She picked one and held it next to the poisonous mushroom. "They all look pretty. If you're ever unsure, throw everything away." She tossed it over her shoulder.

"Planning to poison me?"

"I don't do that kind of thing. And even if I wanted to, I wouldn't be stupid enough to do it immediately after warning you."

Kristina let out a bark of laughter and lifted Gerda to her feet.


Kai listened to the Snow Queen talk as he worked on the mirror. With every match, it became easier to see where the rest of the pieces belonged. He knelt on the ground as he worked and listened to her smooth voice rise and fall like waves.

"I could look for only a few pieces each year," she said. "I had to make certain that winter continued properly—every snowflake, every icicle has to be perfect. I had almost no time to search."

He looked at the thousands of pieces he had counted as he removed them from the chest. "There are so many. How long did it take you to collect all of them?"

Her voice wavered. "A very long time. I knew I had failed again every year when I could feel spring sneaking back. Winter was depending on me and I had failed it. You can't imagine how it feels, to be unable to do anything but wait and plan until it was my time to rule again. Each piece called to me of course, but they became hidden so easily."

She walked to Kai's side and touched the fragment that he held. "This one had sunk to the bottom of an ocean. All water is cold that far down, no matter where you are. I never would have thought water could feel that pleasant; if the rest of my mirror had not still been missing, I might have spent longer down there."

He set the piece into the mirror and picked up the next fragment. "Where did you find this one?"

The Snow Queen took the piece from his hand. "A city where they think they can control winter." Her voice turned smug. "But all the lamps, fires, and closed windows in the world can't keep me from what's mine. This one had lodged in the heart of an old tree. The man-made warmth doesn't leave that city easily—sometimes I could barely breathe. But my mirror had won the tree over by the time I found it. It hadn't taken long to touch the tree's roots with frost. When anybody passes beneath its branches now, they long for the snow to come and dream only of my arrival. I became very fond of that tree."

He watched her fingers tighten as she spoke faster. Before he could stop her, her hand clenched and the mirror's edges sliced into her fingers. He jumped up, but she shook her head and pressed back down on his shoulder. "Not to worry," she said. She opened her hand and there was no blood. He could see the cut in her skin but the mirror was clean. "It's mine. Nothing in this place can ever harm me."

"Don't you worry?" he asked. "The mirror was gone for so long and some of the pieces landed far away from here. Aren't you afraid that some of them might have changed?"

"Look at me," she commanded. She tilted up chin up and looked into his eyes. "Do I seem like the sort to be afraid?"

"No."

"Remember that." The Snow Queen released him. "My mirror is not altered so easily. I don't care how long it was away from me, in all my years of searching I haven't found anything strong enough to change its nature. There is nobody alive who can do that. Understand?"

"Yes."

The next fragment she picked up was the size of her thumbnail and she gazed into it. "Do you remember that family who lived next door to you?"

"No."

"This one was in the possession of their daughter." The Snow Queen chuckled. "The silly girl thought it was just a bit of glass when she found it lying among some rocks. I learned that within days, she had started bringing it everywhere she went. She didn't want to give it back when I found her, but we had a little talk and soon I made her see reason."

"If she was so fond of it, why didn't you keep her?"

"What for? She had no skill with puzzles and she was so dull. The only important thing she did in her short life was to guard the piece until it could be returned to me. You interest me much more than she ever did."

He watched the Snow Queen stroke the side of the mirror. "I'll have it fixed soon," he promised and reached up to touch her arm. "Everything will be all right."

She sighed. "It has to be."


Kristina made her bed on that pile of leaves covered with furs. Another fur served as a blanket against the cold air in the caves. She and Gerda lay there, the dry leaves crackling beneath them with every breath.

Gerda stared at the tree roots covering the ceiling and pretended she was looking at the stars. She had been with the robbers for several days, or maybe it was more than a week. Some days they ventured into the forest, where Kristina continued trying to make Gerda into "a proper robber." Other times they lingered underground. The lack of sunlight in the trolls' rooms disoriented her and she had no idea how much time flowed by. She had continued to search for an escape route but hadn't been able to find one or her piece of the mirror.

"I promised to bring Kai home," she said during another round of their unending argument.

"But what if he doesn't *want* to return?" Kristina argued. "He might be too much like the Snow Queen. You said he was becoming like her already, even before you left. You'll have gone all the way for nothing and then she'll have you."

"You wouldn't say that if you knew him." Gerda dug her fingers into the fur beneath her. "Our grandmother's waiting for us and I'll bring him home."

"Just go to sleep," Kristina said wearily.

Gerda slept. In the beginning she had no dreams. Then it began again: watery light bled through ice behind her eyes. Even when she knew she was dreaming, she could never move or wake before the end. Kai and the Snow Queen stood there, but neither one looked at her. The Snow Queen raised one hand. A layer of ice thin as poppy petals dropped over Kai. She kept her hand up and another layer appeared. And then another. He didn't even try to escape—he only watched the Snow Queen as she slowly froze him within hundreds of layers of ice. Gerda couldn't speak or move. Then the Snow Queen turned to her.

Gerda jolted awake. The room smelled of extinguished candles and the furs were warm around her.

*Please don't let it be true,* she thought. In the aftermath of the nightmare, she sat up and searched for images to block the memories of ice and winter light. Kristina slept on, curled up warm against Gerda with the nyckelharpa in its case by her other side. Even in sleep the other woman was armed: her face was slack and peaceful, but an unsheathed knife lay by her hand.

The nightmare still felt too real for Gerda to immediately fall back asleep. She slipped out of bed and left the room with a candle and a box of matches.

She shielded the light of her candle from the sleeping trolls. If nothing else, at least sneaking across a dirt floor was easier than creeping through dry leaves and twigs. Still, it was too easy to imagine stepping on somebody's tail and rousing the entire band of robbers. She picked one of the hallways she explored seen yet and started walking.

In the beginning she hadn't allowed herself to think about everything that could go wrong when she faced the Snow Queen. As she walked, she rubbed her shoulder that still bore the marks from when the Snow Queen had grabbed her. Even if she reached Kai before he was completely changed and stopped his work on the mirror, she still didn't know how to get away afterward. The Snow Queen might just kill her, and then who would save him?

She forced herself to move even quieter when she heard snores coming from one of the rooms she had been about to enter. Several trolls slept on a bed and she was reminded of hibernating bears.

Gerda continued her stealthy search until she came to a room with several dozen rolled-up carpets standing on end against the walls. She lowered one down and sat on it while she thought. If the reindeer's continued presence was anything to judge by, Kristina was not in the habit of releasing her prisoners. She may have started treating Gerda like a wayward sister but the paired bracelets were a constant reminder of how things really stood. So many things stood in the way even without the Snow Queen: the robbers, finding the piece of the mirror, freeing the reindeer, and coming up with a way for both of them to escape.

At least this time she still had her memories. She smiled grimly.

The walk had helped a little. Maybe if she wandered about for a bit longer, her body would be tired enough to sleep without dreams.

Standing the carpet back up was more difficult than getting it down had been. Her grip slipped; the carpet fell back down, taking several others with it. None of them caught fire from her candle but there were several dull thumps. She froze. As the moments passed, she heard only the beating of her heart instead of feet running in response to the noise.

Why would trolls steal something like this, anyway? She hadn't seen one single carpet used in any of the rooms she had explored. Maybe the trolls didn't care what they stole, just so long as they were able to take it away from somebody else. Yet as she began to tidy the mess, she could have sworn she smelled a hint of fresh air.

When she looked closer, she found a gap in the wall that had been hidden behind the rolled carpets. It led to a tunnel with an uneven floor and piles of stones that were difficult to see in the dim illumination from her one small candle. She almost fell several times. She didn't venture far before she encountered a locked gate. Its bars were set close together but she could smell more fresh air through the gaps.

She examined the gate as best as she could: it was rusty and heavy. She would have to be as small as Nils in order to fit in between any of the bars. A heavy padlock kept the gate shut. She scowled at it. So much seemed to come down to keys: the reindeer's freedom, and now her escape route. Punching the wall wasn't enough to satisfy her anger and she gave the gate a solid kick, despite the need for stealth.

The metal groaned and she froze. The only think she heard was the faint sound of snoring drifting from the closest bedroom.

"Idiot. What were you thinking?" she muttered and turned to leave. Her foot slipped and she fell back against the gate. Something wiggled beneath her hand as she fought to stay upright.

The bar she kicked had started to loosen from the bottom of the gate. It wasn't completely broken free but there was definitely some give in it. She began to smile. It wouldn't be easy to work on the gate without anybody hearing but it was her best chance.

She continued to kick the bar as quietly as she could. After the initial screech, the metallic clinking was quieter and eventually the base of the bar came out of its socket. After that, swinging it loose from the top of the gate seemed almost easy. For the first time, she was thankful that the trolls paid so little attention to parts of their home.

Yet kicking all the bars loose would take time and her candle burned close to its end. She left the tunnel and rearranged the carpets so that they screened the hole in the wall, but so that she could quickly squeeze through. Gerda smiled again and patted a dusty carpet. She would continue work tomorrow.

Dread of the nightmares began to return as she crept back but she pushed it away. She would never stop being afraid of the Snow Queen but she couldn't let that stop her. Even if the nightmares happened every night, she would…

She stopped in the middle of the hall. Laughter bubbled up from her stomach to her throat, and she had to press a hand to her lips so that it wouldn't escape her mouth and wake everybody. It would be the perfect opportunity.

By the time she reached the room, the threads of her idea had begun to weave together. Kristina didn't appear to have so much as turned over in her sleep, much less woken. It was amazing how soundly she slept. Gerda lay down and worked on her plan.

A combination of partying almost every night and the natural inclination of trolls to avoid sunlight meant that the robbers slept for a long time after they finally dozed off. By the time Kristina woke, Gerda was sitting on a rickety chair and worrying at the end of her braid.

She jumped when she heard the rustling of leaves. "Oh! You startled me."

Kristina yawned. "You should work on that." She propped herself up and frowned. "How long have you been up, anyway?"

"A while." Gerda shrugged. "I couldn't sleep."

"Why?"

"I kept having dreams about *her*."

Kristina walked over to her. "You know they aren't real."

"That's not the way it felt." Gerda turned her gaze away and shivered.

They spent the day underground. It passed by so slowly that she had to remind herself not to grind her teeth. It was actually a relief when the robbers gathered that evening. She sat in her usual shadowed corner until everyone was occupied, then returned to the reindeer's cell.

"I found a way out," she said. Even if he didn't understand human language, just saying it aloud filled her with exhilaration.

Remembering how rapidly last night's candle had melted, this time she brought a lamp and set it near the door, away from the straw and careless movements. She stroked the reindeer's coat and waited.

Something scratched in a corner. This time she remained still and watched closely. One of the stones that studded the earthen walls wiggled and pushed out far enough for a small figure to squeeze through.

"I see you're still with us," Nils said.

"That's no surprise," Gerda said dryly. "Listen, we need to talk. I think I found a way out last night."

The tomte's eyebrows shot up. "Where?"

"There's a room in one of the other hallways with a tunnel hidden behind some carpets. I think it leads to the forest but there's an old gate blocking the exit and it's locked."

"I can't believe I didn't know."

"It's blocked really well," she said. "I think even the trolls forgot about it."

"Yes, but I am supposed to know everything about my home. It's who we are."

Gerda sat down next to him. "Don't worry about it. You said that you prefer to spend your time in the fort, not down here."

"I can try to find the key for that gate as well, if you like."

"Look for the one that frees him first." She patted the reindeer's leg. "I can probably break through the gate, so long as I don't get caught sneaking off. Have you had any luck with this one?"

"Not yet but there are still several more places to look. And of course there is Kristina's key ring, if I can ever get to it. She's the sort to keep reminders of her control close by."

"I noticed," Gerda said and looked at her bracelet. "I need you to hurry, though. That troll she sent on the fake ransom demand could come back any time and I want to get away from here before that happens."

"I'll do my best."

"And I still have no idea where she could have put my piece of the mirror, but she's asking for trouble if she's keeping it on her. I think I can get her to trust me more; maybe I can find it that way."

"How do you plan to do that?"

"She's been trying to convince me that it's safer to stay away from the Snow Queen and that I should learn to be a robber. I'm going to let her think it worked."

"It *is* safer to stay away," Nils said.

Gerda smiled wryly. "I know. But nothing's been safe for a long time now. Sometimes I have nightmares about Kai and the Snow Queen. Kristina already knows about one of them. I can let her think they've convinced me to stop searching."

"Do you really think she will believe that?" Nils asked.

"I'm not *pretending* to be scared. The only lie is letting her think that it's stopping me," Gerda said.

"As well as pretending that you want to be one of them."

"It's only for a little while."

Nils shook his head. "Those of us who know trolls know better than to try something so risky."

"Those of us who are going to face the Snow Queen don't have much choice."

Footsteps approached. Nils vanished behind his stone just before Kristina stepped into the doorway. "I see you've met my reindeer," she said.

"I can't believe you managed to catch something so big," Gerda said. "How did you do it?" Even as she spoke admiringly, she noticed that the animal had backed up as far as he could.

Kristina leaned against the door frame and stared at the reindeer. "I hadn't planned it. We were on our way out to the road when I saw his tracks. He must have lost his herd because I saw only the one set of marks. I knew I could find him but he would have run off if he'd heard all of us coming at once. I told the others to wait while I went on ahead." She grinned. "Even the fastest reindeer can't outrun me if he's sleeping. And by the time he woke up, there was one of us blocking every direction he could have gone. That was a fun day."

Gerda wanted to shake her by the shoulders and demand to know where the key was that would set him free. Just being around the wild animal made her long even more for the open sky and the forest. Instead she said, "That sounds amazing. But now you just leave him here?"

"What else am I to do with him? Even with my heaviest chains, if I kept him outside he would find a way to escape to his herd in the north. This way he stays mine." She turned her gaze to Gerda and raised an eyebrow. "Why so curious?"

"I hadn't expected to find a reindeer here and I couldn't help wondering how you'd managed it."

"Now you know. I have to say, it's a relief to hear you finally showing interest in something normal." She smiled and clapped Gerda on the shoulder. "You should come back; you're missing all the fun."

Gerda forced herself not to look back at the reindeer as they left him behind in that cramped, dark room. When they reached the hall, she fought the urge to disappear again and work on breaking down the gate.

That night she sat closer to the activity. Kristina took her usual place by her mother's side. Several of the trolls were throwing daggers for Hedvig's entertainment. One troll stood against a wall and the others tossed blades around his body. The robbers threw the thick daggers as though they were toothpicks. The nicked metal shone in the firelight, flickering and winking as the blades twirled. Most hit the wall a short distance from the troll's body but several struck the edges of his clothing, pinning him like a butterfly on a board. He swore loudly each time it happened and snatched his tail out of harm's way. Hedvig crowed with laughter and clapped her ringed hands throughout.

Later, the robbers dared each other to jump across the fire when it smoldered low. Kristina took a running leap, her long legs driving her high above the flames. Somebody threw a log into the pit as she neared the end and the fire stretched up behind her. Everybody cheered when she landed: not even the heels of her shoes were singed. All the others made it across as well, though there were a few close calls.

Gerda watched and waited for the time when she could leave and go to bed.

She made herself remain awake throughout most of the night. The first time she "woke up", she bolted upright with a gasp and succeeded in throwing off half the covers in the process.

"What is it?" Kristina mumbled, still half-asleep herself.

"Nothing, I—it was a bad dream." Gerda tidied the bed and lay back down.

She dozed a bit and let the next couple of hours pass without incident. Next she tossed and turned without opening her eyes, not a wild thrashing about but a twitching of her arms and legs every few minutes. She could hear the dry leaves rustling beneath her body.

It didn't take long for Kristina to wake up. "Can't you sleep quietly for once?" she grumbled.

Gerda kept her eyes shut and did not answer. Soon she felt her shoulder being shaken. She waited a few more moments for good measure before seeming to wake and asking, "Where is she?"

Kristina looked around the room. Her tangled hair that held bits of leaves snaked over her shoulders. "Gerda, there's nobody else here. Who are you looking for?"

"The Snow Queen. She said she was coming for me."

"She is not." Kristina spoke with more patience than Gerda had expected. The robber's voice was surprisingly soothing. Gerda couldn't decide whether the other woman was truly concerned or whether she just wanted to sleep uninterrupted.

Gerda rubbed her arms through her thick sweater. "She was about to freeze me."

"She's not going to come looking for you here. Try to go back to sleep."

Gerda bit her lip before nodding and rolling over.

It continued like that throughout the night. She repeated several of her actions, such as jumping up. Other times she shivered, or got up to pace around the room. She didn't pretend to talk in her sleep; Kai had said that people tended to babble nonsense while sleeping and she thought it might be a bit much. She did wonder if it might work differently here, as people could visit each other while dreaming and the shadows of their dreams could walk about.

Gerda didn't spend her time solely on dramatics. She didn't think she could search for the mirror without being caught but there was nothing to stop her from planning as she circled the room. Suvi had said that Gerda's piece of the mirror might never return to being like the others. Perhaps she could use her piece to influence the rest. It might be enough to tip the balance away from unending winter.

The plan and its doubts circled in Gerda's mind as she continued her act. Once she wondered if she was tempting fate by faking nightmares when she had been dragged through so many real ones before. She managed to wake Kristina on several more occasions. As Gerda pretended to return to sleep each time, she could tell by Kristina's breathing and stillness that the other woman took longer to fall asleep as things progressed.

By the time Gerda ended her performance, she felt almost as tired as when she had first set out in that blizzard to look for Kai. As she allowed herself to fall into a true sleep, she wondered if she would dream.

When she woke the room was empty of anybody else but the birds in their cage. She remained curled up for a few minutes longer, warm under the furs like a bear unready to come out from hibernation. Then her mind realized what her body hadn't thought of: a lack of Kristina meant opportunity. She rolled out of the bed that looked worse for the wear after the previous night's activity.

There were so many containers and piles of items that she was almost paralyzed by the abundance of places to search. In the end she turned to the closest place: a small table that had two boxes on top of it. One of them held only handkerchiefs. The other contained jewels removed from their settings, broken necklaces, and mismatched earrings. She searched the box, her skin alert for coldness and her fingers wary of sharp edges. Yet she didn't even find any broken glass.

The sound of footsteps in the corridor began just after Gerda finished returning the pile of magpie treasure back to something resembling its original arrangement. She abandoned the box and started tidying the pile of leaves.

Kristina entered the room. Gerda looked up and smiled sheepishly. "Hello," she said. "I'm sorry about last night."

"Good afternoon is more like it."

"I'm sorry about last night."

"A few times I thought you were being attacked in your sleep," Kristina said dryly. "I'm surprised you ever settled down."

Gerda shrugged. "I don't remember a lot of the details but…"

"It was nightmares about the Snow Queen the whole night?"

"Yes. You'd have bad dreams too, if you'd ever met her." Spinning truth and fiction together, Gerda wondered if this was how Nana felt when she told her stories. Gerda returned to tidying the bed. Near the end, she paused and glanced up. She saw at least a dozen places where her tiny box holding the mirror could be hidden, even assuming that it was in this room. "Is it…very hard to be a good robber?"

Kristina had been watching the birds in their cage but turned her attention back to Gerda at this question. "It's not very difficult to be good, especially if you're lucky enough to come across fools. The main trick is finding a good hiding place and waiting for them to come to you. Usually they're too surprised to get very far, so you can catch them without much trouble." She chuckled. "To be a *great* robber like me is much harder, though."

Gerda's amusement at the boasting was unfeigned. The next part was trickier. "Would you try to teach me again?"

"Very funny. Are you by any chance delirious from so little sleep?" Kristina crossed the room and pressed her hand to Gerda's forehead.

Gerda pulled away. "Stop that. Will you?"

"Oh I'll be happy to, certainly. Just to satisfy my curiosity though—what changed your mind?"

"I can't go through another night like the last one."

Kristina nodded. "It's good to hear you talking sense for once. I told you the Snow Queen was best left alone."

She didn't ask about Kai, which was a blessing. So far Gerda believed her lies had been convincing but she wasn't sure she could ever say that she would abandon her brother. She had only ever given him up once, and that had been because she couldn't remember any better.

"Let's get going, then." Kristina jumped up.

"Now?" Gerda asked.

"There's no use in wasting another day. You *do* want to be a robber, don't you?"

Gerda swallowed and nodded. "I'm sure."

They left the fort with the troll named Arvid who had guarded the door the other morning. Gerda tried not to frown as they walked: as if a near-sleepless night and a hastily-crafted deception weren't enough to deal with, soon after waking she had acquired the feeling in her head that meant she was getting a cold. She hoped it would be minor enough to shake off quickly; it wouldn't do to reach the Snow Queen only to be distracted by a need to blow her nose. As it was, she had wrapped a scarf around her neck and filled her pockets with the handkerchiefs she had spotted earlier.

"We won't tell Mother about your decision until after you've robbed somebody, just in case the first try doesn't take. There's no sense in giving her an opening to tease you if you can avoid it." Kristina said. "She'll be impressed when you show her something you took. It will be fine; you learn best by doing."

Gerda nodded and started thinking of ways to "accidentally" fail this test. Perhaps Nils had been right and her plan was too dangerous.

They settled by the road again; Gerda and Kristina remained on one side with Arvid on the opposite hill. "We won't try anything fancy today," Kristina said quietly. "The last time didn't go so well, but just follow our lead and things will be fine."

The scent of damp leaves made Gerda's nose itch as she lay close to the ground and she sneezed several times. Kristina twitched at the noise but didn't scold.

They had been waiting for no longer than a half-hour before Gerda could hear voices approaching. Kristina nudged her and rose to a crouch. "Probably two or three people," she murmured. "It doesn't sound like they're riding horses. Arvid and I will jump down first; if anybody runs off, follow them. We already know you're a fast runner."

Gerda refrained from making a face. Had she been even faster, she wouldn't be in this situation.

Two men and a woman who shared a resemblance walked around the curve in the road. They carried several small bags and chattered freely without looking around for any sign of danger. She wondered if she had seemed that ignorant when the robbers found her.

Kristina and Arvid jumped into the road while yelling fearsomely. The men were startled for a moment but reacted faster than Gerda had expected and ran at the robbers. The woman took off as Kristina had predicted, running back the way she had come. Gerda followed.

The woman ran quickly, but she was hampered by her dress and bag. Although she darted off of the road and wove in between the trees, Gerda easily caught up. The woman gave up the chase and dropped to her knees. "I'll give you whatever I have, but please don't kill me."

Gerda stared while she caught her breath. This traveler had no idea how lucky she was. She seized the woman's arm and said, "Get up."

"What are you going to do to me?" the woman asked.

"Nothing."

Had Gerda not been so worried about Kristina or Arvid catching up, the stunned look on the woman's face would have been amusing. She said, "I'm not interested in whatever you have. I don't care where you go, just get out of here."

The woman didn't need to be told twice. She took off like a rabbit that had just jumped out of a fox's mouth.

Once the woman was out of sight, Gerda sighed and looked around for inspiration. There were plenty of leaves; she scooped up several handfuls and crumbled them over her braid. Next, she rubbed her hands and knees into the dirt. The final touches were unwinding her scarf and tugging her jacket askew.

The men were gone when she returned to the road, but Kristina and Arvid had their bags. "I lost her," Gerda said, scowling.

Kristina stared. "That was perhaps the easiest person you could ever have to practice on. How could you have *lost* her? I thought you were cleverer than that."

Gerda spread her hands. "I tripped in a hole in the ground. She was out of sight by the time I got up. And it's hard to concentrate today." She sneezed again. "I'm sorry. I wanted to show you that I could do it."

"It's not so bad," Arvid said to Kristina in a conciliatory tone. "The travelers weren't a complete loss and now she knows what not to do."

Gerda started at one of the trolls speaking remotely well of her and she almost smiled at him.

"Fine." Kristina threw her hands in the air. We may as well go home— odds are that woman will encounter the next group coming along and tell them to be watching for us. I'd like a larger group before we go after somebody who's at least attempting to be prepared." She sighed.

Gerda had been prepared for anger over her failure, but Kristina seemed more inclined to disappointment. The pressure building in Gerda's head still troubled her but she could tell from experience that it would be no more than a minor illness. Still, she took the opportunity to blow her nose and clear her throat frequently.

They were about halfway back to the fort when a plaintive voice asked, "Can I come home now?" Fredrik stepped out from behind a nearby bush.

"I was wondering when you'd turn up. Did you get anything useful?" Kristina asked.

Fredrik shook his head. "Just a goose and I ate that already."

"Very well. Stay out of sight for one more night. You can come home as soon as I've decided what to tell Mother in the morning."

Gerda felt lightheaded as she listened to the robbers. Her face was hot and the blood roared in her ears. She only managed to stay upright by grabbing onto the tree next to her.

"Don't look so stricken—I'll take care of everything," Kristina said when she looked at Gerda. "I'll make sure Mother feasts well tonight and that I play her favorite songs. It'll put her in a good mood and I can tell her about all the progress you're making."

Gerda nodded. Fredrik returned to lurking among the trees as the other three returned to the robbers' home. Gerda mumbled about not feeling well and retreated to the kitchen. A troll woman was already in there, but she left Gerda alone and kneaded bread dough while humming.

Early on during Gerda's time with the robbers, she had been reassured to discover that even trolls owned a reasonably clean kettle and teapot. She had started to long for coffee as the days grew colder but tea would heal her sooner. She stirred up the fire and sat down at the great table while the water boiled.

Despite the mess, sitting in the kitchen reminded her of the springtime cottage. There had been a number of rainy afternoons when Linnea had showed her to brew combinations of herbs that would cure a headache or soothe a sore throat. It was too bad she hadn't learned how to make the potions that had sent her to sleep again and again. Escaping would be so much simpler if she could put all the robbers to sleep when she wanted to, instead of waiting for them to fall to the ground after drinking barrels of ale.

She remained there until she guessed that the rest of the afternoon had gone by, and that it was now evening. Kristina came to investigate early on but appeared to be convinced by Gerda's show of lethargy, and her claims that she didn't want to move until her head had stopped trying to swell up to twice its normal size. Kristina patted her sympathetically on the shoulder but said, "Just don't pass on your illness to me. I'll kick you into the fire pit if you get me sick with that pitiful sniffling," before she left the room.

Sitting with her head in her hands, Gerda gave it a half-hour for everybody to learn that they would be happier staying away from the diseased human in the kitchen that evening before she made her move. She sneaked off to her tunnel with her latest cup of tea and one of the kitchen's lamps.

Loosening the bars wasn't impossible but it quickly became tedious. Some were more difficult than others. She constantly worried that somebody would investigate the strange noises, but the only sounds were the creaking of the bars and her labored breathing. The faint currents of fresh air blowing through the tunnel dried her sweaty face.

By the time she reached the end of her self-allotted work time for that evening, more than half of the bars were out. Working in the dim light had created a few small injuries despite her best efforts; hopefully neither Kristina nor Arvid had looked closely at her after she "fell" in the forest earlier. Although every impulse screamed to finish it now, she turned away. She could be excused from sitting in the main cavern tonight but even with more freedom, she didn't dare to remain longer in a space she shouldn't know about. Besides, she still had other tasks to accomplish.

Nobody entered the kitchen as she washed her hands and refilled her tea cup. Things appeared the same as every other night when she glanced into the trolls' gathering. After all of Nana's stories about bad-tempered trolls who would turn a human into a statue as soon as they would look at her, she was amazed by the robbers' frequent good moods. So long as there was food, shiny treasure, and somebody to steal from, they were easily pleased. They could be driven to argument with little effort, a thing Hedvig seemed to enjoy, but it meant little. Brawls were as much for entertainment as anything else. Gerda could have almost been convinced to like them, had she not remembered their argument over supper and how they examined her on the day she arrived.

She caught Kristina's eye. Gerda pointed to herself and then down the hall. A sneeze overtook her. Kristina laughed and nodded.

Upon reaching Kristina's room, Gerda looked longingly at the bed but did not allow herself to fall in. She couldn't waste any time now that Fredrik had returned. Soon Hedvig would learn that Gerda wasn't worth anything, and she suspected that greed would win over a daughter's entertainment. She stood at the room's center and turned around, feeling for any hint of cold that did not come from the stone walls or open windows. The bracelet, the reindeer, the piles of treasure, even Gerda herself: everything suggested that Kristina liked to keep the things she valued close by.

Yet Gerda couldn't feel anything unusual. She sighed and started to search once more. If nothing else, she had become impressed by the variety of objects Kristina had squirreled away. There were piles of nyckelharpa strings, clothing, wooden carvings, and furs, but the mirror wasn't to be found among any of them. Various winter weather clothes appeared during her search. She didn't dare to move anything yet, but she carefully noted the location of anything she thought would fit.

Her head grew tired during the search and she continued to sneeze on occasion. She grabbed the last bundle of clean handkerchiefs out of their box while turning to look around the room some more. The careless motion knocked over the little table and all of the boxes covering its surface crashed onto the floor. The one that had held the squares of fabric was easy to tidy, but the jewelry box's contents had spilled in every direction. She swore and dropped to her knees.

When she picked up the box, she found a delicate gold chain strung with garnet beads caught in a gap in between the box's bottom and side. She sighed and tugged gently. The necklace came free. So did the bottom of the box.

The false bottom was a small space containing several coins, a lock of very pale blond hair, and a tiny, unadorned wooden box. She picked it up and heard something rattle.

She stared. It seemed too easy; surely Kristina was trying to test or trick her. She had already examined everything on this table once before. Nevertheless, she picked opened the little container. The piece of the mirror lay inside.

She sank to the floor and giggled until it nearly turned into hysterics. She had used their time apart to work on escaping; why shouldn't Kristina have used the same time to change her hiding places? Gerda held the box tightly in her fist but did not look into the mirror.

Reindeer or no reindeer, she would have to leave in the morning. The thought of breaking her promise made her heart ache, but stopping the Snow Queen came first.

She cleaned up the mess, tucked the box into her sleeve, and lay down. Even though her mind whirled with plans, she still fell asleep before Kristina arrived.

Nils awoke Gerda, patting her cheek until she stirred. He whispered, "I have it!"

She rolled out from beneath the furs, tumbling leaves about. There were no sounds coming from the other rooms, and even the birds in their cage remained quiet. She dressed rapidly in winter clothing and followed him out of the room. Her head still ached a little but she could breathe without trouble.

She made a brief stop in the kitchen and filled a sack with food. Then they were kneeling at the reindeer's feet. Nils showed her a key as long as his arm.

"Where did you find it?" she asked.

"Hidden at the bottom of a well. One of my cousins was dropping stones into the water for fun and heard one hit the key. We managed to pull it up using a hook and line, like we would for fishing. You should have felt how cold it was after being in the dark water for so long."

Gerda smiled at him. The lock was so stiff that she had to use both hands to turn the key, but Nils was able to catch the clasp before it could crash onto the floor. The reindeer shook his leg.

"We'll have to be fast, to get far enough away before they wake up," she said. "Do you want to come with us?"

He shook his head. "I'll see you to the tunnel but no farther. I do not think I could ever bear to leave my home for good. And in any case, I would choose even trolls over the Snow Queen. Were you able to clear the tunnel?"

"Not all of it, but I think there's enough space to squeeze through. If I have to, the reindeer can help kick down the last few bars and we'll make a break for it." She laid her hand on the tall animal's neck. "Let's go."

The gate crashed against the wall. Gerda spun around and saw Kristina in the doorway. "How did you get that key?" the robber demanded.

Once again, Nils had disappeared. Gerda entertained a moment of longing for the ability to vanish whenever trouble appeared. She stood in front of the reindeer and said, "I found it."

"You couldn't have done that on your own. Who helped you?"

"Nobody."

"So you were lying the whole time. You never wanted to be a robber. How could you do this to me?" Kristina asked, continuing to scowl.

"You didn't leave me a choice." She examined the doorway, wondering if she and the reindeer could shove past and get out of the fortress without being knifed in the process.

"You can't leave!" Kristina started to sound more desperate than angry.

"If I don't, the Snow Queen will make it winter forever. Think about it: the entire forest covered in snow and ice, not being able to hide easily when you're looking for people to steal from. Nothing will grow. What will happen to you and your mother? Kai can't finish her mirror but she'll find a way to make it happen if I don't stop her."

"I'm sure she can't do that."

"Even if that were true, how could I leave him to the Snow Queen? You kept telling me to forget my brother but would you be the same if your mother was the one captured? I'm telling you, nobody will be safe if I stay here."

"But there's nothing you can do," Kristina said.

Gerda opened the box and held up her piece of the mirror. "The key wasn't the only thing I found."

"Have you gone mad? You're not really bringing that thing to her?"

"I don't think she can use it anymore. I keep looking and it's less pure winter every time." Gerda held it up to her eye.

Her teeth started to chatter immediately and her lips stuck together from the cold. Yet the mirror had changed once more. As with spring and summer before, traces of autumn had crept in. She could smell autumn leaves and more faint threads of color had appeared in the frozen river. Even though the mirror tried to twist everything, it lacked full strength. Winter still ruled within this piece but she could see faint colors from the other seasons. The cold nipped at her bones but there were smells other than snow, sounds other than wind, and colors other than alabaster and ivory. Even the palace appeared closer.

Somebody was shaking her. She found herself sitting on the ground, slumped against the wall. Kristina tugged at Gerda's wrist and tried to pry the shard out of her hand. Gerda shook away the other woman's grip and stumbled to her feet. She leaned against the blessedly warm reindeer. "I can use it to stop her."

Kristina didn't speak. Gerda prepared to shove past her.

In the end Kristina sighed and said, "You're the only human I've ever met worth being around longer than a few minutes and I could have taught you to be a great robber. If I hear at the end of this that the Snow Queen has won, I'll journey up north and find a way to freeze you myself."

"What?" Gerda heard the words but they made no sense.

"We'll have to sneak you out another way," Kristina continued. "It would be too difficult to get both of you past everybody. But I know of a different route." She left the cell.

Gerda felt certain this must be a trick, but she and the reindeer followed. She kept her lips pressed together as Kristina brought them to the room with the carpets. The robber shifted them aside and led the little group through the gap in the wall. As they traveled down the tunnel she said, "There's a gate blocking the way but I have keys for all the locks—" She broke off as she saw the broken bars piled up alongside the wall.

"I found it like this," Gerda said in a moment of inexplicable giddiness.

Kristina snorted. "Of course you did." Still, the opened the lock and all three of them could walk through comfortably. They proceeded through the tunnel without speaking. It stretched on for far longer than the first tunnel. With every step Gerda wondered if Kristina would change her mind and force them back to the fortress. Yet the robber kept moving forward.

The stars had faded and the sun was rising when they came out from below the earth. When Gerda blinked away the dazzle of light, she saw that they stood near the river once more. The early morning was cool, though the sun came up golden over the hills and spread its light through the trees. The ground began to warm after the dark of night and mist rose from the river.

Making another demand felt dangerous, but Gerda still held out her wrist with the bracelet. "Take it off."

"I don't need to."

"But you said it would let you know where I was, if I ever tried to escape."

Kristina smiled, looking mischievous and sad all at once. "I lied."

"But you caught up with me that first morning when we went out to rob people," Gerda said.

"I don't need magic to find somebody who's still so close by and unused to sneaking through a forest. It seemed an easy way to keep you here." Kristina turned to the reindeer. "He'll have to carry you. Human legs are too slow and I'm not dragging that boat all the way out here." She helped Gerda climb onto his back.

"What changed your mind?" Gerda asked.

Kristina ignored this. "There are some reindeer herders who should be living farther north this time of year. If anybody can tell you how to survive the Snow Queen, it would be them. They must be insane to willingly live so close to her, but they could be useful if you're able to find them."

"Do you know exactly where they are?"

"Does it sound as though I spend much time thinking about the sorts of people who are foolish enough to go that near the Snow Queen? All I know is that they're supposed to camp near the river."

"Thank you."

"You can thank me by not getting yourself killed. Come back here after you get your brother. I want to see if he's worth all this trouble." She waved an arm at the reindeer without waiting for a response. "Go on, then. Shoo!"

The reindeer ran. Gerda didn't know how to properly hold on or ride. She thought that perhaps no reindeer could ever be fully tamed, even one who had been kept indoors for so long. There were no reins or mane for her to hold onto, and the hairs were too short to curl her fingers through. She leaned down and circled her arms around his neck. She wrapped her legs as far around his stomach as they could reach and prayed not to fall.

At last she adjusted to the rhythm of his movements and was able to raise her head without complete fear of falling. The reindeer didn't run in a straight line: he moved in and out of the trees, always zigzagging but remaining within sight of the river.

The sun burned away the mist and they ran through ripe, golden light. The day seemed to last forever. As they traveled farther north, leaves continuously fell from the trees in a pattering shower of bright colors. The forest of birches, maples, oaks, and chestnuts became infiltrated with firs and pines. With more of the sky visible, she could watch the sun slip across the horizon. Time seemed to unwind like a ball of yarn nearing its end. Throughout that long day, she looked north toward winter.

# CHAPTER TWELVE

Kai sat before the mirror in the Snow Queen's chair. Anybody else might have thought the mirror complete: the gaps were filled in and the ivory chest held not even a sliver of glass. There were no cracks. He had polished the mirror with snow until its surface shone like diamonds. Yet one imperfection remained: in the lower right-hand corner, there was a tiny gap. He could barely see it, but he knew it was there. And while the mirror remained incomplete, he knew no peace. Sharp-edged voices clamored in Kai's mind, nagging him to make the mirror whole. He nodded in response to their wheedling and arguments, but he still could not find the last piece that would make the mirror perfect.

He watched his reflection and the reflection watched him. It sneered at him and narrowed its eyes into slits. The mirror did not reflect the walls and doors behind him; instead, it showed the lands surrounding the palace. Winter expanded over the world in the mirror as he watched: Kai saw frost crawl across the earth past the former boundaries of the Snow Queen's domain. It crept into the ground and hardened the soil so that nothing could take root. The cold drew all of the world's animals into a numbing sleep which deepened into a hibernation that would last forever. For as long as the vision lasted, snow fell without ceasing.

He heard the Snow Queen enter the room and looked around. Her dress was as bright as the moon, and her hair and skin were spangled with the cold fire of stars.

This time she ignored him and went directly to the mirror. Her image filled the glass and the Snow Queen smiled at her reflection. She rested her forehead against the mirror and crooned to it in a language he didn't recognize.

Just as her voice was replacing the chidings that had filled his ears, her murmurings and whisperings ceased. Her hand flew to the corner and found the tiny hole. Her entire body stiffened, her back becoming as hard as iron. She turned to Kai.

"It's not finished," she said. Her voice was tight and the words precise. "Why have you left my mirror unfinished?"

He held his hands out to her, palms up. "There aren't any more pieces. I can't do it."

The Snow Queen dragged him out of the chair. One of her nails caught his chin as she grabbed the collar of his jacket. He could feel tremors in her hands as she held him up. "Where is it?"

"It isn't here," he said.

"I can see that, you fool." Now that they were face-to-face, the tremors ceased and she caught her breath. "What happened to your eye?" One of her hands gripped his face. He could feel bruises forming. "You had the last piece. I saw it when we met. Kai, what have you done?"

"I didn't do anything. I thought I had it until I came to the end. But the mirror is almost whole. Won't it be powerful enough?"

She let go and he tumbled onto the floor. He watched her pace around the room. She said, "You think I would settle for an imperfect mirror? This is supposed to be the winter that will last. I mean to bring snow and ice across all the lands and waters forever, but you ruined it. Instead, I have to search once more. How could you do this to me?"

"I'm sure you'll find it soon. I'll help. You told me I could help bring winter back," he reminded her.

"What makes you think I would ever let a human remain by my side?" the Snow Queen asked. She stared out of the window a few moments more before adding, "All I asked you to do was finish the mirror. Only that one task. You've disappointed me, Kai."

She exited the room and the light went with her. Kai was left huddled on the ground, alone in the dark.

It felt as if hours passed yet she did not reappear. Kai searched the room for the missing piece once more. He ran his hands over every inch of snowy floor. When he didn't find it, he returned to the other rooms he had visited and examined them. Yet he still found nothing but snow and ice. He did not see the Snow Queen throughout the search. Now he returned to the mirror.

The whispers kept him company. Whenever he looked away, they reminded him to gaze into the mirror once more. It felt more welcoming each time. If the Snow Queen would not return, he could at least watch winter's progress and see visions of how it would heal the world of damage from the other seasons once it was given the opportunity.

His only fear now was that the Snow Queen would take the mirror away as punishment for his failure. The whispers told him that she would do it easily and never think of him again. As the winter night lengthened and she did not reappear, he began to wonder how long it would be before she cast him out.

Autumn was ending. The first snow came several nights after Gerda left the robbers' fortress. She sneezed in her sleep and batted at her nose. Snowflakes tickled her face, like the whiskers of an inquisitive cat. She woke up long enough to gaze blearily at the white and silver-black world before rolling over so that she faced the reindeer's warm fur.

A thin layer of snow covered the ground when she woke up properly in the morning. The reindeer stirred as she lifted her head. As she moved, she discovered that a clump of snow had fallen down her collar and she twitched as the melting coldness trickled down her back. When she shook herself more snow flew off her clothing and into the air, scattering like powdered sugar.

The bottom curves of tree branches appeared as dark as chocolate. A squirrel jumped onto one branch and sent tiny lumps of snow falling to earth. Only the grass that had been kept warm beneath herself and the reindeer remained bright green. Despite the chill, the river still remained autumn's possession, with its wild current not yet frozen.

Gerda smiled before she could stop herself. Despite the knowledge that soon she would be traveling in land wholly under the Snow Queen's control, she couldn't stop the burst of happiness she had always felt upon witnessing the first snowfall of the season in Vasa. Kai had been fond of winter as well, even before it reached out to take him. She closed her eyes and breathed deeply: past the fragrance of damp snow, she could still smell autumn leaves and the soft earth. The sun was rising and the snow would likely melt before noon. Yet she could tell it would be here to stay before long.

The snow trickled into the river as it melted. Where the sun shone from in between clouds, its rays of light pierced the dark silk of the water. Darker shadows of water weeds and fish swayed beneath its surface.

She saw geese flying overhead often that day as the birds sped away to the south. They flowed in and out of vees that were dark against the sky. Even though she knew the loud honking sounds were the geese calling to one another, she couldn't help imagining that the birds were saying, "Turn back. Come south with us, this is no place for you."

After everything that she had seen, she wondered if there were places where the animals could speak in human language or where people could understand the animals' speech. She didn't know how far the reindeer would accompany her and wished that she knew if he understood when she spoke aloud. Probably he would stay with her only until he could rejoin his herd. Yet the company of another living thing was welcome, even though she could not guess what he might be thinking. She half-expected each day with the reindeer to be the last, and felt a spark of joy each morning that she awoke and found that she was not alone.

She dreamed of Kai again that night. Her sleep had been free of both nightmares and true dreams since the night she set out to fool Kristina, and she had been wondering how long it would last. This time when she saw Kai, there was almost no color in him: he seemed gray and white, like a faded illustration from an old book. She wanted to cry out. He'd always been so much paler than she, but had never seemed so drained of life. Now he was almost as still as an ice sculpture and he didn't speak. She reached for him but was stopped by a wall of ice. She could see every detail but the ice between them was too thick. She pounded at it until her fists bled and her nails broke, but the barrier didn't crack.

"Let me in," she begged. She saw his eyes blink and watched him breathe, but he didn't move forward. He watched her as though she were a stranger.

A white shape stood at Kai's back. It wrapped its arms around his shoulders and held him there. It smiled at her until all she saw were the sharp teeth in its moon-pale face.

Gerda jumped as she awoke from the nightmare. She remained curled up next to the warm reindeer but slept no more that night.

New snow appeared the following day, whiter than any she had ever seen. The last leaves had fallen before dusk arrived, and pines and firs had replaced the trees belonging to warmer seasons. Some of the needles looked as soft as down and hung in long clumps. Others grew in short, spiky bursts and seemed sharp enough to cut.

The snow remained feather-light but Gerda remembered the blizzard the Snow Queen had created. She watched the sky warily, half-expecting dark clouds and screaming winds to descend at any moment. She remembered Lukas's description of the blizzard that had suddenly appeared during the journey with his friends. How far would she be able to travel before the Snow Queen noticed her presence?

She looked for other people as the miles passed and the snow grew deeper. Gerda wished that Kristina had known more about the reindeer herders. Lukas had also said that some people did live in the Snow Queen's territory, but she still couldn't find any suggestions of humans.

The signs of life that she did find didn't appear to be related to humans: on several occasions, clumps of snow dropped onto Gerda and the reindeer, even when they were not walking beneath trees and there was no wind. When she peered at the trees she saw small, white creatures running along the boughs. Yet as much as she concentrated, she could never quite make out the distinct shapes of the little beings.

Although part of her mind protested over any delay, she periodically turned from the river to look a short distance into the forest the reindeer herders. There were still no results but during the last search, the reindeer stumbled on the way back to the river. Gerda dismounted. His leg appeared fine but in the area where he had tripped, the tips of something green and sharp poked out of the snow. Gerda scooped the snow away and uncovered a small holly bush. In that land that was becoming paler with every passing mile, the bush was brighter than anything else in sight. The knife-edged leaves were bottle-green, and berries as red as blood and as bright as summer decorated the stems. It was even free of the ice that had begun to appear as a crust on the snow.

Gerda didn't believe that the Snow Queen knew of the plant's existence. It was easy to imagine the Snow Queen tearing it apart or freezing the whole thing within ice if she had encountered it. Even though the heat of the summer forest now seemed like a dream, Gerda remembered looking into her piece of the mirror on that warm night and willing plants to grow, including a holly bush. She laughed and cupped her hands around a cluster of leaves. A slightly bitter scent prickled her nose.

Knowledge from one of her books on plant lore swam up out of her memory. "'For luck and protection,'" she recited. She also remembered how among the disaster that was Vasa after the blizzard, the conservatory and its plants had remained untouched.

She snapped a cluster of leaves and berries from the bush. Juice dripped from the broken stem as she secured it in her red scarf. She scattered a few handfuls of snow over the little plant before rising. A dusting should be enough to hide it while still allowing the leaves to absorb the light.

Except for the decreasing number of trees, the holly bush was the last plant Gerda saw. She remembered when the forest had been so thick that she couldn't see more than ten feet into its shadows. As she journeyed, the spaces between the pines and firs grew larger, and only snow carpeted the ground instead of undergrowth and broken twigs. During some moments it felt as though she had been traveling forever, yet she still saw no sign of the Snow Queen's palace.

Gerda's and the reindeer's breaths always steamed in the air now and she nestled her hands within her long, fur-lined mittens. The reindeer didn't appear to mind that she rode him most of the time but she still sometimes walked to give him a rest. As the days turned colder, his antlers fell off and were left behind.

Even the deep, fast-moving river began to fall under winter's control: streams still emerged from the thinning forest on occasion but they were frozen solid. The wilder parts of the river grew quiet and ice began to cover its surface.

Sometimes they passed ducks on the river. Most of the birds huddled together on sections of ice that extended from the bank, while others bobbed in the cold water as they sought whatever food remained. A pair of mallards foraged on the bank nearby, their beaks and breasts dusted with the powdery snow. Despite their layers of feathers, Gerda wondered how they could bear to swim in such cold water. Once she paused and pulled one mitten off to dip her fingers into the river. The water was so cold that it burned.

She replaced the mitten and climbed onto the reindeer's back. The time for sightseeing was over.

Aside from the light of the full moon in the sky, Kai remained in darkness.

He wandered the halls of the palace. He stepped through another door that led him in and out of unfamiliar rooms until it brought him to the round chamber where they had looked at the stars together. He remembered her kissing him. Up in that room like the space atop a lighthouse, he watched snow-laden clouds drift across the sky. He walked up and down the stairs with the shuffling gait of an old man.

All throughout this time, he found traces of the Snow Queen. She appeared at the edges of his vision yet remained out of reach. At every corner that he turned, he saw a fold of pearl-edged ivory cloth sliding around the bend. He heard her breathing in rooms just before he entered them.

Kai began to feel as if they were two ghosts who haunted the same place but would never meet.

The day after Gerda saw the ducks, the snow began to fall and didn't stop. The reindeer stepped easily through the growing drifts but the visibility grew poorer and poorer. Soon she couldn't see more than a few feet in front of her face. Listening for the river was little help: the ice grew thicker upon its surface and she could barely hear the current with her hood up.

Still, they were managing until the wind arose. The reindeer stopped walking as it seemed to blow at them from every direction. When Gerda leaned forward to rub his neck, an especially strong gust of wind knocked her from his back.

The deep snow softened her landing but made it difficult for her to stand up. The reindeer patiently allowed her to cling to him as she stumbled to her feet. She didn't have enough energy to climb onto his back once more.

They stumbled forward. It was worse than walking through the blizzard in Vasa. The Snow Queen had known what Gerda was trying to do that time. Had she now noticed Gerda at last and decided to stop her?

The snow and wind pressed down on her until it felt as though she was being drowned by winter. The thin crust was not yet hard enough for her to walk on top of the snow and her legs ached from trudging through it. She knew she would never wake up if she lay down now but she longed for rest. She stopped walking and leaned against the reindeer as she told herself that it was only for a few minutes.

Although the wind continued to shriek and pluck at her hood while they stood still, the falling snow began to lessen. As her dazed eyes stared ahead, in between gusts of snowflakes she glimpsed a cluster of pine trees. A large tent stood below the sheltering branches. Beyond it, there were dozens of dark lumps close together.

She remembered Kai reading to her about mirages in deserts, though she had trouble recalling the exact sound of his voice. He had never said if the same thing could happen to people who wandered in winter wastelands. Regardless, she and the reindeer slowly tramped forward.

Before she could touch the tent, the flap was tugged open far enough for a little head with dark eyes to peer out. "Mama, somebody's out there!" a high-pitched voice shrieked. The head vanished back inside.

After so long with only the reindeer for company, another human's voice sounded almost unnatural. Nonetheless, Gerda stepped forward. She rested her hand on the tent flap; it opened again and she fell in.

"It's only a human," a woman's voice said. Then she added, "What are you doing, wandering around in that storm? You'll catch your death out there!" Before Gerda could lift herself up, a pair of hands reached under her arms and pulled her the rest of the way into the tent.

Strong heat made Gerda pass out. She came as the same hands pulled the sodden scarf from her face and gently pushed back her hood. She lay on fur rugs and stared up at a woman who had cinnamon-colored hair threaded with white. The heat came from a fire in the center of the tent.

"You're the reindeer herders?" she asked, her voice hoarse. As the heat revived her, she realized that the lumps outside must have been their animals.

The faces of two children and a man also appeared above her. "We are," the man said with a raised eyebrow. "And just who are you?"

"Time enough for questions in a minute. Give us some space," the woman said and nudged the other people around her. "Let's get you thawed out first." She pulled off Gerda's coat and boots, and spread her dripping mittens before the fire.

"But my reindeer," Gerda began.

"Will be safe enough outside. He's far more suited to winter than you are."

The man helped Gerda sit up. She had recovered enough strength to strip off her outer sweater and one layer of socks. As he helped her get comfortable, the woman ladled a thick soup into a bowl and handed it to Gerda. The two children, a boy and a girl, watched her with undisguised curiosity. Off to the side she saw a baby sleeping among tightly wrapped blankets.

"You're far from anywhere," the woman said. "Were you separated from your family in the storm?"

Gerda shook her head but before she could say anything, the father said, "She couldn't have been, Mari. Look at her; she's no herder, and we're too far away from anyone else."

Mari sighed. "I was trying to be polite, Johan." Their daughter giggled and Johan flicked one of her braids.

"He's right," Gerda admitted. Mari and Johan's exchange had amused her as well and she found herself wondering if her own parents had affectionately disagreed like this. "I'm alone except for the reindeer and I'm going north."

The baby slept on but the boy and girl had whispered to one another as Gerda spoke to their parents. Now the boy asked, "Why would you want to do that? The only thing farther north is…"

Gerda nodded. "The Snow Queen. I know. That's where I'm going." She turned back to Mari and Johan. "I'm looking for her palace. A friend of mine suggested I look for reindeer herders and said you might be able to give me some advice."

"If you're looking for advice, the best thing you can do is to turn around," Johan said dryly.

"That's what everyone says."

"Then maybe you should listen."

She hoped this would not turn into yet another argument where well-meaning people tried to stop her. Kristina had said the reindeer herders could help but she had also done everything short of locking Gerda up in order to keep her from leaving. The family had been kind so far but part of her started to wonder if reindeer herders were also willing to haul runaways back to the robbers in the autumn forest. She said, "I'd like to turn back but I can't."

"Why not?" he asked. "What could possibly be so important that you would willingly go *there*, of all places?"

"She has my brother. I'm going to rescue him."

"You're looking for that one? We'd heard that the Snow Queen has a new amusement," Mari said.

Gerda bristled. "You make him sound like a pet."

Mari reached forward and rested her warm, calloused hand on Gerda's wrist. "I didn't mean it like that. But you should know that she values our lives less than the smallest snowflake, if you don't already." Her hand tightened briefly before she pulled it away.

"I figured that out early on. But how do you know about Kai?"

"Is that his name? I hadn't known that part. We hear news in the wind. It's not much, but we gather enough bits and pieces to sometimes put together an idea of what she's up to. Margareta hears it clearest, don't you sweetheart?" She smiled at her daughter, who grinned back and played with the ribbons sewn onto the hem of her skirt.

"I can't believe you live so near the Snow Queen. Are you here all year?" Gerda asked. Living on the Snow Queen's doorstep, she thought, must be like walking through a den of hibernating bears, not knowing if they would wake up and strike out at any moment.

Johan shook his head. "We only stay for a few months each year. Later on, we'll go back south with the reindeer and meet with some of the other herders. She tolerates us so long as we don't travel farther north."

"But why doesn't she get rid of you?" They knew they must be in danger, yet it seemed as though they didn't care. Gerda saw the faces of the Snow Queen's false, dead parents in her mind. Even being in another world hadn't saved them. She turned to Mari. "You just told me that she doesn't care about human life, but you're here *every year* and you're all alive."

Mari sighed. She reached into the pile of new logs and dropped one onto the fire. "We're not a threat. She allows us to remain because it amuses her to see how hard we have to work to stay alive in her season. Do you understand? We're like small insects, very far below her, and it's too much work to squash us when she knows that we'll leave on our own. I think that sometimes when she's busy, she forgets us altogether."

"We need her," Johan said. When Gerda stared at him, he added, "She's the reason winter exists. The reindeer couldn't survive if she was gone and we need the reindeer. What do you plan on doing when you find her?" There was a warning in his voice.

"I don't want to kill her. I'm just trying to get my brother back." As Gerda protested, she was amazed to realize that she meant it. She wouldn't cry if the Snow Queen melted into a puddle of water, but what she wanted most was Kai's return and to prevent the mirror's completion. If the Snow Queen could just be kept from following them, it would be enough. Gerda couldn't wait for spring to arrive once more but she also didn't want to live in a world where winter no longer existed. She remembered Suvi saying that the Snow Queen had once admitted that all of the seasons were necessary, even though she didn't care for them herself. And as terrifying as the Snow Queen was, she still had at least one sister who loved her.

"Good."

"Have you ever seen her?" Gerda asked.

Johan shook his head. Before he could say anything more, the little boy opened his mouth. "I saw her!"

Mari and Johan's heads whipped around. For all their talk of needing the Snow Queen and not being scared to live in her realm, their faces turned remarkably pale. "Henrik, why didn't you tell us?" Johan demanded.

"It was only the one time and it was a whole year ago," Henrik said. He squirmed as Johan gave him an eagle-eyed look. "It was! She was flying high above in her sleigh. It was for just a moment, then it started snowing and I couldn't see her anymore. I don't think she even saw me."

"If you ever see her again, you tell us right away," Johan said. Henrik heaved a deep sigh but nodded.

Gerda's limbs still felt sluggish but her mind was more awake every minute. The nearness of the Snow Queen taunted her; she was anxious to be on the move but thought that even the reindeer would have trouble moving through all the new snow. "Do you have anything that could help me get to her palace sooner? I'm worried there won't be anything of Kai left if I keep going like this."

"A sled would be fastest but you wouldn't want to do that, even if we had one to spare," Mari said.

"Why not?"

"Because of the Snow Queen," Henrik said as though Gerda were an idiot. "Your reindeer would need to pull the sled and *she* would kill him. That's why."

"Don't be rude," Johan scolded but the look on his face showed that he thought the same thing.

Her reindeer. Gerda had been so glad for the reindeer's warmth and company while traveling that she hadn't thought what might happen to him when she found the Snow Queen's palace. The Snow Queen probably didn't care for reindeer any more than she liked humans. Gerda had helped rescue him from the robbers but that didn't make a difference if she took him to his death. She glanced at the tent flap. "Would you keep him for me?"

"Are you sure?" Mari asked. She looked surprised.

"I only met him in the first place because he'd been separated from his herd. You have the only other reindeer I've seen since I set out. Even if they're not his herd, it's still better than taking him with me the rest of the way. But…if he stays, will you take good care of him?"

"As if he'd been with us since he was born," Mari promised.

Gerda swallowed the lump in her throat. "Good."

"Can you skate?" Johan asked.

Gerda shook her head. She had tried several times, but it always ended with bruises. Nana could still skate like a young woman, but Gerda couldn't make it once around the skating rink at the college without falling. Kai had made a comment about inherited skills and wondered out loud if Gerda was adopted. She had thrown a snowball at him.

"Skiing, then?"

Gerda smiled. "That I can do." Johan nodded and stood up.

"I have one more thing that might help," Mari said.

It sounded as vague a sentence as possible to Gerda, but something about it made Johan pause halfway through pulling out a set of skis and raise his eyebrows. "Are you sure?" he asked his wife.

"We don't have any plans for it and she needs it more." Mari walked across the tent to where the baby still slumbered, and rummaged through a bag nearby. When she turned back, she held a length of thick blue cord that had been twisted into a knot the size of her hand.

"What's so special about that?" Gerda asked.

"I traded with a witch earlier this year. There's a good wind bound up in here; I'll unwind it after you get onto the river and it should help to push you along for a little while."

Johan still looked as though he didn't completely agree but he didn't say anything more against Mari's decision. He returned to Gerda, and set down a set of wooden skis and poles.

"Thank you," she said. "Do you know anything else about the Snow Queen that might help?"

"You already know how powerful she is," Mari said as she rubbed one finger along the looped cord. "She'll be even stronger when you get closer and sometimes humans entertain her. She doesn't understand us and she doesn't *want* to, but she likes to watch and play with us. If you can catch her interest, it might buy you enough time to find your brother."

Gerda nodded. "I'll remember."

Margareta crawled to the tent flap and peered out into the cold world. "Mama, the storm's over."

"Good. Did you hear anything interesting during this one?"

Margareta shook her head.

"All right, then. If you get bundled up, you and Henrik can come outside with us."

The children shrieked with delight and chattered a mile a minute as they bounced around the tent in the process of dressing to go outside. Gerda put her own outdoor gear back on, which was now wonderfully dry and warm after lying beside the fire. The first blast of cold air outside made her gasp, but she secured her hood and moved on.

Her reindeer didn't appear to have moved from the tent's entrance during the whole storm. His coat was thick with snow but he readily lifted his head as she emerged from the tent. She threw her arms about him. He patiently allowed the gesture, as he had done all the other times since they met. "You can't come with me anymore," she whispered into his ear. "She would kill you and Nils would never forgive me if he found out. If you stay here, at least you'll be safe." She resisted the urge to say, "Be good." He had been a friend of sorts but never her pet. Even now, she wasn't completely sure if the reindeer would stay behind. She didn't own him and after his time with the robbers, she had a feeling he would only remain in a place that he chose. She didn't let herself cry—she knew the tears would freeze.

Mari helped Gerda balance as she strapped the skis to her feet. Her first movements were clumsy but soon her body remembered how to use the objects. The new, deep snow scattered like powder in all directions as the family stepped through it. The adults trudged along, but Henrik and Margareta tossed snowballs at one another. The brief, weak sunlight had faded as they waited out the storm. Now the sky was scoured of clouds and the moon had risen.

Arriving at the river, Gerda saw that the same wind that had tormented her earlier had now swept the crystal-like river clean. She had trouble remembering how it appeared when she had first landed in it, the wild water woven through with weeds and minnows. So long as the river stayed clear of snow, it would be easy enough to follow.

She smiled as she turned back to the family. "Thank you for everything. I'll never forget what you did."

"Good luck," Johan said. "But remember—we need her even though she doesn't care about us."

"I will."

The children stopped playing long enough to wave. Mari smiled and began to pull apart the knot in her hands. Gerda waved back at them. Then she was off.

She wished that she could have watched exactly what the cord did, for a light wind immediately started to blow behind her. It felt like a pair of comforting hands on her back. She skimmed so fast across the snow that it seemed as though she was flying.

The frozen river reminded her of watching ice fishers as a little girl: uncaring of the cold, they sat on chairs around holes drilled into the ice. Even during the harshest winters she had lived through, they had always found fish swimming in water far below. As she continued traveling, she wondered if any fish that had dared to venture this far north were now suspended forever in the ice.

The world was quiet, disturbed only by the noise of her skis and the whispering wind that blew north. Her eyes were so focused on the river that she missed the Northern Lights' initial appearance. When a flicker of lime green overhead caught her attention, she looked up so fast that she nearly fell. But the view overhead was the same as before and the crowds of stars twinkled innocently. She was about to return her gaze to earth when the lights returned.

Banners of color spun across the sky. Long ago, she had read a description of the aurora borealis and imagined hours of unending lights; instead, these came and went. One moment the sky was colored like a box of oil paints and the next, the colors vanished like ghosts. She thought they had ended but several minutes later traces of pale blue reappeared, almost invisible against the moon.

The lights wavered like seaweed or a gossamer veil. Gerda's neck ached from looking up so long. Skiing so fast through the cold air caused tears to spring to her eyes and she had to wipe at her face so that her eyelashes wouldn't freeze. For one moment the sight made her think well of the Snow Queen, seeing that winter here contained at least one thing that was colorful and lifelike.

Kai returned to the mirror and left it no more. He could see everything in it: the visions in the mirror took him around the world. It showed him land covered in ugly shades of green and brown beneath too-hot sunlight and dirty rains.

The people were even worse. Everyone he looked upon was hideous. Unaware that he watched, they laughed in voices harsher than ravens, sneered when they meant to smile, and plodded along like toads. The humans were terrible and Kai despised them.

He felt at peace only when the mirror showed places belonging to winter: mountain tops that had snow all year long, where no one could live; frozen lakes and harbors; caves where the temperatures plummeted until icicles coated the stone. He grew anxious for winter to cover the rest of the world and searched for signs of the creeping frosts. Everything must be under winter's control, or else it would never be clean.

He still did not see the Snow Queen. Sometimes he felt her presence so strongly that he turned and was surprised when she didn't stand behind him. Once he thought he saw her riding away in the sleigh past the windows. At other times a cold breath stirred his hair. Only when he suspected that she might be truly gone did he cry out, his voice almost frozen from lack of use.

The Northern Lights didn't last forever. Eventually the brilliant colors faded and there was no proof that they had ever existed. It was always night now and the only illumination came from the moon.

She caught glimpses of water weeds and leaves frozen deep within the clear ice as she skied. She remembered that Kai would once have been fascinated by fragile objects so perfectly preserved.

After so much travel, she had difficulty believing that soon she would see him again. She thought about him often. She remembered him at every age: a little boy before he needed the owl-like glasses; several years later, when his fast-growing limbs caught the legs of chairs and corners of tables and she had teased constantly, even as she sprouted up like one of the seedlings in the conservatory; and the tall, brilliant, almost-man he was becoming when that winter came and broke him apart from her and Nana.

But now there was no reindeer for company, and she had little to distract her mind from what might happen when she reached Kai and the Snow Queen. With the Snow Queen's palace closer each minute, Kristina's arguments were loud in her head: What if he had been with the Snow Queen too long? What if he didn't want to return to Vasa? "What if" a million times over.

Desperate for hope and distraction, Gerda sang Christmas songs. There was no festivity in this winter, but she clung to the music. She whistled the tune for, "The holly and the ivy, when they are both full grown, out of all the trees that are in the wood, the holly wears the crown." Into the cold, unwelcoming air she sang, "God Rest Ye Merry, Gentlemen" and the bright melody that went with, "Mark my footsteps, good my page, tread thou in them boldly; thou shall find the winter's rage freeze thy blood less coldly."

Such cold air wasn't conducive to deep breathing and strong singing. The frosty air burned her lungs and the wind whisked the words away as soon as they formed upon her lips. Often she got out only a hint of sound. Yet she still sang. More than the pretty tunes, she clung to the lyrics. Again and again, she sang songs that were full of cheer and promised that good things were emerging from the dark of winter.

The now-featureless land stretched out from either side of the river. If she ventured even a half-mile from the river, she would be lost forever. The sun vanished for good before she reached the palace. She looked gratefully upon the moon that provided some light, and continued skiing. Eventually the enchanted wind faded away and the snow became free to settle where it pleased. She continued north for as long as she could follow the river, but soon it was hidden entirely by snow.

She looked back; the falling snow had filled the tracks she left behind and she couldn't tell if she was moving straight. There was still no sign of a palace ahead. It wouldn't have surprised her if the Snow Queen had learned of Gerda's approach and had sent her traveling in circles until a time when she might fall and not be able to stand.

The fragment of the mirror remained in her pocket. Gerda hesitated before opening the box but there was nowhere else to go for help. Holding the bit of mirror as though it was a compass in her left hand, she slowly swung the arm from left to right.

At the beginning it seemed motionless like any normal mirror. Just as she started to think of putting it away, she felt twinges in her fingers. She moved a little farther and cold burst underneath her fingernails. Gerda cried out but managed to avoid dropping the mirror into the snow where she might never find it.

She tucked the mirror back into her pocket, where it was surrounded by her bits of flower blossoms, seeds, and herbs. She flexed her fingers constantly but the motions remained clumsy. Still, it had given her a direction.

She used the mirror several more times. On most of the occasions when she checked her direction, she had wandered only a little astray. Once however, the mirror revealed that she had turned almost completely around. Her hand felt colder and stiffer after every use.

Thoughts of what might happen to her piece of the mirror now that it was surrounded by winter constantly worried her. Suvi had thought it would never return to its original nature, but she hadn't known for certain. Would one piece really be enough to change the rest of the mirror? Had Gerda been in any of the other seasons she would have looked into it for reassurance, but now she was so cold that she couldn't bring herself to do that again.

The palace appeared in the midst of the darkness. Its walls were made from thick slabs of ice and snow as polished as marble. At intervals on the upper floors she saw shining objects that were either mirrors or more windows cut from ice. The building was so tall that she almost fell over when she leaned back to take it all in. On the roof she could see the gleam of a little room made entirely of ice. The whole place shone so brightly that her eyes watered. Everything was dreadfully silent in that spellbound winter.

She didn't approach the palace yet. She was so mesmerized by its steady light that she didn't immediately notice when snow began to swirl up around her. It tumbled and spun in the otherwise still air, still making no sound. It was unlike anything she had seen since setting out with the reindeer. Without warning, it stopped. The silence felt different.

Gerda turned around.

The Snow Queen stood behind her.

# CHAPTER THIRTEEN

She looked even more beautiful than Gerda remembered. In Vasa she had pretended to be a human; now she did not bother. She was winter merely dressed in the costume of a woman.

"You have good timing," the Snow Queen said in the contemplative tone a person would have used upon realizing that she had forgotten to close a door before leaving her house. She took a few steps closer. "I was just about to leave and do some more of my season's work when I felt you sneaking up. I was even more surprised after I remembered telling you not to follow me."

All of Gerda's instincts screamed at her to run away. She bit her chapped lips and continued to face the Snow Queen. "You did. But I want my brother back."

"He's just another human. Why do you care, when there are so many of you?" The Snow Queen almost looked confused. It was the most human-like expression Gerda had ever seen on her face.

"I care because he's my family. You don't get to take him away from us."

The Snow Queen chuckled. "You always did become worked up over the smallest things. He came with me to fix my mirror so that I can make the world perfect. He *wanted* to do it. You should be content to leave him to such a worthy goal."

"No."

"And there is the single-mindedness that made you so boring the last time I saw you. But we might be able to fix that—let's see if your begging has improved." The Snow Queen raised her hands.

Thick snow began to fall once more. Instead of swirling around as the Snow Queen had done, it settled in piles surrounding Gerda. The quiet snow began to crunch as ice was added to the mixture. Arms and legs grew out of the piles. The things pulled themselves out of the ground, even as they were still taking shape.

Gerda saw creatures that she had never imagined, even in her nightmares. One thick-bodied figure bristled with spikes made from icicles with serrated edges. Another was similar to an armored knight, but it had a featureless circle of ice where the face should be. One of them had a bear's head, but the legs were distorted and it was far larger than any normal bear. As she turned around, she saw that several of the creatures pointed spears at her, the tips a mere hands-breadth away from her face. There were no gaps in the circle large for her to ski through. Even if she did, how could she escape in this featureless land where the Snow Queen would find her instantly?

The Snow Queen stood outside the circle and smiled. "What do you say now?"

Gerda's voice lay like a stone in her throat.

"I will grant you one gift: you may choose your death," the Snow Queen said. "I can freeze both you and your brother, and you can stand on either side of my mirror. Or I can kill you quickly right here. Or you may leave and wander through my realm alone until you no longer want to live. This is far more than I offer most humans. Which will it be?"

Gerda tried to ignore these choices. "Kai hasn't finished your mirror, has he?" Her voice rasped but she got the words out.

The Snow Queen's face twitched. The monsters stepped apart enough for her to enter the circle. "Why do you say that?"

"You said you would freeze both of us. You wouldn't do that to Kai if he was still working on the mirror. He *can't* finish it."

"How do you know that?"

Gerda took a deep breath. It was time to gamble with the only thing she had to offer. "Because I have the last piece."

The Snow Queen laughed. "You do not."

"I do." Gerda touched her pocket.

The Snow Queen grew as still as the frozen river. She did not even appear to breathe. "A pathetic human like you should never have been allowed to touch any part of my mirror. Give it to me." She stepped closer until no more than an inch separated them. Gerda hadn't been warm since leaving the reindeer herders' tent, but the cold drifting off of the Snow Queen sank into her skin and bones until she thought she would never feel warm again.

Gerda stared into those iceberg eyes and waited for the Snow Queen to snatch the piece from her. Yet the moments stretched on in that silent place. The monsters surrounding them didn't so much as shift their weight. Had she not been too terrified to look away, she would have missed the

Snow Queen's gaze flicker to the cluster of leaves and berries at Gerda's throat. She had been so focused on finding the palace that she had almost forgotten about the holly. Yet somehow it had never fallen out of her scarf, even after all the wind, and skating, and tumbles into the snow. Her eyes widened. "You can't take it. The holly is protection."

"Continue to try my patience and we'll find out how much protection that weed really offers."

Gerda shook her head, even as she raised one hand and cupped it over the little plant.

The Snow Queen's mood changed as rapidly as the flickering colors of the Northern Lights. "If you give the mirror to me, I can reward you. You did bring it all this way and now I won't have to waste another year searching. Help me now and you won't have to die. I can even make it so that you will enjoy my new winter."

"How?"

"You would have to change—you humans are so frail—but it takes only completing the mirror and a kiss. Then you could live anywhere you want and do anything you like. Winter is the most beautiful season and there are so many wonderful things that can be done during it."

Gerda caught herself nodding dreamily. Her hand had dropped from the holly and rested on the pocket where her piece of the mirror lay hidden. It was true that she rejoiced at seeing the first snowfall each winter and even during the coldest times, she hated staying indoors all day without stepping outside for at least a few minutes. The frost on the windows was beautiful and she enjoyed looking upon the frozen lake.

The Snow Queen stepped closer. Her pale, smooth hand hovered a mere inch away from Gerda's as she murmured into the human woman's ear, "You must be tired. All you have to do is hand it to me. Just one little thing and all of this can be over."

Even though Gerda's fingers were always stiff now and she had looked into the mirror shard too many times for its effects to ever fully go away, she still did not have a piece of the mirror within her body. There was no ice in her heart that the Snow Queen could call upon. She thought about sunlight and plants that remained green, even in the middle of winter. All of that would be gone if she surrendered now. She stepped back. "I want to see Kai."

The attempt at a pleasant expression melted from the Snow Queen's face. "Why should I let you do that? He belongs to me now and I do not give away my possessions. He thinks of nothing but carrying out my wishes. I only had to set him before my mirror and he immediately devoted himself to it. Do you really think he would care about you any longer, even if he remembers who you are?"

"But you're bored." Gerda spoke faster. Mari's advice was strong in her

174

mind. If Kai has changed so much, maybe he doesn't entertain you any longer. You would have just frozen me right away if he was still so interesting. And if the mirror is still broken, you can't use it. Letting me talk to Kai will give you something to watch."

The Snow Queen tapped her chin with one finger. "I'm impressed—you've learned how to create a halfway tempting offer."

"If you let me leave with Kai and swear never to bother us again, I'll even finish the mirror like you want. Why not give me only a few more minutes when you know you can make up for lost time after it's finished?" Gerda had heard enough of Nana's stories to know that loopholes could be found in almost any promise, but this was the best one she could think of.

The Snow Queen was silent as Gerda fought to keep from trembling underneath her heavy coat. At length, she nodded. "If you finish the mirror and convince your brother that he *wants* to leave, the two of you may go. But know this: try to fool me and holly or not, I will freeze all the blood in your body, one vein at a time."

"I know."

Gerda unstrapped her skis and stepped forward. A gust of wind swept through, scooping up the narrow pieces of wood and ski poles, and tossing them out of sight.

The Snow Queen led her past the monsters to the glasslike walls of the palace. As they stood there, thick lines appeared in the ice and created the outline of a door. The door opened and, with the Snow Queen at her back, Gerda entered the palace.

# CHAPTER FOURTEEN

Gerda looked around the room they had entered: it was a large space walled with ice on three sides, and with a series of closed doors along the fourth. The only objects in it were the mirror and a chair made of snow, which Kai sat upon. She rushed over. "Kai!"

He didn't even blink. All he did was continue staring into the mirror. When she dared to take a brief look at it, all that met her gaze was plain silver glass. She waited to feel the pain that occurred whenever she had used her piece, but nothing happened. She stepped in front of him and shook his shoulders. "Look at me."

Kai slowly looked up at her then, but it was without recognition. His body seemed drained of all color. He still wore the same clothing as when he had disappeared, yet even that looked faded. The coldness of the palace nipped at Gerda's exposed skin but Kai showed no signs of feeling the chill, as though he were already made of ice. "Who are you?" His voice was flat. There was nothing of his usual curiosity in the words.

"You don't know me?" She sank to her knees. A quiet sound that might have been a laugh floated from across the room. Outside the palace it had been possible to believe that the Snow Queen was lying about how Kai had changed. Now she knew Kristina was right—he didn't remember anything and he belonged to the Snow Queen, all because Gerda hadn't gotten there soon enough. If he had been turned into a raging monster, it still would have been easier to deal with than this emptiness.

For a few moments he gazed down at her, his face impassive. Then he looked past her and became animated for the first time. The little attention he had been giving to Gerda vanished. "You came back. I *knew* you wouldn't leave me forever." He stepped past Gerda and walked to the Snow Queen. Just as he was getting close, she raised one hand and he

176

stopped in his tracks.

"Don't count your blessings just yet. I haven't forgotten how you failed me," she told him.

"If you'll give me just one more chance—" he began.

"There will be no more chances."

Kai stood motionless at this answer.

She turned her attention to Gerda, who still sat on the snow-packed floor. "You're doing an excellent job so far. I've never met anybody so persuasive."

"Stay out of this," Gerda said.

The Snow Queen laughed. "I never promised to make it easy for you."

Anger won out over despair as Gerda struggled to her feet. She herself had forgotten everything important in the springtime garden. Even when Eva had appeared in her dream, she still hadn't remembered right away. Memories didn't have to be lost forever. Even if he couldn't be saved in the end, she wouldn't let the Snow Queen win this easily.

Gerda stepped in between them. Turning her back on the Snow Queen made her flesh crawl but she did it all the same. Kai's gaze had drifted to the mirror during the brief argument. "Kai—"

"Look at it," he interrupted and held up a hand speckled with thin scars. "Something wonderful is appearing again. See?" He seized Gerda's arm and pulled her over to stand before the mirror. It was almost the same tone he had used whenever he was talking about the end of a particularly good book. She shivered to hear him speak about something of the Snow Queen's in that way.

Gerda looked at the mirror once more. For a moment it seemed as though its surface glimmered with half-formed shapes, but she saw nothing more.

Yet Kai was enraptured; his eyes flickered back and forth, and he smiled faintly. His too-pale face glowed with the light cast forth by the Snow Queen in the palace and the moon outside. "Isn't it perfect?"

Gerda sighed. "Yes, it's perfect. I have to tell you something." He didn't seem to be paying attention but she continued, "I'm sorry I didn't get here sooner."

This time when Kai looked at her his gaze was filled with impatience. "What are you talking about?"

"Don't you remember *anything*?" she asked.

He sighed and, in that patronizing tone he had always used when lecturing and that she had always hated, said, "I remember everything important: I work on the mirror and live here with her," he said and gestured at the Snow Queen, who had taken Kai's place in the chair and watched them with a little smile on her face. "What I *don't* remember is you. You obviously have me confused with someone else. You should leave now and look for him somewhere else; you're very annoying."

"I will not go away," Gerda said. "You're my brother. You used to live far away from here with me and our grandmother." She felt as though she were picking her way across a frozen river while the ice had started to crack around her as she tried to keep from tumbling into the cold water. She laid a hand on his arm.

He yanked his arm away, looking distastefully at her mittened hand. "I did not. I've never seen you before in my life." He stalked back to the Snow Queen's side. "Why did you let this person in? All she does is lie and it's not even interesting."

The Snow Queen tapped a finger against her chin. "I would say it's at least a *little* interesting. And I must admit that I'm curious as to what lies she'll try next."

"Would you just listen to me? She doesn't care about you; she's just using you to fix her mirror," Gerda pleaded.

Kai shook his head. "It's an honor to be allowed to work on the mirror. And she does care about me; I wouldn't have been chosen if she didn't."

"Chosen? That means you came from somewhere else." Gerda's heart raced as she found her first opening since laying eyes on him. The chance was as slim as a piece of the mirror but it was more than she'd had before.

He looked confused, although he hid it well behind that icy mask. "You're trying to trick me but it won't work. I belong here."

She sighed and took one of his hands. He didn't break away this time, though he made no returning gesture. "Okay, let's say you belong here. Do you like stories?"

"I used to tell her stories." He nodded at the Snow Queen. "I forgot them but that's all right; they were no good, anyway."

"I have a much better story," Gerda promised. "Will you listen to it for at least a little while?"

He glanced at the Snow Queen, who nodded. Gerda's heart twisted: in their old life, Kai wouldn't have asked for permission to listen to a story or do anything else he thought was interesting.

She took a deep breath. "Not long ago, a grandmother and her two grandchildren lived in a town called Vasa.

"The granddaughter was named Gerda. What she loved to do most was to be around plants, so she worked in a glass house where she could be with things that grew every day. Her twin brother was named Kai. He was very clever and wanted to learn everything. His tongue could be sharp but his family knew that he cared about them. The grandmother told stories about trolls, elves, treasures hidden in caves, heroes, and wise animals. The three of them were very happy.

"Then, at the start of one winter when the twins were grown up, they met somebody new in town who called herself Eva. She was very beautiful

178

and made Kai believe that she was in love with him. But nobody knew that Eva was really the Snow Queen, and that there was only ice inside of her instead of blood and warmth."

Kai's fingers twitched in Gerda's grasp. She continued speaking, and tried to keep from showing any sign of hope in front of the Snow Queen.

"Many years ago the Snow Queen had a magic mirror that made everything reflected in it believe that it was ugly and horrible. She could also use it to make her power even greater, and she wanted to reflect the whole world in it so that winter would never end. But the mirror broke before she could do that and its pieces were scattered. One went into Kai's eye and that's what brought the Snow Queen to Vasa. He had the last piece that she needed to collect.

"Kai changed after the mirror found him. He lost interest in the things he had cared about before and became cruel to his family. The only things he enjoyed now were being with Eva and looking at the snow. And then in the middle of a blizzard, the Snow Queen took him away so that he could fix her mirror.

"But as clever as the Snow Queen was, she didn't know that Kai had found out about the piece of mirror in his eye. He got it out and gave it to his sister before he was stolen away." Gerda heard the Snow Queen's dress rustle behind her at this revelation but she refused to look away from Kai. "She wanted her brother back so much that she made her way to another world and traveled through a whole year, always going north to find the Snow Queen and Kai. After all the other seasons had passed, she arrived at the Snow Queen's palace. She went to her brother and now she says, 'I'm here to bring you home.'"

Gerda pressed her lips together and watched. Kai frowned a little, as a person might when waking from a strange dream. He looked *at* her for the first time since she had entered the palace. "Gerda?"

*"Finally."* She lunged forward and wrapped her arms around his neck.

"You're really here," he said, as though he was still trying to believe what he was seeing.

She couldn't stop herself from smiling for what felt like the first time in years. Even in that dim room she could see that he no longer appeared drained of all color: his gray eyes seemed less faded and there was the ghost of pink life in his paper-white face.

The Snow Queen stepped forward. Her face was impassive but Gerda had the feeling of a great storm brewing below the surface. "What an unexpected success."

Joy made Gerda reckless. "Thank you."

"Don't forget the rest of our bargain."

"We made a deal," Gerda said to Kai when he looked confused. She wanted to hug him and keep him safe forever, but she forced herself to let go. "I promised to finish the mirror if she let us leave." She dipped her hand into her pocket and held up the last piece of the mirror.

"Are you crazy?" Kai demanded as the Snow Queen rushed forward with hunger in her eyes. "I didn't give you that thing just so you could return it to her!"

"Be quiet," the Snow Queen commanded. Kai clutched at his throat and fell silent. "So *that's* how you got it."

*He sounded like Kristina just now,* Gerda thought. *I'll have to tell him all about her.* She ignored the Snow Queen long enough to smile at her still-mute brother and squeeze his hand. "It's going to be all right."

"I'm waiting," the Snow Queen said.

Gerda approached the mirror. It now reflected herself and the Snow Queen standing side by side. She still couldn't see any of the images that had mesmerized Kai and she wondered what the Snow Queen saw in it. Gerda immediately found the space where the last piece should fit. She looked away from the desire in the Snow Queen's face and reminded herself how much that piece had slowly changed throughout her journey, like hyacinths creeping inch by inch out of the ground. She remembered finding a holly bush growing in the middle of the Snow Queen's land, where it had seemed as though nothing could survive. But would it be enough?

"Wait!" the Snow Queen commanded.

Gerda paused, her hand inches away from the last hole. "What is it?"

The Snow Queen pushed herself in front of the mirror and peered at Gerda's hand. "What did you *do*?"

Gerda automatically stepped back from that searing cold. "Nothing."

"You've changed it somehow. You've tainted my mirror." For the first time since Gerda had met her, the Snow Queen sounded appalled.

"And now I'm going to do what you wanted—put it back where it belongs." Gerda couldn't see a point in pretending ignorance any longer. She reached forward.

"You can't!" The Snow Queen spread out her arms.

Gerda took a deep breath and grabbed the Snow Queen.

The cold shot through her but she didn't let go. The Snow Queen tried to seize the last piece of the mirror from Gerda's other hand. Even though the holly had kept Gerda from being attacked outside the palace, it seemed that even the plant's strength couldn't protect her entirely. Gerda clenched her teeth and held on.

Kai leaped forward and grabbed the Snow Queen's shoulder. She was distracted for only a moment, but it was long enough for Gerda to reach forward and finish the mirror.

Gerda collapsed onto the floor and curled into a ball. The pain from holding onto the Snow Queen made her want to scream. How had Kai endured it for so long?

The silver glass rippled with waves as if Gerda had dropped a stone into Linnea's well. When the surface cleared, falling snow surrounded the Snow Queen's reflection. Gerda stopped breathing. Kai knelt beside her.

Yet the images in the mirror continued to change. Color bled slowly into the white background and the snowflakes melted together to form pale green vines.

"You've ruined everything," the Snow Queen whispered.

Now the Snow Queen's reflection was completely gone. The sky in the mirror turned blue and glowed with the light from a sunrise. With a bird's view, they passed over a forest where leaves unfurled from the trees' branches like the rippling of waves. A sapphire river appeared. At last, the mirror settled on the image of a garden where plants were in the midst of sprouting from the soft earth. Hawthorn trees started to bloom and forsythia shrubs grew up around a cottage. Gerda thought she could even smell the fresh grass.

Kai pulled Gerda to her feet. When they looked at the Snow Queen, they saw that she still stared into the mirror and appeared to notice nothing else.

"Now we can leave," Gerda said.

Kai examined the Snow Queen. She remained motionless and silent as she stood in front of the mirror, no matter how long he stared at her. He remembered the way she had walked around the palace and how he had thought her voice was the most wonderful sound in any world. He cleared his throat and found that he could speak again. "What did you do?"

"After I started searching for you, I could see traces of the other seasons when I looked into your piece of the mirror. I didn't want to break the mirror just so that she could start over but this piece had changed. It kept changing when I was looking for you. I talked to another queen and she said that this piece might never go back to the way it was, and that it might be able to change the rest. So I decided to do what the Snow Queen wanted and finish her mirror."

He laughed shortly. "I think that's a plan she never would have expected from anybody, especially you. I wonder why she looks like that."

"You were here for a whole year. Her season's over for now. That other queen also said that even the Snow Queen used to accept the need for other seasons, even though she hated it. A year spent watching the mirror like it is now should remind her of that. I think when it's time for winter again she won't be able to do anything more powerful than the other seasons."

"I hope so." He looked at Gerda properly for the first time since he began to remember: her face was weathered and the fur-lined coat she wore was tattered. She looked older but he *knew* her now and was amazed how he had forgotten so easily. He wondered how his own appearance had changed.

He noticed a new door carved into out of one of the icy walls, one that led out of the palace. Gerda walked through it without hesitation but Kai paused at the threshold. This palace and the Snow Queen had become all he knew. Some part of him wanted to wake her up so that they could walk to that little room at the top of the palace and look at the stars together once more.

"I really loved her, back when she was Eva," he said, mostly to himself.

"She never really existed," Gerda said. Her voice was kinder than he would have expected when speaking of the Snow Queen.

"I know." He drew a deep breath and forced himself to turn around. He did not look back again as he stepped out of the palace. The snowy wasteland stretched out before them and the land remained under cover of night.

"How are we going to get home?" he asked. *The palace is home,* his mind whispered.

"I didn't think about that much," Gerda admitted. She started walking and he followed. "Most of the time I was too busy worrying about what to do when I found the Snow Queen. We might be stuck with walking back for a while. I was captured by a group of robbers when it was autumn; if we find them we could ask Kristina—the leader's daughter—for help. She always had ideas even though most of them involved trying to turn me into a robber. Or there's the other queen I mentioned; she has visions in her dreams and I'm sure she could think of a way to send us home."

Kai stared at his sister. "What *were* you doing while I was here?"

She smiled. "I'll tell you everything. It'll be a new story for you and Nana. And by the way—trolls *do* exist."

It was good to hear her talk. If she kept telling him about her adventures, it would be easier to stop thinking about the Snow Queen. "I— Gerda, look."

She turned where he pointed to the east. The sun had begun to creep above the horizon as they spoke. As it climbed higher the sky lightened from black to watery gray, then was stained with pink and gold, every moment pushing away more of the night. All that color seemed almost unnatural. He put up a hand to shield his eyes from the unaccustomed light, even as he turned his face toward the fragile warmth. There was nothing wrong with the sun; it was all right to feel happy when it appeared. "I thought I'd never see the sun again."

"So did I."

He shivered a little. He had been numb for so long that it was amazing to notice the difference between cold and warmth now. Gerda gave him her scarf and mittens. His fingers were unaccustomed to the softness of the fabric after knowing only the slickness of the mirror's surface, hard-packed snow, and the Snow Queen's frozen touch for so long.

He caught a glimpse of Gerda's hands before she tucked them into her pockets. The skin on her left hand had turned almost white. "What happened to you?"

"A lot," she said before she saw where he was looking. "Oh. I was starting to get lost near the end. I...had to use the piece you gave me to find the palace."

"Why would you do that? You saw what it did to me!"

Gerda scowled. "I didn't have many options. My hand got a little cold, that's all. Look." She pulled it out and clumsily flexed her fingers. "I'll be fine."

Kai gave her a look but he bit his tongue. They resumed walking. "I still can't remember everything," he confessed after a short time. "It's hard to stop thinking about *her*."

"All right, I can help with that," Gerda said. She began with Nana: how their grandmother looked, all the years she had raised them, and how she changed voices when telling stories. Gerda continued with every room of their house, next moving on to the conservatory until he remembered the scents of its different plants.

The sun continued to rise and he saw a frozen river appear from underneath the snow. He saw pine trees growing, with sap shining on their trunks. He allowed himself to look back for the first time when they stopped by the river to rest. The palace was out of sight, though he could still see a frozen land of pure white snow in the distance. Winter still remained where he and Gerda stood, but here it was softer.

"I can't figure out why it's like this," he said, frowning.

She said, "When I was traveling I found out that there are places where it stays the same season forever but the farther you go, the more it starts to change. The Snow Queen would want her palace to be at the center, but here must be one of the in-between places." She tugged on his hand as he continued to look back. "Come on, let's keep going."

Kai saw a flicker of movement among the trees when he turned to start walking again. He jumped, still half-expecting the Snow Queen to come flying after them in her sled. Instead it was an enormous, brown-and-cream reindeer peering at them. He laughed weakly with relief and pointed. "Look, I think we have a new friend."

He wasn't expecting Gerda's hands to fly to her mouth or for her to stumble through the snow as she tried to run to the reindeer. It amazed him even more when the wild animal didn't leap away but instead allowed her to throw her arms around it.

"You know it?" he asked.

"I helped rescue him from the robbers. I wouldn't have made it here without him. I left him with some reindeer herders before I got to the palace, but he must have run away."

A spark leaped in his mind and another piece of his memory fell into place. "He's like the reindeer statue."

Gerda's head snapped up at these words. She had a strange look on her face as she watched him. Kai was puzzled until he realized he was grinning for what felt like the first time since he had met the Snow Queen.

"He is," she said and turned back to the reindeer. "What do you think? Can I talk you into helping me out one more time?"

The reindeer stood patiently as Gerda climbed onto his back. When she reached down Kai asked, "Are you sure he's strong enough?"

"He's strong enough. And do you really want to continue on foot until we find somebody who can help us get home? I don't know about you, but I could use a rest from walking."

"If you say so." He sat behind her and kept a tight grip around her waist. It felt like he would fall off any moment.

The reindeer started out walking yet, even with the heavy load on his back, he was soon running. He swerved in and out of the trees that became even more common around them. When they passed near the river Kai heard loud cracks that he came to realize were the sounds of ice breaking on the river. The cool air grew warmer. It tickled his face and tugged at his hair, turning into a balm against memories of the Snow Queen's touch. As they ran faster and faster, he caught glimpses of greenery among all the snow.

"Where's he taking us?" Kai shouted.

Gerda laughed. "I don't know!" It was the first time he had heard her laugh since he started remembering. In between wondering how they could be moving so fast and worrying about falling off, he wondered what had happened on her journeys that had weighed on her.

The reindeer ran even faster until it seemed as though his hooves barely touched the ground. Kai shut his eyes as the world swirled around them.

The reindeer's hooves clattered against something hard instead of thumping into the softening snow. Kai opened his eyes and looked around. The three of them were in Vasa's town park, next to the reindeer statue. It was early morning and he couldn't see anybody else about.

"How did he do that?" he asked as he dizzily slid to the ground.

"I don't know." Gerda laughed again and followed him.

"The sun's already up; our statue is supposed to come alive only at night."

"Maybe it's different because this one is already alive. Anyway, he's been special from the beginning."

The reindeer was examining the statue and Kai could have almost sworn that he looked puzzled. The reindeer wheeled about and darted through a space in between the hedges. As they watched, the reindeer raced down the street and out of sight.

"I'm going to miss him," she said.

"I know." Kai continued to look in the direction the reindeer had gone. "Do you think he'll be stuck here?"

"He went from that world to this one. Why couldn't he go back if he wants?" Then she said, very quietly, "Maybe he can take me back someday."

Kai looked around. The icicles on buildings dripped as they melted and green sprouts poked out of the low mounds of snow that covered the ground. He could hear sparrows chirping somewhere nearby. "Do you think we were gone a whole year here, too?" he asked.

Gerda didn't seem to be able to stop smiling as she looked around. "I don't know. After you went away she kept a blizzard going until the snow was high everywhere but now..." She squeezed his hand. "Let's go find out."

The melting snow and ice ran down the sidewalks in rivulets, until it seemed like all the world was melting and they had to walk in the street to keep from sloshing through cold water. Kai stared at the town around him. The memory of it had slipped away from him while he lived with the Snow Queen, one bit at a time, until he didn't even recall that it had existed. Now it was like a dream had come to life. He looked at the buildings as they walked past and remembered what the stores contained, how he had walked these streets almost every day of his life, and how he had once known he could find his way around Vasa blindfolded. Yet the part of him that had been the Snow Queen's creature marveled at the bright colors of the buildings, and how so many people lived so close together, and the idea that winter could be something that did not last forever.

After the first block, they started to run. Sticking to the roads took too long, even for the relatively short distance left, and they cut through yards without looking around to see who might be watching.

The house where the Snow Queen had lived while pretending to be human still stood as it had before. Kai spared it only a quick look but he could still tell that it felt empty now. Even if he lived in Vasa for the rest of his life, he would never set foot in that place again.

Seeing their own house made his heart ache. As they approached, Nana opened the door and stepped outside. Her laughter sounded like a young woman's and she called out, "I *knew* you would come home; I saw it in my dreams." Gerda and Kai ran to her. As the three of them embraced, they were surrounded by crocuses blooming amethyst and gold on the snow.

Winter was over.

# ABOUT THE AUTHOR

As a Western New York native, Amy Aderman has experienced a number of winter storms that may have been caused by an enthusiastic Snow Queen. She has a lifelong passion for fairy tales; one of her favorite parts of writing "The Way to Winter" was researching Scandinavian folklore and stories. You can learn more about her at her blog:
http://amyaderman.livejournal.com